# THE SINS OF
# RACHEL
# SIMS

## DENNIS M. CLAUSEN

BROWN POSEY PRESS

an imprint of Sunbury Press, Inc.
Mechanicsburg, PA USA

an imprint of Sunbury Press, Inc.
Mechanicsburg, PA USA

For information about special discounts for bulk purchases, please contact Sunbury Press Orders Dept. at (855) 338-8359 or orders@sunburypress.com.

To request one of our authors for speaking engagements or book signings, please contact Sunbury Press Publicity Dept. at publicity@sunburypress.com.

ISBN: 978-1-62006-207-4 (Trade paperback)

Library of Congress Control Number: 2018942417

FIRST BROWN POSEY PRESS EDITION: May 2018

Product of the United States of America
0  1  1  2  3  5  8  13  21  34  55

Set in Bookman Old Style
Designed by Crystal Devine
Cover by Lawrence Knorr
Edited by Lawrence Knorr

*Continue the Enlightenment!*

# CHAPTER ONE

*May 1952*

Rachel Sims parted the thick brush and weeds as she walked across the ancient, muddy riverbed to Hodges Island. It had been an early spring, and the weeds and brush were already well above her head in many places. Tangled heaps of dead vegetation that had accumulated over the years were piled high on all sides of the area where she was walking, as were the shattered remains of granite rocks that had been dynamited years earlier when the northern channel of the Lonely Willow River was closed. High above the marshlands, where the river had once flowed, a hawk extended its long wings against the sky as it glided along the air currents.

She had been down to the riverbed before to pick wild berries or retrieve lost cows, but this time she had another reason for venturing so far from home.

She chose her path carefully as she made her way across the muddy riverbed, trying whenever possible to step on rocks or dynamited fragments of the granite boulders that littered the area. As she approached Hodges Island, she paused next to one of the many puddles that had been formed by the heavy spring rains, and she watched as tadpoles darted across the shallow water. She removed the tiny combs that held her hair in a neat bun on top of her head, and her long black hair fell to her shoulders, where it swayed gently in the breeze that swept across the riverbed. As she watched the tadpoles, she removed a pink ribbon from the pocket of her dress and placed it in her hair.

Rachel Sims was a young woman in her mid-twenties, but her blue eyes revealed a sadness that made her look older and wiser. She possessed an independence of spirit that was evident in her firm jaw and eyes that seemed to be fixed on something that was troubling her. She had high cheekbones and full breasts, but her hands were calloused from years of hard work. Under other circumstances, she might have been considered beautiful, but her beauty was concealed and muted by the gray cotton dress that hung loosely on her shoulders.

A deep underlying passion was reflected in her entire demeanor, even though it was a passion that was out of place in the church community in which she had been raised. The church was comprised of grim, humorless men and women who saw human passions as the most obvious evidence of Satan's presence in the world.

*There is so much here that is new to the sun and the sky*, she thought as she watched the tiny, brown tadpoles dart swiftly back and forth across the shallow puddle of water. *So much that makes one feel alive and courageous enough to resurrect old dreams.*

She knew she had to harden herself against the desire to resurrect old dreams. Sometimes, she knew it was best that old dreams be put to rest and never revived.

*Still, with all this new life, there is hope. And with hope comes the overwhelming desire to relive a passion that had never died.*

Suddenly, she heard a loud noise in the thick brush behind her. Apprehensively, she watched the tall weeds bend and sway as something charged across the riverbed, moving relentlessly toward the area where she was standing. Abruptly, the noise stopped, and she could once again hear the breeze blowing gently through the brush that covered the riverbed.

*If it's Grant, what will I tell him?*

A cow suddenly stepped into the clearing next to the puddle of water. The cow's huge brown eyes stared at her. Then it bellowed and plunged back into the brush. She listened to the fading hoof beats until they disappeared in the distance. She took a deep breath and continued walking toward Hodges Island.

As she unbuttoned the tight collar of her dress, she glanced at the blossoming lilac bushes that grew wild on the island. The air was heavy with the smell of the lilacs. As the beautiful purple flowers caught the first rays of the early morning sun, they shimmered and glistened in the sunlight.

For centuries, the Native Americans living in the area believed the island was populated by the spirits of warriors who had never been allowed to leave this world. They gave the island a name, which meant "The Island of Lost Spirits." Later, the first European settlers in the area claimed they would see strange human forms walking on the riverbank at night. They called them "Heaven's

Outcasts." Even in recent years, the dead and mutilated bodies of small animals were sometimes found along the riverbanks, all of which added to the evolving legend of Hodges Island.

Although those stories had caused her some fear and apprehension when she had ventured over to the island for the first time, she had nonetheless decided it was the best place for her to meet Jesse. She knew that Hodges Island was the one place where they could be completely alone, and where no one would find them.

As she walked past a large granite boulder and plunged into the thick brush that fringed the island, she thought about what she was planning to tell Jesse. It would not be easy. She had kept the secret to herself for much too long. But she had decided it was time for Jesse to know what had happened to her, and why she made the decisions she had made. She knew it would cause him much pain. But, in time, maybe it would help him get on with his life.

*Maybe if Jesse knows the truth, he will understand. And maybe the hopeless feeling of being pulled and torn in two different directions will end.*

She soon found the dirt road created by the horse-drawn wagons that had once hauled granite rocks out of the quarries that had been dug on the island. The quarries were shut down when it became too expensive to ship the granite downriver. It was much cheaper to mine the granite elsewhere and ship the rock by railroad or in trucks.

The entire island was overgrown with vegetation that had accumulated over the years. She knew it was not wise to venture too far off the path. Once before, she had almost stepped on some dead brush that concealed a huge hole in the ground. She stepped back just in time, but that experience had taught her never to wander too far from the dirt road.

All around her, she could hear small animals rustling through the underbrush. In the wetter areas, a thin haze hovered a few inches above the ground. From somewhere in the dark shadows cast by the tall trees that hovered high overhead, she heard what sounded like a lone whippoorwill still singing its mournful lament, seemingly unaware that night had passed and the early morning sun was rising in the east.

A few feet ahead of her, a large black garter snake suddenly slithered across the path and disappeared into the hollow end of a

rotting tree trunk. Startled by the snake, she stepped off the path
and almost stumbled over the grayish-white skull of a horse or
cow that had perished on the island.

Finally, she arrived at the center of the island, where several
moss-covered stone and wooden structures—the remnants of the
old quarry buildings—were partially concealed by weeds, blossoming lilac bushes, and climbing vines.

To her right, on a slight elevation, she could see some small
granite stones protruding out of the earth. She knew they marked
the graves of the quarry workers who died when a mysterious epidemic swept across the island at the end of the previous century.
Later, itinerant laborers who died or were killed while working in
the quarries were also buried in the company cemetery.

To her left, a stone structure protruded out of the side of an
embankment. An elderly member of the church who had worked
in the quarries told her the stone structure was used to store per-
ishable foods for the quarry workers. He said it was abandoned
when snakes and other wildlife took it over and used it as a place
to hibernate for the winter.

Suddenly, she heard a sound from behind a pile of broken
boards. Startled, she held her breath as a rat's fat body and long,
thin tail disappeared into a hole in a crumbling stone wall.

*What was taking Jesse so long? He had said he would be here.*

Beneath one of the trees that surrounded the decaying buildings, she saw a bird's nest that had been dislodged by the wind
or some predator. The mutilated bodies of two baby birds were
lying in the thick grass a few feet away from where the nest had
fallen to the ground. Hearing a soft chirping sound at her feet,
she dropped to her knees and parted the weeds with her hands.
Another baby bird was trembling with fear in the shadows where
it had sought refuge.

"Oh, you poor thing!" she whispered softly. She picked up the
tiny, trembling bird and cupped it in her hands. "You must be
terrified. Where is your mother?"

She picked up the nest and lodged it firmly in one of the lower
branches of a tree. She placed the tiny bird in the nest and gently
stroked its head.

*How could a mother abandon her young, even in the most hope-
less of situations?*

While she waited for Jesse, she walked over to one of the lilac bushes and gently removed several of the purple flowers. She

removed the pink ribbon from her hair, wrapped it around the flowers, and tied it into a bow. When she was finished, she held the bouquet in the air and admired her handiwork.

*Would Jesse ever be able to understand? And if he did, would he be able to accept what had happened? He needs to know. She should have told him earlier. That way if anything happens, he will . . .*

As she stared at the bouquet of lilac flowers, she became aware of a strange noise coming from behind some thick bushes next to a toppled wooden shed. From where she was standing, it reminded her of the creaking sound a wooden floor joint makes when someone steps on it.

"Who's there?" she yelled apprehensively. "Is someone there?"

Very cautiously, she walked over to the decaying wooden structure and peered into the tangled layers of brush. Suddenly, two large birds burst out of some tall weeds and soared awkwardly into the sky.

Startled by the sound of the flapping wings, she tripped and almost fell down a small embankment. She reached for a low-hanging tree branch and regained her balance. Then she heard the creaking sound again.

"Jesse?" she asked. "Is that you?"

When there was no answer, she took another step to peer into the brush and vines. She paused when she heard another strange sound. She waited for it to reoccur, then took another step . . .

*The long, black whirlpool enveloped Rachel Sims for what seemed like an eternity. Drifting and rolling and spinning ever downwards. Pulling her ever deeper into the vortex. Beyond time, beyond space.*

*On all sides of her, there were misshapen reptilian forms seemingly trapped and floating in the black, spinning walls of the whirlpool. And always there were the voices whispering seductively to her from the darkness.*

*Then she saw the light at the end of the vortex. The light that beckoned to her with its comforting presence. The light that encouraged her to end the struggle or risk losing her spirit to the misshapen forms that surrounded her. But as she held out her hand to the light, she saw that she was still clinging to the bouquet of lilac flowers.*

*From somewhere in the darkness, she heard strange voices begin a haunting, mournful lament that built to a crescendo pitch and faded away altogether. Then she drifted deeper and deeper into a dark, silent world where the light could not reach her. A dark, silent world filled only with the beautiful purple flowers of the blossoming lilac bushes.*

><><><

Shortly after Rachel Sims disappeared, her husband Grant Sims showed up in town with a bouquet of lilac flowers that was tied together with a pink ribbon he claimed belonged to his wife. He said he found the flowers and the ribbon on Hodges Island when he was searching the area for his wife, who had vanished that morning. He claimed a neighboring farmer, who had been chasing a cow across the old riverbed, had seen her walking over to Hodges Island earlier that day. So, he went over to that foreboding place to look for her.

Grant asked almost everyone in town if they had seen his wife or knew of her whereabouts. Then he retreated to his farm and had nothing more to do with the townspeople until he died one year later. Some of the townspeople believed he died of a broken heart. Others speculated that he knew more about his wife's disappearance than he was willing to admit.

The disappearance of Rachel Sims was overshadowed by an even more ominous event. Earlier that year, Senator Norbert Samuelson, who represented Archer County in the state legislature, drowned when his boat overturned while he was fishing on the Lonely Willow River. His body, battered against rocks and granite boulders by the current, was found miles downstream. After an appropriate period of mourning, Samuelson's death touched off a frantic political scramble as several candidates positioned themselves for the special election to be held in November.

With such an important election on everyone's mind, Archer County residents were not overly concerned about the disappearance of a poor farmer's wife, especially one who was rumored to have been last seen in "the company of a well-dressed gentleman who drove an expensive car with Iowa license plates."

As the years passed, the events of that spring day in 1952 gradually faded in the minds of all but a few of the farmers and townspeople. Indeed, the story of Rachel Sims would quite possibly have been forgotten altogether, had it not been for the reports of Charlie Flanigan, the caretaker who lived in the cemetery on the southern side of the Lonely Willow River.

According to "Crazy Charlie," every spring when the lilac bushes blossomed, he claimed he could hear strange noises drifting across the river from Hodges Island. If the moon was full and the fog was not too thick, he said he would see a young woman holding a bouquet of flowers as she glided gracefully through the trees and bushes that fringed the riverbank.

Charlie even gave the young woman a name. He called her the "Lilac Lady," and he swore she came out in spring when the smell of the blossoming lilac bushes was heavy in the air. Always the next morning, he said he would find lilac flowers on some of the graves in the cemetery on his side of the river. When the lilac flowers disappeared on Hodges Island, the young woman also disappeared, not to return until the next spring when the first purple flowers appeared on the lilac bushes.

*And so it was that Charlie Flanigan's crazy ramblings created the legend of the Lilac Lady who walked the riverbanks at night, with flowers in hand, for reasons known only to her and the wind.*

# CHAPTER TWO

*May 1974*

Laura Fielding stood in the open doorway, waving goodbye to the last of the people who had attended her mother's funeral earlier that day. Then she closed the huge oak door and turned to face the empty house. During her mother's long, lingering battle with cancer, she had prepared herself for everything, or so she had thought. The one thing she hadn't prepared herself for was the loneliness she felt the minute the door thudded shut.

She had just about decided to wait until morning to clean up the downstairs area where the reception was held, when she heard a knock on the door. "Laura, it's me," she heard her friend Annie's muffled voice on the other side of the door.

Laura unlocked the door and swung it open. "What did you forget this time?" she asked.

"Nothing," Annie shrugged meekly. "I just wanted to make sure you were okay."

"I'll be fine," Laura reassured her. "I just have to get used to living in this big house by myself until I can start taking in renters again. It'll take time, but I'll get used to it. I'm seeing Dr. Herschler tomorrow. That'll help."

"Okay. Call me tomorrow, so I'll know you're okay."

Although Laura and Annie were both graduate students at the University of Minnesota, they were as different as two friends could possibly be. Annie, a blonde, blue-eyed Scandinavian, was impulsive and unpredictable. Laura had dark hair and brown eyes, and she was more methodical and contemplative. Annie was also more outgoing and gregarious, whereas Laura tended to be a loner. Still, the two young women had forged a friendship during the time they had known each other as graduate students in the English Department.

Laura shut the door and quickly switched off the downstairs lights before walking up the staircase to her bedroom on the second floor. As her feet shuffled across the carpeted hallway, she paused in front of her mother's bedroom. From the dim greenish glow of a nightlight she had placed near the baseboard, she could see the tray of medications on the nightstand next to her mother's bed.

As she stared at the bed, she remembered the many conflicting feelings she had after she took a leave of absence from the university to care for her mother. The many hours she had sat by her mother's bedside were still very vivid memories and always would be. A part of her had wanted to savor every moment, every word, knowing it would all end very soon. Another part of her had wanted it to end quickly, so her mother would no longer have to suffer.

*She had suffered so terribly in this room. How would it ever be possible to walk down this hallway again without seeing her lying on her bed next to a tray of medications?*

Laura almost walked into the room, but she decided that was not a wise thing to do. It was too soon after the funeral. There would be too many memories. Memories that needed to be dealt with when the bright sunlight was pouring through the windows, not in the middle of the night when the smell of death was still heavy in the air.

She quickly walked down the hallway to her own bedroom. After she undressed and crawled into bed, she pulled a pillow close to her chest and tried to think of something, anything that would take her mind off the funeral that afternoon. Her thoughts shifted to the poet Emily Dickinson, who had struggled to recommit herself to life every time she lost another friend or family member. Laura tried to envision her mother, like the narrator in Dickinson's poem "Because I could not stop for Death," on a casual carriage ride into the Hereafter. She knew the poem probably had a darker undertone, but the image of her mother travelling through the clouds in a carriage with a kindly travelling companion named "Immortality" gave her some comfort.

She silently repeated the opening lines until she fell asleep.

*Because I could not stop for Death—He kindly stopped for me— The Carriage held but just Ourselves—And Immortality. We slowly drove—He knew no haste and I had put away my labor and my leisure too, For His Civility . . .*

><><><><

Laura awoke the next morning to the smell of the blossoming lilac bushes in the back yard. As the fragrant smell poured through her open window, she sat up in bed and stared outside at a beautiful spring day. It was a welcome respite from the previous afternoon when the graveside service had almost been cancelled because of thunderstorms that were moving through the Minneapolis-St. Paul area.

As she brushed her teeth, she studied herself in the mirror. Her brown eyes were tired from the many sleepless nights she had sat by her mother's bedside. She had given up on trying to do anything with her hair. She just didn't have the time or energy. It was much easier to part it in the middle, pull it back, and tie it with a rubber band. Because her hair was short, the ponytail did not fall to her neck. Instead, it angled to her right, and the end curled slightly upwards.

She knew that most people who first met her thought she was shy and introspective, which she was. They didn't know she was fully capable of being strong, even stubbornly aggressive when she had to be. Still, she was more comfortable as an observer of life. Relationships, especially, often drained her of energy, and she avoided most of them. Her friendship with Annie was an exception. There was something about Annie that enabled her to be open without feeling exposed and vulnerable. Her relationships with men were another thing altogether. They never ended well.

*Maybe things will change now that Mother is gone, and I can start to think about my own life? Maybe things will be different? Maybe . . .*

Later, Laura ate a bagel and cream cheese for breakfast while she drank a cup of coffee and watched the news on television. The weather report predicted an entire week of clear skies and bright sunlight. The national news focused on the investigation into the Watergate affair.

She finished eating and quickly walked back upstairs to begin the difficult task of cleaning out her mother's room. She knew she had to get rid of the medications, or every time she walked past the open doorway, she would see her mother's thin, emaciated form lying on the bed, staring at the ceiling.

She paused in the hallway and peered into her mother's bedroom. The shades were still closed, and the entire room was covered with gray shadows. The shadows reminded her of the color of her mother's skin in the weeks before she finally succumbed to cancer. The thought of her mother lying in that bedroom, surrounded by gray shadows, was overwhelming.

*I'm not ready yet. I can't go into the bedroom. Not yet.*

She stepped backward, never taking her eyes off the bedroom door, until her back touched the opposite wall of the hallway. She slid down the wall until she was sitting on the floor, still staring into the bedroom. She slowly lowered her head and buried her face in her arms. The feelings of being completely alone suddenly overwhelmed her, and she started to cry softly.

Laura let her eyes wander around the office while Dr. Herschler neatly rearranged some papers on his desk. Outside the window behind his desk, some reddish brick university buildings were visible in the distance. On the sidewalk, two students strolled past the window and their muffled voices filtered into the room.

To Laura, everything in the office seemed to have been organized to maximize efficiency. Nothing was out of place. She had often wondered if Dr. Herschler was slightly obsessive-compulsive. Everything about him was too neat. His manner of dress, neatly trimmed beard, contents of his desk—everything was too symmetrical. It seemed as though he was struggling desperately to bring some order to the disorderly and often unfathomably complex human minds he was exposed to every day.

It had also occurred to her that Herschler looked like a stereotypical psychiatrist. Even his full name, "Dr. Jerome R. Herschler," sounded like a psychiatrist's name. She was convinced if any ten people were placed in a lineup, and another group of people were told to pick out the one who was a psychiatrist, they would all point to him. His eyes reflected empathy and deep intellectual curiosity, while his dark hair and beard seemed trimmed to perfection. He was the consummate professional, yet he was also kind and generous with his time. He had agreed to continue seeing her even after she dropped out of the university to care for her mother. He charged her very little for those visits, even though she was no longer eligible for the university health care plan, and for that she was very grateful.

Herschler placed the papers on his desk into a folder and looked up at Laura. "I was reviewing some of the things we talked about before," he said, folding his arms and leaning back in his chair. "We haven't met for over a month. How have things been going for you?"

"My mother passed away. I've been pretty busy taking care of her."

"I'm sorry to hear that," Herschler said sympathetically. "I knew she was very ill. I believe that is why you dropped out of the university."

"Yes, that's why I left."

"How are you dealing with your mother's passing?"

"It's been difficult. There's some relief, now that she's no longer suffering. But she was all the family I had."

"Do you have any kind of a support system?"

"Not really. I have one friend, Annie, another graduate student. But that's about it."

Herschler tapped the file folder he had just set aside. "We've talked before about your problems with relationships. The difficulty you have with them, even when you want them to last. Why do you suppose this friendship with Annie has lasted, but others haven't?"

"I don't know."

"It makes it especially difficult at times like these," Herschler said sympathetically.

"Yes, it does."

"You told me before that you even felt alone in your own home."

"From the time I was very young, I spent most of my time in my room reading. I didn't have any real friends. I've broken more relationships with men than I can count. When things become serious, I retreat back into my private world."

"But you were close to your mother?"

"Oh, yes."

"And you do miss her?"

"Very much."

"It is so important for you to reach out to others, especially at times like this. I'll continue meeting with you, of course, and hopefully your friend will be there for you. But you need to continue expanding your relationships. We all need an extended family."

"I'll try. But it's difficult for me. It always has been."

"Do you know why?"

"I've always felt there is something different about me," Laura said softly. "I can't explain what it is. But I've always felt like I had something else inside of me, something that belonged somewhere else. I can't explain it. It's very confusing. I've struggled with it my whole life. Yet, I can never get any closer to understanding it.

As she sat at her desk, Laura glanced at some branches on an elm tree that were swaying gently outside her bedroom window. Then she looked back at the books and piles of typing paper that had accumulated on top of her desk. One pile contained the various drafts of an essay she had been working on for several months, during the time she was caring for her mother. The essay had given her something to do while her mother slept or lay in her bed, staring at the ceiling.

Laura loved the research. She had become somewhat of an expert on finding information other researchers had managed to overlook. For that reason, two of the professors on campus had hired her to do research for them. One of them also recommended her to a law professor who specialized in reexamining the case histories of prisoners who had provided compelling evidence of their innocence. She worked as an intern on some of those cases. She learned a great deal about criminal investigative procedures, and even considered pursuing a legal career, but she found the daily interactions with people she interviewed to be emotionally exhausting. She soon retreated into her bedroom office, where she could pursue safer, more scholarly research into literary classics.

She read a few pages of the most recent draft of the paper she hoped someday to turn into a doctoral dissertation. It was a paper based on Hawthorne's *The Scarlet Letter*, one of her favorite novels. Ever since she read the story of Hester Prynne in high school, she had related to it on a deeply personal level. From the very first sentence, she felt like the story was inside of her, not on the printed page. She always marveled at how Hawthorne had accomplished something so remarkable. She wondered how a writer, any writer, could get so deeply into a character's mind that the character became more real than the people who shared the reader's life.

Those personal feelings for the novel had eventually been transformed into an academic paper that explored the subtler implications of Hawthorne's story. She was convinced the plot was an allegory, or series of allegories, that concealed a deeper, more profound message for future generations of readers, especially women.

*Hawthorne clearly intended to send a message across the ages when he wrote at the end of the novel, "The angel and apostle of the coming revelation must be a woman, indeed, but lofty, pure, and beautiful; and wise . . ."*

A distant creaking noise in the hallway suddenly caught her attention, and she glanced in that direction. It was the kind of noise her mother often made when she turned slowly in bed.

Laura glanced again at the cluttered contents of her desk and then looked back into the hallway. She knew she had to face what she had avoided earlier that day. She had to clean out her mother's bedroom so she could start her own life all over again.

*I can't put it off forever!*

She walked swiftly down to her mother's bedroom. Without pausing in the doorway, she walked over to the windows and pulled on the cord that was attached to the shades. As sunlight poured into the room, she opened the windows and allowed a fresh spring breeze to carry the smell of new life into a room she associated only with pain and death. When the breeze touched her skin, it felt pure and cleansing. It immediately renewed her spirits and gave her the strength to walk over to the bed where her mother had died.

*Try not to think about it. Just do it.*

She threw the medications in a trashcan and quickly stripped the bed. Then she decided that maybe it would be a good idea to move the bed to the far corner of the room. If it was in another location in the bedroom, perhaps it wouldn't remind her so much of her mother's long, painful battle with cancer.

The mattress was heavy, but she managed to drag it across the floor and lean it against the far wall. When she returned to the bed, she saw something lodged in the area between the box spring and the sideboard. Puzzled, she reached into the narrow opening and extracted an envelope.

She sat down on a chair and studied the envelope carefully. From the handwritten return address, it was clear that her mother had written the letter, but for some reason she had never mailed it.

*It's mother's writing. But why would she hide the letter? Why didn't she give it to me to mail?*

When she pulled the letter out of the unsealed envelope, she saw that it was undated. She surmised that her mother had probably written it a few weeks before she died. The handwriting was barely decipherable, as though the act of putting pen to paper was an excruciatingly difficult chore.

"Dear Selma," Laura whispered softly, reading the letter out loud, "I know I promised you many years ago never to contact you again after we finished with our affairs, but times have changed. I have kept that promise, but now I don't know how much time I have left. I find myself lying in bed, wondering if we did the right thing. As you requested, I have never told Laura. She knows nothing. But before I die, I want your permission to tell her everything. I would greatly appreciate it if you would write back as soon as possible. Everyone has a right to know who they are. Harold and I denied Laura that right. Now I believe I owe it to her to be more forthright about who she is. I look forward to your reply. Sincerely, Margaret Fielding. P. S. I thank you for doing everything you did for us so many years ago."

"Annie," Laura exclaimed breathlessly, "you have to see this!"

"What's wrong?" Annie asked.

Laura thrust the letter into her friend's hands, and the two women sat down at the kitchen table in Annie's small upstairs apartment near the university.

"Just read this!" Laura insisted.

Annie stared at her friend for a few seconds before reading the letter. Then she leaned back in her chair and looked across the table. "What's this all about?" she asked.

"I found it hidden away in my mother's bed," Laura explained. "She must have written it shortly before she died. Maybe she forgot about it. Or maybe she was too weak to finish it. Or maybe she had second thoughts about sending it. I don't know. But the letter seems to suggest that I am not who I think I am, whatever that might mean."

Annie studied the address on the envelope. "Who is this 'Selma Madison'?" she asked.

"I don't know. I don't remember my mother ever mentioning that name to me."

"Is it possible your mother was delirious or hallucinating? I know that happened to my aunt during the last weeks of her battle with cancer. She started talking to friends who had been dead for many years, and she thought I was someone else when I visited her."

"Mom was very weak the last few weeks of her life. But she never became delirious or started hallucinating. She always knew exactly what was going on around her."

"Maybe it was just a poor choice of words on your mother's part," Annie speculated. "She was very sick. Maybe she was trying to say something quite innocent, and it just came out all wrong."

"I thought about that, too. But she was coherent, right up to the end. I think she said exactly what she wanted to say."

Annie read the letter again. "Is there any chance that you were kidnapped?" she asked, scratching her temple. "I've heard about those things happening."

"I don't know what it means. I only know that it's very strange."

"Maybe you should drive over to Baxter, Wisconsin, where this woman lives and see what she can tell you about this letter," Annie suggested.

"Maybe," Laura agreed.

Later that day, Laura sorted through more of her mother's belongings. She concentrated on trying to find something that would tell her more about the Selma Madison her mother had written to shortly before she died. Laura found some old letters and a handful of photographs, but she found nothing about a Selma Madison who lived in Baxter, Wisconsin.

She did find a photograph of her mother, father, and her standing near a lake. Someone had written the year 1953 in the bottom right hand corner of the photograph, but the location where the picture was taken was not identified.

*I've never seen a photograph of the three of us when I was so young. And only a couple when I was older. Why didn't they take more photographs of me shortly after I was born? Most parents do that.*

She also knew that her mother and father had never taken many photographs of themselves. She had never seen a wedding picture or any pictures of them when they were dating. Nor had there been any pictures of relatives. Although her parents had explained that they both came from the east, they never talked about brothers, sisters, cousins, or other relatives. She had taken all of that for granted when she was growing up, but now it seemed to have more ominous implications.

Another thought occurred to her as she studied the photograph of her mother and father standing by the lake. Her father was tall, and he had blond hair. Her mother was shorter, but she also had blond hair.

*I don't look like either one of them. Why hadn't I thought of that before?*

She was aware that different generations could be very different in physical appearance, but after reading her mother's letter, she was suspicious of many things that had never seemed to her to be unusual or peculiar.

Before turning in for the night, she picked up her mother's well-worn Bible from the nightstand. She liked the feel of the black leather cover against her palms. She remembered how her mother would prop herself up in bed and read the Bible every night before she became too ill to sit up anymore.

As she idly flipped through the first few Chapters of the Book of Genesis, she noticed that her mother had underlined some favorite passages in pencil. She read some of the passages out loud. They made her feel closer to her mother.

Suddenly, she felt exhausted. The stress of caring for her mother, the funeral, and the sense of loss seemed to drain her of all energy. She placed the Bible on her mother's nightstand, then had second thoughts and decided to put it on the nightstand in her own bedroom. That way she wouldn't feel so alone.

Before falling asleep, she continued to think about the strange letter her mother had written. It was hard to know what to make of it. Perhaps, she decided, the thing to do would be to call information to see if someone named Selma Madison lived in Baxter, Wisconsin. If so, maybe she could clear up the mystery with a brief telephone conversation. If not, she would just have to drive over to Wisconsin and try, as best she could, to figure out what her mother was referring to in the letter. The implications were too important to be ignored.

*Is it possible that I'm not their child? Is that the great secret Mother referred to in her letter?*

As Laura stared into the darkness, she felt more alone than at any other time in her life. Her mother's death had made her feel completely isolated. Now, she was faced with the possibility that she might not even be Laura Fielding. She might be someone else.

She impulsively reached for the Bible and held it against her chest. For the first time since she was a little girl, she cried herself to sleep.

><><><

Laura drove her 1966 blue and white Chevrolet across the St. Croix River Bridge and entered Wisconsin. Her purse and an open map were on the passenger seat next to her. The landscape on the other side of the bridge was not that different from what she had just passed through on the Minnesota side of the border. It was still mostly rolling prairie, although the forested areas became thicker the deeper she drove into Wisconsin.

Before leaving home, she had called to see if there was a telephone number for a Selma Madison in Baxter, Wisconsin, but the operator told her there was no such listing. She decided to drive to Baxter anyway. She was determined to find out what her mother meant by the cryptic letter she had hidden in her bed.

*Maybe it'll all turn out to be very innocent. Maybe there's a simple explanation.*

The more she thought about the letter, the more she realized that Annie might be right. Perhaps her mother was more delirious than she appeared to be, and she had written to some old acquaintance she had known much earlier in her life. It might even be someone who died a long time ago, but who still lingered on in her mother's memories.

*Maybe that's all there was to it.*

A sign outside of Baxter indicated that it was a town of 2,143 people. As she entered Main Street, she stopped an elderly man and asked for directions to Sutter Street. She turned left on Main Street and soon pulled up to a small frame house with the numbers 103 above the front door.

*Well, at least Mother was right about one thing. There is a 103 Sutter Street in Baxter, Wisconsin.*

As she walked up to the front door on a pitted concrete sidewalk, she noticed that sun-bleached curtains covered all the windows. The yard was weed infested and looked like it hadn't been cared for in some time. She knocked on the door, waited, and knocked again. When no one answered, she walked around the house to the back door. As she walked past the side windows, she saw that they too were covered with faded curtains.

*This place looks like it's been abandoned.*

The back yard was even more weed infested than the front yard. She knocked on the screen door, waited, and knocked again.

As she was standing on the back stoop, not sure what to do next, an elderly woman in bib overalls appeared from around the corner of the house. "Looking for someone?" the woman asked somewhat suspiciously.

"Yes," Laura said, stepping down from the stoop. "I'm trying to find out if a Selma Madison lives here."

"What's she to you?" the woman asked.

"I believe she's someone my mother knew," Laura tried to explain. "My mother died last week. After the funeral, I found a letter she had written, but never mailed to Selma Madison." She pulled the letter out of her coat pocket and showed it to the woman. "I don't know why my mother wrote the letter, but I wanted to ask Selma about it."

"Well, Selma lived here for a long time," the elderly woman replied more warmly. "But they took her away about a year ago."

"Took her away?"

"The county put her in the retirement home on the other end of town. The Lake View Retirement Home."

"Is she still there?"

"Far as I know, yes. But if you go out there, you should know one thing. She was real sick when they took her away. Kind of touched in the head, if you know what I mean. She's been there ever since. County is trying to sell her house to pay the cost of keeping her in the retirement home."

"Does she have any relatives who live nearby?"

"Not that I know of. She kept pretty much to herself. She was always real pleasant, and we swapped garden vegetables and things like that. But we never really did get to know one another, even though we were next-door neighbors. I've never even been inside her house. She never invited me to come inside. What's more, I've never seen anyone else go in there either."

The Lake View Retirement Home was located next to a small lake on the northern end of town. As Laura walked across the parking lot, she realized the building was an old three-story resort building the county had transformed into a retirement home.

Inside the lobby, a short, overweight woman with thick, puffy, dark-brown hair greeted her from behind the front counter. The word "Receptionist" was inscribed on a nametag pinned to the woman's blouse. "Can I help you?" she asked cheerfully.

"I was hoping to see one of your patients," Laura explained. "Her name is Selma Madison. I'm told she lives here."

"Selma Madison?" the receptionist said. "I don't think anyone has come by to see her since the county brought her over here about a year ago. Are you a relative?"

"No. Before she died, my mother wrote her a letter, but never mailed it. I wanted to give it to her."

"Well, I'm sorry about your mother. Selma's on the back lawn, sitting in a wheelchair. But you probably won't get much out of her. Dementia. I doubt that she'll remember your mother. She doesn't even remember what happened yesterday."

"What does she look like?"

"There are only three patients sitting out there in wheelchairs. She's the one without a left leg. Diabetes." The receptionist slid a lined, open-faced guest register book across the counter. "Please sign this and indicate who you're visiting."

Laura quickly signed her name and Selma Madison's name in the spaces provided. As she walked down the hallway, she glanced into an adjacent room and saw several hospital employees gathered around a television set. She spotted Selma Madison sitting under an elm tree, looking across the lake. A male caretaker sat on a bench nearby, reading a newspaper.

Selma Madison was an unusually small woman with thinning white hair. As Laura approached the wheelchair, she realized diabetes appeared to have also robbed the elderly woman of much of her eyesight. Although Selma stared at something in the distance, her eyes were vacant, seemingly uncomprehending of anything going on around her.

"Excuse me," Laura inquired gently, leaning down. "Are you Selma Madison?"

The elderly woman's lips twitched slightly, but she continued to stare across the lake, while her right forefinger tapped a slow, steady beat on the eating tray attached to the wheelchair. Her head was propped up slightly by a pillow.

"Selma, I'm Margaret Fielding's daughter, Laura. Do you remember my mother?"

"Nice day. Windy. Horses would run in the fields," Selma replied. She stared at her index finger as she spoke. "Sometimes birds fly out of the trees."

"Selma, do you remember anything about Margaret Fielding? She's my mother. She wrote you a letter before she died. I wanted to ask you some questions about it."

Laura placed the letter on the eating tray, but Selma ignored it. She stared back at the lake and muttered more incomprehensible, disconnected words and phrases.

The caretaker suddenly looked up from where he was reading his newspaper. "You're not going to get anything out of her," he said. "She hasn't carried on a conversation with anyone for some time. She just mutters words that don't mean anything."

Laura picked up the letter from the tray and placed it in her pocket. "Selma, I just wanted you to know that my mother thought about you in the weeks before she died. She wanted to ask your permission to tell me something. It had something to do with a promise she made to you many years ago. Her name was Margaret Fielding. Do you remember Margaret Fielding?"

Selma looked down at her index finger and watched it beat a slightly faster rhythm on the eating tray. "Car crash. Bad car crash. So many times," she muttered softly. As she spoke, her head slowly settled into the pillow and she fell asleep.

Laura stared at the elderly woman as she slept peacefully in the wheelchair. Whatever Selma Madison knew that was so important was obviously lost forever in the maze of acute dementia.

Greatly disappointed that her trip to Wisconsin had yielded no explanations for what her mother had written in the letter, Laura walked back into the retirement home. She paused briefly in front of the receptionist's desk. "What do you know about Selma Madison's background?" she asked. "Did she have any friends? Any relatives?"

"I don't know anything about that."

"Would anyone here have that information?"

"They might. But it would probably be confidential. Like I said before, no one has ever come by to see Selma. That is, until you showed up today asking about her. I do remember someone saying she once worked in the County Recorder's Office in Hastings, eight miles east of here. That's all I know about her."

Laura climbed the granite staircase to the third floor of the Stearns County Courthouse. The County Recorder's office was in the middle of the hallway. Recently mopped and polished gray granite tiles glistened on the hallway floor. A woman who reminded Laura of Eleanor Roosevelt was standing by the front counter.

"Can I help you?" the woman asked in a very professional tone of voice.

"I was told that Selma Madison once worked here," Laura replied. "I was trying to find out if anyone she worked with could tell me more about her."

"Yes, Selma started working here in the early 1950s. I worked with her for almost twenty years."

"What do you know about her?"

"Not much. Selma wasn't unfriendly. But she was one of those people who kept everyone at a distance when it comes to their private lives. She never socialized with any of us outside of the office."

"My mother's name is Margaret Fielding," Laura explained. "I don't know exactly what her relationship was to Selma. But before she died, she wrote a letter to her. It was never mailed. It said some things about our family that were troubling. I've been trying to find answers to the questions that were raised in that letter."

"Margaret Fielding?" the woman mused softly. "Why does that name sound familiar to me?"

"You've heard that name before?"

"Yes, I have. But it doesn't have anything to do with Selma. I've seen that name someplace else. Wait just a minute. Let me look something up in the vault. I'll be right back."

While she waited, Laura listened to the sounds filtering into the room from the hallway. Minutes later, the woman returned. She was reading a death certificate as she stepped up to the counter. "It took me a while, but I finally figured out why I remembered the name Margaret Fielding. I do volunteer work for the historical society, and I remembered coming across an old newspaper article about a woman by that name who was killed in a car accident outside of Baxter in the early 1950s. This is her death certificate."

She placed the death certificate on the counter, and Laura quickly read through it. "I don't understand," she stammered. "I don't understand this at all."

"What's wrong, dear?" the woman said in a more comforting tone of voice.

"This Margaret Fielding has the same middle name as my mother. Same birthday, too."

><><><

Before leaving the County Recorder's Office, Laura asked for a copy of the death certificate for the Margaret Fielding who had died in a car accident in the early 1950s. She also asked for directions to the country cemetery where Margaret Fielding was buried. As she drove over to the cemetery, questions raced through her mind so quickly that she could not find answers to a single one of them.

*How was it possible for mother and the other Margaret Fielding to have the same middle name and birth date? Why did Selma Madison, who apparently had forgotten just about everything else in her long life, somehow remember the car accident that killed Margaret Fielding? Nothing, absolutely nothing about this entire affair made any sense!*

Laura parked the car outside the gates of a small rural cemetery that was enclosed by tall pine trees. The trees cast huge shadows across the ground as the late afternoon sun descended into the western horizon. She walked up and down the rows of gravestones until she found a granite stone with the name "Fielding" partly exposed beneath some dead leaves. She brushed away the dead leaves and exposed the name "Harold Fielding."

*Dad! How can that be? He's buried in a cemetery in Minneapolis!*

She quickly brushed away the dead vegetation that covered the adjacent stone and exposed the name "Margaret Fielding."

*Mother!*

The two gravestones were inscribed with the years, but not the months and days when Margaret and Harold Fielding were born and died. As Laura glanced to her right, she saw a third stone concealed in the dead grass.

She scrapped the dead grass off the inscription on that stone, revealing the name "Laura Fielding."

*Me!*

# CHAPTER THREE

Laura stayed awake most of the night in her motel room, perplexed by what she had learned that day. She finally concluded that there was only one possible explanation for her mother's letter, the fact that Selma Madison had worked in the Stearns County Recorder's Office for many years, and the names on the three gravestones.

*Selma Madison must have helped Mother and Father establish new identities! But why was it necessary to take such drastic measures? What had they done to apparently fear for their lives so much that they changed their identities? And why did Selma Madison help them? If her role had been exposed, she would have faced a prison sentence!*

Laura was convinced that it did not involve a kidnapping, as Annie had speculated. None of the people involved—her mother, father, and Selma Madison—seemed like the type to do something that criminal. It had to be something else.

*They must have been hiding from someone! But who?*

In the morning, she drove back to the Stearns County Recorder's Office. The woman who had reminded her of Eleanor Roosevelt was standing behind the counter, reading some documents, when she walked into the room. "Back again?" she smiled warmly, but professionally.

"Yes," Laura explained. "I was wondering if I could get copies of death certificates for two more people."

"Did you ever figure out what the problem was with the death certificate you got yesterday? The one for the person who had the same name as your mother."

"Apparently it was a coincidence," Laura lied. She did not want to share what she suspected with anyone else. "But could you see if you have death certificates for Harold Fielding and Laura Fielding? I believe they also died in the car crash that took the life of Margaret Fielding."

"Just a minute," the woman said. She disappeared into the vault and reappeared a few minutes later, carrying two documents.

"Here they are. And yes, you're right, they were killed in that same car accident."

While Laura was paying for the copies of the death certificates, she decided to play a hunch. "Could I also get birth certificates for these people and for the Margaret Fielding who was killed in that same accident?"

"Well, you can if they were born in Stearns County," the woman replied. She glanced at the two documents. "These two were born in this county. Was the other one born here, too?"

"Yes," Laura said. "I believe Margaret Fielding was also born here."

The woman disappeared once more into the vault. Minutes later, she reappeared with a puzzled look on her face. "I can't find birth certificates for any of these people," she said. "That's very unusual."

"Could they be misfiled?" Laura asked.

"Possibly. But it wouldn't be like Selma to do something like that." The woman checked the spellings of the names and quickly disappeared back into the vault. She reappeared minutes later, shaking her head. "I can't find them. Maybe Selma's mind was slipping, and she accidentally placed them in the wrong file."

"Was she in charge of all birth and death certificates for Stearns County?"

"Oh, yes. For over twenty years, Selma cared for those birth and death certificates like a mother caring for her children. The system we still use to file those certificates is the one she developed."

Before leaving the County Recorder's Office, Laura asked for directions to the Stearns County Historical Society. She wanted a copy of the newspaper article describing the deaths of the Fielding family. She also asked if there was a public administrator or public guardian who was handling the sale of Selma Madison's home. She hoped that perhaps she could pose as a prospective buyer and get someone to let her into the house to see if there was anything there that might tell her more about Selma Madison's relationship to her parents.

She picked up the copy of the newspaper article in the basement of the county building, where the historical society was housed. She made another stop on the first floor to speak to the public administrator. A receptionist offered to place a call to a retired county employee in Baxter who had keys to the house. He agreed to meet Laura at the house later that morning.

Afterwards, she found a picnic area in a park on the edge of town. She sat down at one of the concrete tables and placed the death certificates and newspaper article on the pitted tabletop.

Once she had learned that the birth certificates for Harold, Margaret, and Laura Fielding were missing, and that Selma Madison had complete control of those records for many years, she was convinced that Selma had helped her parents set up new identities for themselves. Selma Madison would have been in a perfect position to falsify and forward any requests employers, insurance companies, or government agencies made regarding her parents' birth certificates.

The death certificates confirmed her suspicions. The birth dates for all three members of the Fielding family corresponded to the birth dates for her father, mother, and herself. Everything on the death certificates was identical to what her parents had told her about her own family's birth records.

*Selma Madison must have used her position in the county re-corder's office to protect our family. But why was she so devoted to Mother and Father? And who was she protecting them from?*

The newspaper article did not contain much in the way of new information, except for the details about the accident that killed the Fielding family. The accident occurred on "an icy stretch of Highway 63 on November 11, 1950." According to the article, "The car driven by Harold Fielding apparently hit ice and skidded into the path of an on-coming truck, killing all the occupants." The driver of the truck was uninjured. Harold Fielding "was 34 years old at the time of the accident, his wife Margaret was 32, and their young daughter was 18 months old." The article added that Laura Fielding "was the couple's only child."

*Once she learned that the Fieldings were all dead, Selma Madi-son must have stolen their identities and allowed Mother, Father, and me to use them. So, what were my parents' real names? And why did they agree to such an elaborate scheme? Were they in a witness protection program, and was Selma Madison working for the government to protect them? No, that made no sense either. None of it made any sense. It was too bizarre to make any sense.*

Laura glanced at her watch and realized she was due to meet the retired county employee in front of Selma Madison's house in fifteen minutes. She quickly got in her car and drove to Baxter.

The retired county employee was waiting for her on the front stoop when she parked next to the curb.

"I'm Sam Hanson," he said warmly. "I understand you might be making a bid on this house when it comes up for public auction?"

"I'm thinking about it," Laura lied. "But I need to see the inside first. I don't know if it's exactly what I'm looking for."

"Well, that can be arranged," he said, reaching into his pocket for the key and walking her to the front door. "Real estate market in this town is pretty soft. Mostly retired people living here now, and they don't buy homes. They live in the ones they've lived in all their lives. You moving to Baxter?"

"Maybe," Laura lied, "although I'm thinking of it more as an investment property."

"I'm not too sure this would be much of an investment property," he replied. He swung the door open and gestured at the sheet-covered furniture. "I covered everything myself so it wouldn't get too dusty. I suspect they'll be selling the furniture in a separate auction."

"Are public auctions held when the owner has no relatives or no one is named in the will?"

"Yup, that's the only time you would have a public auction. If there was someone named in the will, or if someone stepped forward and could prove they were a relative who had a legal right to the property, there would be no need for a public auction. But Selma Madison didn't will this property over to anyone, and no one has stepped forward to lay any claim to this house."

As she walked through the house, Laura saw that the furniture in the bedrooms was also covered with sheets. The only things in the entire house that were not draped in sheets were some photographs in the hallway that connected the back bedrooms to the living room. Laura paused in front of the photographs to study them carefully. "Do you recognize any of these people?" she asked, pointing at one of the photographs. "Or where this picture might have been taken?"

"No. Don't know any of them. That picture wasn't taken around here, that's for sure. Looks more like parts of Minnesota than Wisconsin."

"Why do you say that?"

"Well, for one thing, this lake here in the background. It looks more like the area around eastern Minnesota, in the middle of the state. I've been through there many times. I would swear it's one of the lakes I fished on east of the Mississippi River."

"What about these people?" Laura asked, pointing at another photograph of a tall man in a poorly fitting suit, his wife who looked equally uncomfortable in a dress that was several sizes too big for her, and their young daughter who was staring shyly at the camera.

"Nope, never seen them before. But it looks like the picture was taken in the same area as the other one."

Laura thought about saying something more, but she decided against it. Until she knew what she was dealing with, she decided not to tell anyone that the three people in the photograph were her father, mother, and her when they were all much younger.

"Where do you go from here?" Annie asked.

The two women were sitting on wooden lawn chairs in the back yard of Laura's home in Minneapolis. The gables of the huge three-story Victorian home cast long shadows across the lawn. A long line of thick lilac bushes ran parallel to the alley.

"I don't know what to do," Laura admitted.

"How important is it to you?"

"Well, it's my whole life," Laura replied a little sharply. "Suddenly, everything about my life is part of some monstrous lie. I have no idea who I am anymore."

"I guess you're right," Annie agreed. "But aren't you a little scared? Your mother and father were hiding from something or someone. Maybe whatever it was is a threat to you as well."

"Yes," Laura admitted, "it does concern me. But not as much as never knowing who I am, and why my whole life has been a lie. That concerns me even more."

"You never talked much about your father. How did he die?"

"He was killed in an industrial accident when I was about five years old. The only thing I remember about him is how this tall man in dirty work clothes would walk into the house at the end of every day."

"You've lived here all your life?"

"Yes. After he died, Mother used the insurance money to buy the house from the elderly couple who owned it. This is the first year we didn't have any renters. Mother was too sick."

Annie was silent for a moment, and then she said, "I don't know much about insurance, but I would guess an insurance company would need a birth certificate before issuing a policy to your father."

"Yes, I would think so," Laura agreed. "Selma Madison undoubtedly sent the insurance company a copy of the birth certificate for the Harold Fielding who was killed in the car accident."

"What about Social Security numbers?"

"They didn't have Social Security numbers. Neither of them signed up for it."

"It's all too bizarre," Annie exclaimed, shaking her head.

"Yes, it is," Laura agreed.

Annie looked up at the gables at the top of the three-story home. "Laura, you need someone in your life," she said. "You can't live in this big house all by yourself."

"You know my track record with relationships," Laura replied. "I've had a string of them. They all end the same. I pull out as soon as they get serious. It happened with Phillip. Then Tom came into my life. He was one of the sweetest, kindest men I have ever met. But I pulled away from him too. I can't seem to help myself. I don't want to be alone, but everything I do seems to guarantee that I will be alone. It's just the way I am, even if I don't want to be that way."

"I just don't like the idea of you living here alone," Annie insisted. "It's not healthy. Not with everything you're going through."

After Annie left, Laura continued to sit in the back yard, staring at the shadows creeping across the lawn. The back yard had been her favorite place ever since she was a young girl. She was especially fond of the lilac bushes. Every spring, when the lilacs blossomed, she would pick bouquets off the beautiful purple flowers and have her mother put them in a vase on the dining room table. She loved it when the fragrance of the lilacs drifted through the house and into her bedroom. It always made her feel so alive and excited about life. Now, even the lilac flowers could not lift her spirits. She felt herself slipping slowly into a deep depression—and she knew she could not let that happen. Her emotional state was already too fragile.

*How could Mother have kept the deception from me for so long? At some point when I was growing up, wouldn't she have wanted to tell me the truth—so I could protect myself after she was gone? Or maybe that's why she wrote the letter!*

><><><

Laura awoke that night in a panic. She sat straight up in bed and stared into the darkness. She listened to the sounds of the night just outside her bedroom window. She struggled to remember what it was that had frightened her so terribly.

*It's the dream! The one that would wake me up in the middle of the night when I was a child! I would be crying and Mother would come into my bedroom to comfort me!*

She remembered the reoccurring dream from when she was a young girl, and again when she was a teenager. Then, for some reason, the dream had disappeared into the depths of her subconscious mind, where it apparently lay dormant.

*Until now! Something brought it back to life!*

She struggled to remember the details of the dream. She remembered that she was surrounded by darkness, with flashes of sunlight, movement, and unrecognizable faces surging across her memories. Somewhere on the other side of that darkness, it seemed there was a memory so early and so traumatic that it had seared its imprint on the deepest levels of her subconscious mind. Mostly, it was the pervasive sense of fear that surrounded and enveloped her in the darkness.

Memories of the dream had motivated her to be tested at the university as part of a psychology experiment. She was told she had an unusual memory, and perhaps the dream was connected to the way she remembered things. She did not have a photographic memory, and she did not remember everything in vivid detail. But the things she did remember often came back to her in pictures. When her memories involved traumatic or emotional experiences, she was told, "Your visual recall is off the charts."

*Somewhere in my past there are memories hidden behind an impenetrable black veil, and I cannot see through that veil no matter how hard I try.*

Another thought suddenly occurred to her as she listened to the sounds outside her bedroom window. Always before, she had accepted the fact that she was a loner. After what she had learned in Wisconsin, she felt a different kind of loneliness. She felt like she had no connections to the rest of the human race.

*I have no family or relatives who truly define my place in the world. If I am not Laura Fielding, somehow I need to find out who I really am. I must break through the darkness that covers whatever and whoever are on the other side of the dream.*

# CHAPTER FOUR

Dr. Herschler read through the letter Laura's mother had written. Then he studied the death certificates for the Fielding family and the other materials Laura had collected in Wisconsin. When he was finished, he placed them on his desk and looked up at Laura. He seemed to be studying her face, as though seeing her for the first time.

"Have you gone to the authorities with these?" he finally asked. "Stolen identities are prosecutable."

"I don't have anything there that would be considered real evidence. Besides, I don't want to involve the authorities. At least not yet. I need to find out more about what I'm dealing with before I bring anyone else into this bizarre puzzle."

Herschler read through some of the documents again. "The last time we talked you said you always felt like there was something else inside of you, something that belonged somewhere else. Maybe this explains what that something else is."

"What do you mean?"

"Maybe you *were* someone else before you became Laura Fielding. Maybe that's what's still inside of you."

"Dr. Herschler," Laura said hesitantly, "there are some things I've never talked to you about. Things that I didn't feel comfortable discussing with you before."

"What are they?"

"I've had a dream, a couple of them actually, that kept coming back when I was very young. They went away when I was a teenager. But I've just started to have them again."

"What kind of dream?"

"I'm surrounded by darkness, with flashes of sunlight, movement, and unrecognizable faces surging across my memories. I feel very afraid. Why? I don't know. They are very clear, vivid memories. I feel like I knew those people at one time in my life. Yet, I do not know who they were."

"It sounds like you need someone to help you explore those memories to determine where they might come from."

"Are you able to do that?"

"I'm afraid that's somewhat outside my range of expertise. But I do know someone who has made a career of studying early childhood memories and how they relate to our development as adults. His name is Dr. Ned Finley."

"Think he would help me?"

"He might. But you need to know that he is very eccentric. He lives and does all his research at the Farmington State Mental Hospital. He moved his practice and everything he owns into one of the patient's rooms. Some of his ideas are also pretty farfetched. But he has done some important work on human memories."

"How are they farfetched?"

"Well, for one thing he believes human memories may be transferable from one generation to another generation, not intact of course, but enough so they can significantly affect individuals who are susceptible to those kinds of influences."

"Do you think I'm one of those people?"

"I don't know. It can't hurt to talk to him about your dreams and see if he can help you."

A light rain started to fall as Laura approached the Farmington State Mental Hospital. When she turned on the windshield wiper, the water mixed with the dust the car had accumulated during her trip to Wisconsin. One streak of water and dust created an image that looked like a tiny twig with a single leaf at the end. The very next swipe of the wiper blade smeared the image across the windshield, and the next swipe eliminated it.

Through the streaking mixture of water and dust, she saw Farmington's huge walls and tall brick buildings towering above the prairie. She knew that Farmington was an ancient structure, one that had been built in the previous century and renovated periodically throughout the twentieth century. Despite repeated efforts to modernize Farmington to make it look less like a nineteenth century "insane asylum," it continued to look more like a prison than a mental hospital for people with serious psychological disorders.

She parked her car just outside the huge, towering stone walls and quickly passed through the security gate. As a heavier rain fell, she rushed up the granite stairs and into the first floor. A receptionist just inside the front door pointed down an adjacent hallway and said, "Dr. Finley is in room 112, right over there."

Babbling, incoherent voices from somewhere overhead greeted her as she walked down the hallway. A few heavily sedated patients with dazed, expressionless faces sat on wooden benches along one wall of the hallway. The rooms on the other side of the hallway had name plates for various medical personnel attached to the doors. When Laura turned into room 112, she was confronted by a scene that reminded her of television documentaries she had seen of hoarders who filled their homes with everything they had ever accumulated throughout their lives. There were piles of books and papers everywhere. Two rusty filing cabinets were piled high with boxes that almost touched the ceiling. Unhung pictures leaned against the walls and on top of cluttered bookcases.

Dr. Finley was seated behind a desk that was also cluttered with piles of books, files, and papers. Finley was dressed in a green t-shirt and tan pants, and he wore a baseball cap with a faded, indecipherable logo on the front. Even seated he appeared to be a tall man, well over six feet. He had been studying an open file on the desk in front of him when he looked up at Laura.

"Can I help you?" he asked.

"I'm Laura Fielding. We have an appointment."

"Oh, yes, of course," Finley said, pushing the file off to the side. He stood awkwardly and limped over to one of the chairs in front of the desk. He quickly removed a stack of old newspapers on the chair and gestured for Laura to sit down. Then he retreated behind the desk.

"Now, what can I do for you?" he asked warmly as he sat down.

"Dr. Herschler suggested I meet with you," Laura explained.

"Yes, I talked to him yesterday, and he described your situation to me. He said you've been having some very disturbing memories that do not seem to be connected to anything you have ever experienced. How long has this been going on?"

"It started when I was a little girl. Then they went away during my teenage years. After my mother's recent death, they've come back again."

"Dr. Herschler also said you've learned some things about your past that are quite disturbing."

"I found a letter my mother wrote before she died," Laura explained, handing Finley a large envelope. "It's in there, along with some things I gathered in Wisconsin when I tried to locate the woman the letter is addressed to. The letter, the birth certificates, and the newspaper article all indicate that my mother and father switched identities with a couple who were killed in a car accident in the 1950s. They apparently had me assume the identity of their only child. So, I am someone else. Someone who has been living under a false identity for most of my life."

As Finley opened the envelope and read through the contents, Laura surveyed the room. In the back, a small cot and chair were tucked into a space next to the window. A framed pencil drawing of an elderly man who looked very much like Albert Einstein was positioned prominently on top of a reddish-brown wooden book-case near the cot.

As Laura glanced around the room, she concluded that Finley seemed to be the very antithesis of Dr. Herschler. If Herschler was almost obsessive-compulsive in his need to organize and neatly arrange everything in his office, then Finley was obviously some-one who could not stand the very thought of organizing anything into neat, manageable components. She was also convinced if Finley was placed in a line-up of ten people, no one would identify him as a psychiatrist. They might conclude instead that his ec-centricities and manner of dress were more consistent with some-one who was under a psychiatrist's care.

Finley looked up from what he was reading and saw that Lau-ra was studying the contents of his office. "I suppose you wonder why I live like this," he said. He raised his left leg in the air and lifted his pant leg, revealing a prosthetic lower leg strapped just below his knee. "I lost my lower leg in a car accident. A very bad car accident. While it was healing, I decided it was time to sim-plify my life by moving the contents of my office and apartment to Farmington. It's much more convenient for me. I get to observe the patients on a twenty-four-hour basis, and that has been in-valuable to my work. I haven't been outside these walls in over three years. I don't know that I will ever go out again. Everything I need is here."

"I guess it wasn't what I was expecting," Laura replied awkwardly.

"Nor should you have," Finley replied sympathetically. "As for that drawing on top of the bookcase, the one you were looking at earlier, that's an old friend of mine. His name is Aurther Schle-pler. It's a self-portrait. He drew it himself."

"He looks like Albert Einstein."

"Indeed, he does," Finley agreed. "Aurther lived in this very room for many years. Then a few years back, he just stopped communicating with everyone. They moved him to the third floor where he spends most of his time sitting in a wheelchair staring out the window. I visit him every day and talk to him, but he does not respond to me or anyone else."

"Dementia?" Laura asked.

"We don't know what it is," Finley said, shaking his head. "Aurther has been retreating from the human race for as long as I've known him. Maybe this is his final retreat. Aurther's a psychic. He once worked with police on high-profile murder cases. He saw too much. I don't think he wanted to see anything more about the cruelties the human race is capable of inflicting on one another. So, he just checked out, maybe permanently."

Finley read through the materials in the envelope again. Minutes later, he raised his prosthetic leg and rested it on the desk. He leaned back in his chair and looked at Laura. "This is indeed quite ominous," he said. "What do you want from me?"

"Dr. Herschler said you were an expert on human memories. He thought maybe you could help me find out how my memories are connected to everything in that envelope."

"Shouldn't you go to the police with what you have here? It sounds like you could have been kidnapped as a young girl and raised by a different family than your natural parents."

"I thought about that. But it doesn't really make any sense. If I was kidnapped, why would the people I thought were my parents change their names, too? That involved a very elaborate scheme that wouldn't have been necessary if they had simply brought me into their home and changed my name, while keeping their own names."

"Yes, it would have been much easier," Finley agreed.

"They must have been hiding themselves and me from someone. That's the only explanation I can come up with."

Finley stood and walked slowly over to the cot in the rear of the room. He glanced out the window and then turned to face Laura. "I've had many patients who have memories that don't seem to come from anywhere in their lives," he speculated. "Most of them are psychotic. But in your case, there seems to be a more logical explanation. Apparently, you *were* someone else before you became the person you are today. The memories you have are undoubtedly based on the experiences you had before you became Laura Fielding . . ."

"I would have been very young," Laura interjected.

"My research with the patients in this hospital has revealed that we have memories from the moment we enter the world. Maybe even earlier than that. They are just not very well defined. But they are there."

"If they are deeply troubling memories, how do people get to the source of them so they can be resolved?"

"Regressive hypnosis is one way, but I wouldn't recommend it yet."

"Why?"

"It can dredge up all kinds of memories, some that would probably be better left buried in the maze of your subconscious mind. Before we do that, I would recommend you take what you have learned from the documents in this envelope and do some detective work to see if you can follow the path they are illuminating for you. I would also like you to leave them with me for a few days so I can look at them more closely. If that doesn't work, we can try hypnosis."

"Did Dr. Herschler also tell you that he believes I have a bonding disorder. I have struggled with relationships all my life."

"Yes, he did tell me that," Finley admitted. "Do you have any friends?"

"Just Annie, another graduate student. None of my other friendships ever lasted. At some point, I start pushing people away."

"Why do you think your friendship with her has lasted, while the others didn't?"

"I don't know."

"I'm a bit of a loner myself," Finley admitted. "I only have one close friend. The elderly fellow who drew that self-portrait of himself over there. But my reasons for being a loner are different than yours."

"Do you think a bonding disorder could be connected to whatever happened to me when I was very young?"

"Absolutely," Finley replied, tapping on his pant leg. "A bonding disorder can grow out of early childhood traumas and be just as debilitating as the car accident that resulted in the amputation of my lower leg. I can still feel my foot, even though it is no longer there. So, too, adults feel the effects of childhood traumas, even if they no longer remember them on the conscious level. The human mind is as complex as the cluttered contents of this room. But there are generally connective patterns that we can see if we look deeply enough into our own lives and the lives of those who preceded us."

><><><><

Later that day, Ned Finley stood at the bottom of the first-floor staircase pondering whether to take the elevator or walk up the stairs to Farmington's third floor. He often joked to the hospital staff that he didn't know which he missed more: his foot or the 1953 Studebaker that had been destroyed when a truck hit him head on. When he had to climb stairs, however, it was no longer a joke. The prosthesis worked well on flat surfaces, but it was awkward and clumsy on stairs. Still, he tried to walk Farmington's staircases whenever possible, just to get the exercise and to become more comfortable with walking on different surfaces.

Deciding this was not one of those times, he turned and walked over to the elevator near the receptionist's desk. He tucked the envelope Laura had left with him under his arm and pushed the call button. He could hear the elevator rumble and creak as it neared the first floor. Like everything else at Farmington, the elevator was part of an earlier renovation project, and it was not aging well.

Finley stepped into the elevator and pushed the button for the third floor. The groaning and creaking of the cable system was even louder inside the elevator. He watched the lights on the control panel as the elevator passed the second floor, where Farmington's most dangerous patients were isolated, and approached the third floor, where patients with extreme dementia or catatonia were housed.

The elevator door opened slowly on the third floor, and Finley made his way past several patients in wheelchairs who were staring idly at their hands or the floor. In a lobby at the end of a hallway he spotted a small, white-haired man sitting in a wheelchair next to a large window. Aurther Schlepler's demeanor did not change in any way as Finley approached. He continued to stare out the window at the dark prairie and the twinkling farm lights on the horizon.

"So, how are you this evening, Aurther?" Finley asked cheerfully, walking over to Schlepler and patting him gently on the shoulder. "Anything new up here on the third floor? Not much going on down below, except that I do have a new case that I thought you might be interested in."

Finley removed the contents of the envelope and placed the letter, death certificates, and newspaper article on Schlepler's lap. "A young woman named Laura Fielding came into my office today," he explained. "She brought these with her. It seems the people she thought were her parents have lied to her. For some reason, they changed their own identities and her identity when she was very young. She's asked me to help her find out who she really is."

Finley leaned forward and looked into Schlepler's eyes, but there was nothing that indicated the elderly psychic had heard him. "Aurther," Finley said, "I know you're no longer interested in these kind of things. I know your interests are elsewhere. But if you change your mind, I'll leave this envelope with you. I'll be back tomorrow to talk about it." He carefully put everything back in the envelope and placed it on Schlepler's lap. "I think the young woman in this case is really very much alone in the world. I think she could use our help."

Finley patted Schlepler gently on the shoulder again. Then he walked over to the nurse's station. A young nurse looked up at him as he leaned his elbows on the counter.

"I left an envelope with some important documents on Aurther's lap. I know it's a long shot, but I was hoping he might develop an interest in them."

"I haven't heard him say anything or read anything in all the time I've been working here," the nurse replied.

"I guess there's always a first time. When you take him back to his room, would you place the envelope in the top drawer of his vanity? Just remind him that it'll be there if he wants to look through it. I'll pick it up tomorrow."

Finley immediately walked over to the elevator. As he waited for the door to open, he looked back at the area where Aurther was sitting in the wheelchair. Schlepler had not moved. He was still staring out the window at the dark Midwestern prairie.

By the time Laura returned from Farmington, it was early evening. She was still tired from her trip, so she decided to go to bed

early. Before turning off the light on her nightstand, she reached
for her mother's Bible and paged slowly through the *Book of Genesis*. She continued to get some comfort from holding the Bible
and reading the passages her mother had thought were important enough to be underlined in pencil.

There didn't seem to be any connecting threads to the passages her mother had underlined. They were a mixture of passages that focused on ancient biblical events and other passages
that contained little seeds of wisdom that summarized the morals
of biblical stories. Nothing seemed unusual or different, until she
turned the page to Chapter Twenty-nine of the Book of Genesis,
which described how the biblical Jacob met and married Rachel.
On that page her mother had underlined a long passage:

> Now Laban had two daughters; the name of the older was Leah,
> and the name of the younger was Rachel. Leah's eyes were weak,
> but Rachel was beautiful and lovely. Jacob loved Rachel; and
> he said, "I will serve you seven years for your younger daughter
> Rachel." Laban said, "It is better that I give her to you than that
> I should give her to any other man; stay with me." So, Jacob
> served seven years for Rachel, and they seemed to him but a few
> days because of the love he had for her.

In the right margin next to the passage, her mother had written in bold pencil, "So many lies!!!"

*Lies! What kind of lies?*

Perplexed as to why her mother had commented on that particular passage, especially in such strong language, Laura paged
quickly through several other books in the Old and New Testaments to see if there were other comments. Her mother had underlined other passages throughout the Bible, but she had not
commented on any of them except the passage about Jacob and
Rachel in the *Book of Genesis*.

At the end of the Bible, something on the cardboard insert
attached to the back cover caught her eye. What was most likely
a name and date had been erased, leaving only a smudge mark.
But she could see the faint traces of two words that had not been
so thoroughly deleted.

She retrieved a magnifying glass from her desk on the other
end of the room and held it over the cardboard insert. The handwritten words, "Point Tyson," were faintly visible on the yellowish-brown surface.

Playing a hunch, she rushed down the hallway to her mother's room. She had seen a map of Minnesota in the closet when she had been going through her mother's things. She retrieved the map and rushed back to her bedroom.

She placed the map under the light on her nightstand and read through the index. Point Tyson was listed under J-22. She quickly spread out the map on the bed. She located the letter J in the left-hand column and the number 22 at the bottom of the map. They intersected in an area some forty or fifty miles east of the Mississippi River, not too far from the Wisconsin border.

*That's where the retired county employee who showed me Selma Madison's home said he thought the photograph of Mother, Father, and me was taken.*

# CHAPTER FIVE

Puddles of water lingered in many of the ditches and adjacent fields as Laura left the interstate highway and drove north on a succession of state and county roads. Tractors and plows were moving up and down the countryside. In some of the fields, small green cornstalks were protruding out of the glistening black furrows. In other fields, cattle and dairy cows were grazing on plush green grass that covered the pastures.

Laura had some mixed feelings about her decision to spend a few days in Point Tyson. She had no plan whatsoever. She was casting her line into unknown and muddy waters. She knew the likelihood that she would catch anything was extremely remote.

*This could easily be a wild goose chase, but it's all I have to work with. Maybe the thing to do is to start out by asking if the name Selma Madison means anything to the residents of Point Tyson. If not, I can try something else.*

Earlier she had stopped by Farmington to show Dr. Finley the strange marginal comment her mother had written in the Bible next to the story of Rachel. The receptionist said he was working elsewhere in the hospital and would not be able to see her until later in the day. Laura decided to leave the Bible with a note referring to the passage her mother had commented on so vehemently. She also informed Finley that she was on her way to Point Tyson. The receptionist said she would make sure he received the Bible and the note as soon as he returned to his office.

An hour after Laura left Farmington, she approached a sign that indicated she was crossing the "Archer County Line." Next to the sign, a huge farm dog with matted red fur was plodding wearily alongside the shoulder of the road. For the next ten miles, she drove on a county road that angled off in a northeasterly direction. She saw a sign next to a bridge indicating she was about to cross the "Lonely Willow River." On the same wooden post, a black arrow on another sign indicated, "Point Tyson City Cemetery, 2 miles east."

Laura parked on the shoulder of the road and glanced down at an open map on the passenger seat. She saw that the Lonely Willow River flowed in a southerly direction, except for a three or four mile stretch that angled sharply east, before flowing south again. She realized she was crossing the river at the precise point where it started to flow east.

The bridge was constructed out of iron beams and posts that were rusty with age. Climbing vines filled with blossoming yellow flowers covered the support beams that were anchored near the adjacent ditches. The road across the bridge was constructed out of thick wooden planks that groaned and rumbled under the weight of the car.

The car had just crossed the bridge when Laura sensed a blur of activity to her right. She watched as a huge buck deer bolted out of the ditch and leaped across the road thirty or forty feet in front of her car. She hit the brakes and the car came to a screeching halt as the deer disappeared into a grove of trees on the other side of the road.

*That was too close!*

She took a deep breath and continued driving at a slower speed. She passed through an area with large granite boulders protruding out of a pasture. As she watched three cows trudge slowly across the pasture, a thin human figure in bib overalls walked out of the ditch and stood on the shoulder of the road. The man's eyes were fixed on the ground, and he seemed oblivious to his surroundings. After Laura passed the area where the man was standing, she glanced in her rear-view mirror and saw him cross the road and shuffle into the adjacent fields.

On the outskirts of Point Tyson, the Lonely Willow River curled around the western edge of the small town. The river widened considerably in that area, creating the impression that Point Tyson jutted out into a small lake.

Spotting a service station on the edge of town, Laura decided to get gas and ask for directions to the nearest hotel or motel. The station attendant, a bearded middle-aged man in grease-stained bib overalls, was sitting in a lawn chair, gazing into the distance. When she pulled up to the pump, he pushed himself wearily from the chair and shuffled over to her car.

"Please fill it up," she said, slowly getting out of the car to stretch.

Without speaking, the attendant inserted the nozzle into the gas tank, placed it in the locked position, and began to clean the windows of the car with a large sponge. A small white ball bounced around inside the gas-filled, glass chamber of the pump, while the meter obediently clicked off the gallons of gasoline as they flowed into the gas tank.

"Tell me," Laura said, "where is the nearest motel or hotel in Point Tyson?"

"We don't have a hotel anymore," the attendant replied, looking up at her from the rear of the car. "Closed many years ago. Never did have a motel."

"Where do visitors stay for the night?"

"Well, actually, most of them don't. They drive over to Pelican Lake, about nine miles north of here. It's the county seat. It has two motels and one hotel."

"So, there's no place in Point Tyson where you can rent a room for the night?"

"I didn't say that. I just said we don't have a motel or hotel. We do have a bed and breakfast. It's on the other end of town. Gunda Arneson runs it."

Laura looked in the direction of Point Tyson. "Tell me something. Have you ever heard of a Selma Madison who might have lived around here?" she asked.

"Nope, never heard of anyone by that name," the attendant replied.

Sensing that the attendant did not want to talk any more than was absolutely necessary, Laura paid for the gasoline and drove into Point Tyson. Small stores and shops, some with empty second-story apartments and curtainless windows overlooking Main Street, were lined up along both sides of a city park in the very center of town. Most of the stores were boarded up and unoccupied. Others had been demolished, and the bricks and lumber hauled away. One empty lot was littered with two abandoned automobiles and a pile of old wooden beams, apparently left behind after the building had been demolished.

Many of the remaining buildings had been constructed out of red granite blocks like the ones Laura had seen protruding out of the pastures on the outskirts of town. Three of those buildings—a general store, café, and small grocery store—appeared to be the only functioning enterprises left on Main Street. An apparently abandoned telephone booth was located next to a mailbox that had weathered and rusted until it had turned a greenish-brown color.

Several huge, towering elm trees were scattered around the park. Other trees had Dutch elm disease. Their blackened, leafless branches had stiffened with age and remained motionless in the breeze that swept through the small town.

A few elderly people were sitting on the benches and chairs that were organized around a small bandstand and concrete dance floor in the middle of the park. Thick weeds grew out of huge cracks that zigzagged across the concrete surface of the dance floor.

*There's not much left of this town. If what I'm looking for is in Point Tyson, it's probably going to be awfully hard to find.*

Spotting a historical marker in a large granite boulder in the middle of the park, she decided to park her car and walk over to read it.

*This is as good a place as any to start learning more about Point Tyson.*

As she approached the marker, an elderly man wearing a faded blue work cap looked up at her from where he was reading a newspaper on a park bench. He nodded politely at her as she paused in front of the historical marker.

The marker, which was badly tarnished from wind and water erosion, read: "Welcome to Point Tyson, the Granite Capital of America. Since 1880, granite mined in this area has been shipped downriver to be cut and polished for building stones and cemetery stones. Point Tyson granite is considered some of the highest quality granite in the upper Midwest." At the bottom of the marker, the words "Point Tyson Chamber of Commerce, 1926" were engraved.

"Not that way anymore," Laura heard a voice behind her say.

Turning, she saw that the elderly man sitting on the park bench had walked over to join her. "What do you mean?" she asked.

"That marker was placed there when Point Tyson was a prosperous little community. Not anymore. As you can see, Main Street's just about all boarded up."

"What happened to Point Tyson?"

"Other parts of the state started finding high grade granite closer to the railroad lines and highways. Companies set up processing plants right there. It was cheaper and much more convenient. Pretty much put our local granite companies out of business."

She looked up and down Main Street at the many boarded-up shops and stores. Then she looked back at the marker. "How . . ."

"Pete Solvie's the name, by the way," he said, extending his hand.

"How long have you lived in Point Tyson?"

"All my life."

"Did you ever hear of someone by the name of Selma Madison who might have lived here?"

"Nope. Never heard of anyone by that name. There were some Madisons who lived here, as I remember, back in the 1930s and 1940s. But no one by that name. Why do you ask?"

"I was just wondering," Laura replied evasively.

Laura spotted a restored Victorian home with yellow siding and white decorative trim on top of a small hill on the northern edge of town. A wooden sign next to the road read, "Gunda's Bed and Breakfast." Laura turned into a gravel-covered driveway and drove up to the house.

She parked the car and was greeted at the front porch by an elderly woman who smiled warmly at her. The woman, who wore a white apron and a yellow dress that matched the color of the house, leaned on a cane with one hand and a guardrail with the other. "Welcome to Gunda's Bed and Breakfast," she greeted Laura cheerfully. "I'm Gunda."

"I'm Laura Fielding," Laura replied, joining the elderly woman on the porch. "I'm looking for a room for a couple of days. Do you have one?"

"Oh, my, yes. There's been no rush on these rooms. Not since I opened. Always nice to have company, though."

"Where do I register?"

"We can deal with that later," Gunda said with a gentle wave of her hand. "Why don't you just sit down out here on the porch? I'll get some cookies and coffee, and we can visit a little first." She hung the cane on the guardrail. "Don't need this all the time," she explained. "Only when the arthritis acts up. I'll be right back."

Gunda limped into the house and returned moments later carrying a tray with a coffee pot, two cups, and a plate filled with oatmeal cookies. "Just baked these," she explained, placing the tray on a small wooden table next to two chairs. "It's best to eat them when they're warm. How long you staying?"

"I'm not sure," Laura replied.

"Here on business?"

"No. I'm doing a research project on the old granite quarries," Laura lied, deciding it was wise not to reveal her real reason for being in Point Tyson, at least for a while. "I'm a graduate student at the University of Minnesota."

"Didn't think you were here on business," Gunda said, slumping slowly into the wooden chair. "Not much business left in Point Tyson, I'm afraid."

"How long have you lived here?"

"Well, I was born and raised here. Worked here, too, until the quarries closed. Then I moved to Chicago and lived there until I retired. I got kind of a hunger inside of me to come back to this small town. I thought maybe it would be nice to have a bed and breakfast, just to keep busy. But it's not the town I remember."

"When did you leave Point Tyson?"

"1946. Didn't come back until 1966."

"Does the name Selma Madison mean anything to you?" Laura asked. "I was wondering if she ever lived around here."

"Madison? Hmm. Well, there were some Madisons who lived around here when I went to school. But they're long gone. Along with everyone else, I'm afraid. But I don't remember that any of them was named Selma."

Laura looked out at the Lonely Willow River and the open fields beyond. The man in bib overalls she had seen outside of town was walking slowly, methodically next to the river. His eyes were fixed on the ground, while he shuffled steadily across a small pasture.

"Who is that?" she asked. "I saw him at the other end of town, just before I drove into Point Tyson."

"That's Sheldon Andert," Gunda replied, reaching for another cookie. "He does that every day."

"Does what?"

"Just walks. He circles the town twice, just like a clock. You can set your watch by him. Sheldon's always been different. He was born that way. But he didn't start walking around this town until he was older. Something must have happened to him, and he just decided to start walking. People in Point Tyson are so accustomed to seeing him circle the town that no one pays attention to him anymore."

><><><><

Gunda Arneson assigned Laura a bedroom above the front porch, where she would have a view of the sunset. Laura sat in a padded easy chair and looked out the window until long after the sun had disappeared behind the horizon.

She felt a little foolish for having driven so far without any clear plan. It seemed like such a long shot. The mere fact that she had been able to identify the words "Point Tyson" on the cardboard insert of her mother's Bible didn't really mean much of anything. Still, it was the only clue she had to work with, and she was determined to find out if it was relevant in any way to the deep mystery that shrouded her own past.

*At least it's a start. If Selma Madison lived in Point Tyson, then there's a good chance Mother and Father also lived in this small town. If I can find out who they were before they changed their names, maybe I can also learn why they changed their names. And maybe I can figure out why it was so important for all of us to go into hiding.*

She had decided that she would not ask any direct questions about her parents until she knew more about what had motivated them to assume new identities. She would inquire about Selma Madison first. She was apprehensive that whoever her parents were hiding from might still pose a threat to her.

*Whoever Mother and Father were hiding from might still be in this small town!*

><><><><

Finley stepped out of the third-floor elevator and walked over to the window where Aurther Schlepler's wheelchair had been parked the previous evening. Seeing that Schlepler was not there, he walked down to his friend's room. Schlepler was asleep on his bed, his small frame covered by a single sheet. He slept peacefully, his breathing deep and quiet.

Finley opened the top drawer of the vanity next to the bathroom and saw that it was empty. He opened the next drawer down and found the envelope he had left with Schlepler the previous evening. On the way back to the elevator, he decided to stop at the nurse's station where the young nurse was making notations on some charts.

"Do you know if Aurther looked at this envelope?" Finley asked.

"No, he didn't," the nurse replied. "The envelope was unopened and sitting on his lap last night when I went down there to take him back to his room. I put it in the top drawer of his vanity and told him it was there, as you requested."

"Are you sure you placed it in the top drawer?"

"Yes. Why do you ask?"

"Because it was in the second drawer from the top."

"That's not where I left it," the nurse said emphatically. "I put it right where you told me to put it."

"Is it possible somebody else might have moved it?"

"Not very likely. There would be no reason for them to move it."

A puzzled look spread across Finley's face as he turned slowly and looked back in the direction of Schlepler's room.

In the morning, while Laura ate breakfast on the front porch of the bed and breakfast, Gunda told her about a local businessman who knew a lot about Archer County history. She said his name was Sibley Fields, and he had converted an old icehouse he had inherited into an antiques warehouse.

As Laura pulled up to the barn-like structure near the river, she saw the faded words, "Point Tyson Ice House," painted across the top of the front door. A newer sign advertised the ancient structure as "Sibley's Antiques Warehouse." Several partially submerged, rotting wooden posts protruded out of the water, the last decaying remnants of a dock that had once extended out into the river.

When she walked into the building, she had the immediate impression that Sibley Fields had somehow managed to collect every marketable item that could be salvaged from all the other enterprises on Main Street. There was furniture of every size and description, two old pool tables, a long wooden bar with a brass rail, a hand-cranked printing press, and many other items that had undoubtedly once been used by downtown businesses during more prosperous times.

She spotted a thin, balding man examining a reddish-brown mahogany chest of draws in the rear of the warehouse. Sibley

Fields had unusually long, thin fingers. As he ran them along the grains of wood in the chest of drawers, she was reminded of the way a concert pianist gently coaxes music out of a piano keyboard.

"Are you Sibley Fields?" Laura asked.

"Yes, I am," he replied, looking up at her. "What can I do for you?"

"Gunda Arneson sent me over. She said you might be able to help me."

"Are you an antiques dealer?"

"No. I'm a graduate student. My name is Laura Fielding. I'm doing a research paper on the old quarries in this area. I'm also interested in some people who once lived around here."

"Well, I've lived here all my life. What do you need to know?"

"Have you ever heard of someone by the name of Selma Madison who might have lived in this area?"

Sibley leaned his elbow on top of the chest of drawers and looked at the other end of the room. "Nope," he said, shaking his head. "Can't say I've ever heard that name before."

"Think anybody by that name might have lived in Point Tyson?"

"I can pretty much guarantee you no one by that name ever lived in Point Tyson. Now, did someone by that name ever live in Archer County? That, I don't know. There are several other towns in the county you know."

"Yes, I know that. Do . . ."

"Tell you what you might do, though," Sibley said, interrupting her. "You might go over to the newspaper office and read through some of the old *Point Tyson Chronicles*. It was more of a local gossip sheet than a newspaper. There was so little news in this town that whenever someone visited someone else, they wrote it up in the paper. If this Selma Madison ever lived in Point Tyson, her name would have to pop up on one of those pages."

Laura glanced out one of the dusty windows. "I didn't realize you still have a newspaper. Your Main Street looks pretty abandoned."

"We don't have a newspaper anymore," Sibley said, gesturing at the printing press Laura had noticed earlier. "I've already sold most of the equipment, except for that printing press over there. But the newspapers from years back are still stacked around the floor of the building where the Chronicle was published. Nobody wants them, and I don't know what to do with them."

"Where is it located?"

"On a side street, a few doors down from the bank." Sibley walked over to a roll-top desk, opened one of the drawers, and pulled out a key. "Here," he said, handing the key to Laura. "Just return this when you're done with it."

Laura looked around the room at the many antiques that cluttered the warehouse floor. "Looks like there are a lot of memories here," she said. "Did all of these antiques come from the stores in Point Tyson?"

"Ya, they sure did. That scale over there used to be in the drugstore. And that sign was above Dr. Warner's Office. That popcorn machine was in a little soda shop that belonged to Tom Wozniak. Rumor was that he was running from the Chicago mob, and he came to Point Tyson because he figured no one would ever come looking for him here."

"Do you think the rumor was true?"

"Nah, small town people gossip. Pretty soon they've taken something that has the tiniest grain of truth in it, and they use it to bake a whole bread of lies. Tom was a sweet, gentle old man. No way that he was involved with criminals."

"What was the 'tiniest grain of truth' in the gossip?" Laura asked.

"I don't know," Sibley replied, shaking his head.

Laura studied the popcorn machine for several seconds. "I'll bring the key back later," she said, turning to leave.

"You know, you are right, though," Sibley mused softly.

"About what?"

"What you said about memories. This icehouse was one of the first businesses in Point Tyson to go under. Way back in the 1940s. Modern refrigerators put my father out of business. Everyone felt sorry for him. Then the quarries closed and other businesses started folding, one by one. Since then, I've been selling off what remains of the town piece by piece. Now, this old icehouse has been converted into an antiques warehouse, and it's once again a profitable business. I don't feel good about it. But I guess someone has to dismantle a town after its time is up."

Laura parked on a side street near the abandoned bank building and walked up to the front door of another building that had been constructed out of red granite blocks. *Point Tyson Chronicle* was stenciled in faded letters across both front windows. When she turned the key in the lock and opened the front door, she was greeted by a dank, moldy smell from somewhere in the semi-darkened room.

The abandoned newspaper office was empty except for one small table and chair that had been placed next to a window over-looking the alley. Other than that, the room contained nothing but piles of yellowish-brown newspapers stacked around all four walls.

*This seems more impossible than it did before. Where do I even start?*

She wandered from pile to pile until she settled on one that contained newspapers from the late 1940s to the early 1950s, none of them arranged in chronological order. The *Point Tyson Chronicle*, a weekly newspaper, had been treated rather shabbily by whoever had dumped the newspapers on the floor before abandoning the premises.

She hauled several of the newspapers over to the table and used the light streaming through the back window to read them. For almost three hours, she worked her way through the pile of dusty newspapers. Front-page stories sometimes addressed national events pertaining to the Eisenhower-Stevenson presidential campaigns, the rising presence of Senator Joe McCarthy in national politics, and news regarding the Korean War. Mostly, as Sibley had said, the newspaper focused on local news and community social events.

As she skimmed through the social columns, she realized Selma Madison might not even be the elderly woman's real name. Maybe it was a married name, although that did not seem very likely from what people in Baxter, Wisconsin, had told her about the elderly recluse. But if it was necessary to find new identities for her mother and father, Laura speculated that Selma could also have changed her own name. If so, she realized her search would be futile. Still, she plodded through paper after paper, searching for any reference to Selma Madison.

She spent the rest of the day rummaging through old copies of the *Point Tyson Chronicle*. She learned a good deal about the local culture of the small town, but there was no mention whatsoever of anyone by the name of Selma Madison. She was reading an article about a social event in some elderly matron's home, when she sensed a slight, shadowy movement to her left. Looking up, she saw what looked like a face appear and disappear in the corner of the dirt-stained window overlooking the alley.

She quickly leaned forward and tried to look through the dirty windowpane to see into the alley. The late-afternoon sunlight reflecting on the window made it impossible to see much of anything. She tried to open the window lock, but it was so rusty and corroded it would not budge. Shielding her eyes from the sunlight, she glanced once again up and down the alley, but could see nothing unusual. Finally, she turned and stared into the shadows that covered the abandoned newspaper office.

*Don't let your imagination get the best of you, Laura!*

# CHAPTER SIX

Laura returned to the newspaper office early the next day. She spent the entire morning and much of the afternoon reading through the old editions of the *Point Tyson Chronicle*. Nothing she read shed any light on Selma Madison. But she did find some interesting articles on local events. The May 6, 1952, edition of the *Point Tyson Chronicle* had headlines that announced the tragic death of State Senator Norbert Samuelson. An accompanying news article described how Samuelson had drowned when his boat overturned on the Lonely Willow River. Samuelson's body, which was described as having been "battered against rocks and granite boulders by the current," had been found miles downstream.

A June edition of the newspaper described the intense political maneuverings that followed in the wake of Samuelson's tragic death, as various candidates positioned themselves for the vacated seat in the state legislature.

Laura had just about decided to call it quits for the day, when she discovered a May 20, 1952, edition that described an unusual incident that had occurred on May 15th of that same year:

Rachel Sims, wife of local farmer Grant Sims, mysteriously disappeared on May 15th of this year. Although Mrs. Sims's current whereabouts is a deep mystery, Albert Felstuhl, who farms in the area, claims to have seen her walking across the riverbed near Hodges Island shortly before she disappeared. Others have claimed they saw her in the company of a well-dressed man who was driving a car with Iowa license plates.

Grant Sims, husband of the missing woman, says he has found a pink ribbon belonging to his wife on Hodges Island near the old quarry buildings. Mr. Sims says the ribbon was tied around some lilac flowers, most likely picked by his wife before she mysteriously disappeared.

Mr. Sims has offered a reward of $10 to anyone who can lead him to his wife's whereabouts. Persons with information regarding Mrs. Sims are requested to contact Mr. Sims or this newspaper.

Laura leaned back in the chair and stared out the window at the alley. Then she read the newspaper article again.

*Was this the "Rachel" Mother was referring to when she wrote, "So many lies," in her Bible?*

><><><

"Find what you were looking for?" Sibley asked as Laura walked into the antiques warehouse.

"No," she replied. "But I found something else that was interesting. Did you ever hear of a Rachel Sims who disappeared near a place called Hodges Island in 1952?"

"Yes, I remember that incident," Sibley said, nodding.

"Did they ever find her?"

"No."

"Did anyone ever figure out what might have happened to her?"

"No. There were a lot of rumors. But I don't know if any of them are true. Most people thought she left her husband for another man."

"What do you think?"

"I don't know. I hate to accept small town gossip, but this time they just might be right."

"Why do you say that?"

"Doesn't seem to be any other explanation for what happened to her."

"Does she have any relatives who still live around here?"

"I don't know. She was part of that church community a few miles east of here. The First Sentinels of God is what they call themselves. There are only a few of them left."

"Think any of them would remember her?"

"They might. But I don't know what you'd get out of them. They kept to themselves. Never mingled much with the townspeople. They were a strange lot. Didn't believe in electricity or photography or cars or anything they associated with the modern world. I tell you what, though. There is one fellow who would definitely remember Rachel Sims. But you probably can't trust his word on anything. His name is Charlie Flanigan. For years, people around town called him 'Crazy Charlie' 'cause he was always kind of different."

"Where can I find him?"

"Far as I know, he still lives in his shack in the Point Tyson City Cemetery, about two miles east of here, on the banks of the Lonely Willow River."

"And you think he would still remember this Rachel Sims?"

"I know he would. But like I said, you can't trust anything he tells you. For years after she disappeared, he claimed he could see her wandering on the opposite riverbank, which is Hodges Island. I don't know if he still tells people that story. But he swore it was the truth. He said it was Rachel Sims. He called her the 'lilac lady' and he swore she came out every spring when the lilacs were in bloom."

A flood of unanswered questions rushed through Laura's mind as she got into her car and drove out of town toward the cemetery.

*Rachel Sims? Is that the connection I'm looking for? When mother wrote, "So many lies," in the margin next to the story of the biblical Rachel, was she referring to the story of Rachel Sims's disappearance as it was described in the Point Tyson Chronicle? Or is all of this just coincidence, and I'm deluding myself with trying to find connections where none exists.*

Laura turned left at the sign that indicated the Point Tyson City Cemetery was located two miles east of the main highway. As she drove on a narrow gravel road, she could see the Lonely Willow River at the bottom of a long, sloping embankment. Through the trees, she caught glimpses of a dam-like structure. The undulating glimpses of the dam through the openings in the trees made her feel strangely uneasy, almost like it was a sinister presence slithering through the openings in the trees.

*Why am I feeling this way about a place I've never been before? Or maybe I have been here before?*

Several tall, moss-covered tombstones protruded out of the grass and weeds as she approached the cemetery. Huge elm and maple trees were also scattered around the cemetery, their branches swaying slowly in the afternoon breeze.

An ancient stone fence constructed out of granite rocks enclosed the cemetery. Many sections of the fence had fallen to the ground or tilted at awkward angles to the earth, almost as though imitating the tombstones, very few of which stood erect.

She parked the car on the shoulder of the gravel road and walked into the cemetery through a wrought-iron gate that hung by one hinge from a concrete fence post. The path was overgrown with weeds and grass, and some sections were wet from a previous rain.

The marble and granite surfaces of the tombstones on both sides of the path were darkened from exposure to wind and rain. Most of the names and inscriptions were still legible, some dating back to the 1870s and 1880s. Some of the inscriptions indicated that the graves were for soldiers who had fought and died in World War I and World War II. A few of the stones indicated the graves were for veterans of the Korean War.

In the middle of the cemetery, the statue of a young World War I soldier towered above the other gravestones. The soldier was carrying a rifle in one hand, while he glanced over his shoulder and gestured for his fellow infantrymen to follow him into battle. His other hand had broken off, however, and the young soldier appeared instead to be gazing horror-stricken at the stump that was once his arm.

Near the river's edge, Laura spotted a tiny white cabin that appeared to be a storage shed some enterprising person had converted into a home. On the other side of the cabin, the embankment sloped down to the shoreline, allowing for a clear view of the Lonely Willow River.

An elderly man was cleaning fish on a plank nailed to the trunk of a huge fallen tree near the river's edge. The roots of the tree dangled above a large, black hole in the earth. The trunk and some of the longer branches extended out into the river. A rowboat, tied to one of the branches, bobbed up and down in the water as the river's current lapped against the shore.

"Looks like you've had some strong winds over here," Laura said, walking over to the fallen tree. "I take it you're Charlie Flanigan."

"Yup," Charlie muttered without looking up.

Charlie's forearms were covered with fish scales, and his fingers were smeared with blood. A faded, blue stocking cap was unraveling on top of his head, and his flannel shirt was open, revealing thick tufts of gray hair on a muscular chest.

"Tornado?" Laura asked, gesturing at the uprooted tree.

"Thunderstorm," Charlie replied. He stood more erect and nodded toward the cemetery stones on top of the embankment. "If you're tryin' ta find a grave, I can prob'ly help ya. I know just 'bout everyone who's buried in this cem'tery."

Laura noticed that Charlie's spine was slightly curved, bending him forward. It reminded her of some of the cemetery stones she had just seen. Nothing, it seemed, in the cemetery was erect anymore, not even the caretaker. "No, I'm not trying to find a grave," she explained slowly. "I'm trying to see if anyone in Point Tyson can help me locate some people my mother knew."

"Who is it you're lookin' for?"

"Selma Madison. Do you know if anyone by that name ever lived in Point Tyson?"

Charlie shook his head slowly. "Nah, I've never heard of anyone by that name. But I'm not the one ya should be askin'. I haven't had much to do with the people in Point Tyson for many years. They leave me 'lone, and I leave them 'lone."

Laura stared across the river at the thick trees and blossoming lilac bushes on the opposite riverbank. "There's someone else I'm curious about, too."

"Who's that?"

"Rachel Sims. I read about her disappearance in an old *Point Tyson Chronicle* article."

"I don't know her either," Charlie replied tersely.

"That's not what Sibley Fields told me," Laura said gently. "He said you've told people you still see her walking on that riverbank over there."

"I suppose he also told you I'm crazy, and that some people call me 'Crazy Charlie'!" Charlie replied angrily. He stabbed the knife into the plank and looked up at Laura. "I suppose he told you that, too!"

"Yes, he did," Laura admitted. "But I came out here anyhow. I wanted to see what you knew about Rachel Sims."

"What's she to you?"

"I honestly don't know. But I have a hunch that maybe my mother knew her. And maybe her disappearance is connected to my parents in some way. My mother just died," she added almost as an afterthought.

Charlie knelt to wash his hands in the river. "Come with me," he said, wiping his hands on his shirt. "I'll show ya somethin'."

Laura followed Charlie over to the cabin, where he placed the bucket of cleaned fish on a drain board next to the front door. He proceeded to walk briskly up a winding path to the cemetery. "I just don't have the strength ta keep this place up anymore," he lamented as they passed several tombstones that had fallen to the ground. "Frost goes outta the ground every spring and does this. Used ta be I'd go out and set 'em upright. But I can't do it anymore. Maybe after I'm gone the county'll take over this place an' do somethin' ta fix it up." He suddenly dropped to his knees and started feeling into the dead vegetation with both hands. "Yup, here they are." He tore at the grass and weeds until he had exposed two gravestones set level with the ground.

Laura leaned over to read the inscriptions, both of which were fringed with lilac flowers engraved on the gray granite surfaces. One gravestone was inscribed, "Grant Sims, Husband, March 14, 1910–July 28, 1953." The second stone had faded, darkened letters that bore the inscription, "Rachel Sims, Beloved Wife of Grant Sims, March 23, 1928–May 15, 1952."

"I don't understand," Laura said. "If Rachel Sims is buried here, why is there such a great mystery about her 'disappearance'?"

"Well, that's the whole point," Charlie explained. He stood up slowly and looked down at the gravestones. "Ya see, she's not buried here. Jus' before he died, her husband Grant Sims asked us ta place this stone in the ground next ta where he planned ta be buried. He didn't know if his wife was alive or dead, so he jus' had the date she dis'ppeared put on it. I guess he hoped that maybe someday, if she was still alive, she might see this and decide ta be buried next ta him."

"That's kind of an unusual last request," Laura speculated.

"The unusual thing is that he decided ta be buried over here in the first place," Charlie replied, pulling a blue handkerchief out of his pocket and wiping his forehead. "He was one of those Sent'nels of God. Those church people have their own cem'tery a few miles east of here. Jus' about all of 'em are buried in that cem'tery."

"Why do you suppose he decided to be buried over here?"

"I don't know," Charlie replied. "But he musta had his reasons."

Laura spent the rest of the afternoon and early evening talking to Charlie Flanigan, while they sat together on the tree trunk that extended out into the river. The sunlight from the descending sun glimmered and sparkled on the water as the sun dipped into the western horizon. The blossoming lilac bushes caught the rays of the departing sun and shimmered beautifully on the opposite riverbank.

"Do you think Grant Sims had anything to do with his wife's disappearance?" Laura asked.

"Nah, I can't believe that was the case at all. No one would murder his wife and then do what he did on top of that hill. 'Sides, there's sumthin' else. Sumthin' I didn't tell ya."

"What's that?"

"The day Rachel Sims dis'ppeared, some farmer saw her walkin' 'cross the old riverbed on the other side of the island, an' he told Grant 'bout it. Grant went over there, an' he found some lilac flowers tied together with a ribbon that he said belonged ta his wife. But he couldn't find any trace of her. He asked us ta bury him with that ribbon and those flowers. An' we did. He's still holdin' 'em."

"That doesn't sound like someone who murdered his wife," Laura agreed.

"No, it doesn't."

"I read in the newspaper account of her disappearance that some people in town said they saw her leaving town with a man who drove a car with Iowa license plates."

"Ya, they said that," Charlie replied, a note of disgust in his voice. "But it jus' ain't true."

"Why do you say that?"

"'Cause it jus' ain't true," he said even more angrily. "Those people will gossip 'bout anyone jus' ta make themselves feel better'n the rest of the human race. I don't put no stock at all in that story."

Laura glanced to the west as bright streaks of crimson and orange began to streak across the sky, making it appear that the clouds were on fire. "Did anyone ever come out here to visit Grant Sims's grave?"

"Ya, one fella did. Fact is, he came out here a lot."

"What's his name?"

"Jesse Willert."

"Is he still alive?"

"I don't know. I haven't seen him in years. But he made many of the granite stones in this cem'tery. Every time he came out with a new stone, he'd walk up on that hill. I'd see him up there, lookin' down at those two gravestones. Then he'd sit for a time on the riverbank an' stare 'cross the river at Hodges Island. Jus' like we're doing now. He even asked me a couple times 'bout what I'd seen over there on Hodges Island."

"What'd you tell him?"

Charlie sighed deeply, as though it was a story he had told many times, but did not want to tell anymore. "I told him every spring I'd hear strange sounds driftin' 'cross the river. An' if the moon was full and the fog was not too thick, I'd see someone wandrin' 'long the riverbank. In the mornin', I'd find lilacs spread 'cross those graves I jus' showed ya. Lilacs grow wild over there on Hodges Island. But there are none over here. So, someone had to bring 'em 'cross the river an' put 'em on those graves. An' spirits are the only thing I know of that can walk on water."

The headlights on Laura's car illuminated the blossoming yellow flowers that covered the support beams of the bridge that spanned the Lonely Willow River. As she drove across the bridge, the headlights swept across the rusty iron beams and railings. She listened to the thick wooden planks groan and rumble under the weight of the car.

As the headlights continued to probe into the darkness, she pondered what the old cemetery caretaker had told her that afternoon. If Charlie was delusional, as some townspeople believed, he certainly didn't show it. He appeared to be perfectly rational, and he was clearly convinced that he still sees Rachel Sims walking along the opposite riverbank on dark spring evenings.

From what Laura had learned, she realized that nothing about Rachel Sims's life was simple. The missing farm wife disappeared in a way that was most unusual. She was married to Grant Sims, and yet another man seemed interested enough in her to visit her gravestone and stare across the river at the island where she vanished. Yet, some of the townspeople were apparently convinced she left the area with a well-dressed gentleman from Iowa. If all of this were true, Rachel Sims must have been a very unusual member of her church community.

*More importantly, what, if anything, does this all have to do with me?*

On the way back to town, Laura drove into the gas station where she had filled her car the day she arrived in Point Tyson. She had felt the car pull slightly to the left, and she thought that perhaps one of the front tires might be low.

When she drove up to the area designated "Water/Air," she noticed a small, box-shaped white truck parked next to the gas pumps. The right fender of the car was badly dented, and it looked like there were red blood streaks across the hood. She wondered if perhaps a deer, like the one she had seen the day she arrived in Point Tyson, had jumped out in the path of the truck, and the driver had been unable to avoid it.

"Do you have a tire gauge?" she asked the attendant when he walked out of the station and joined her by the air pump. "I think one of my front tires is low."

The attendant tapped his boot against the left front tire. "Looks like this one right here," he said. He leaned down and tested it with a tire gauge he pulled out of his grease-stained shirt. "Yup. It's down about five pounds. You probably have a slow leak."

As the attendant filled the tire with air, Laura watched the box-shaped white truck pull away from the gas pumps and disappear in the direction of Point Tyson. She looked back at the attendant, who was checking the other tires.

"I don't think it's a nail," he said, standing up. "Probably a leaky valve. You should have it replaced. But it's no hurry."

"What do I owe you?" Laura asked.

"Nothing. Air's free."

"Thank you."

"You know, last time you were here you asked me if I ever knew of a Selma Madison who lived in this area. The more I thought about it, the more I thought that maybe I had heard that name before. So, I've been asking some people who gas up here if they'd ever heard of her. But none of them could remember anyone by that name living in these parts."

"Well, thanks for trying," Laura said. She started to get into the car, but then turned and looked back at the attendant. "There's another person I've been trying to learn more about, too. Rachel Sims. Have you heard that name before?"

"Wasn't she the woman who disappeared around Hodges Island back in the early 50s?"

"Yes, that was her."

"I remember," the attendant said, nodding. "What are you try-ing to find out about her?"

"I think my mother might have known her. I was trying to figure out if anyone knows what might have happened to her."

The attendant rubbed his dirty fingers across his brow. "Seems to me folks thought she left her husband for another man."

"What did you think?"

"Well, it really wasn't none of my business. But it wouldn't surprise me if she did take off with another man."

"Why do you say that?"

"Seems to me there was some talk about her being a little loose and out of control, if you know what I mean. She stood out among those other church people. They were so grim and rigid about everything. She didn't fit in with them, I guess."

"Think . . ."

"There's something else, too. You got to remember that the life of a farm wife twenty years ago was tough. It was nothing but hard work. For the wives of those church people, it was tougher yet. They had no modern appliances, no electricity, no in-door toilets, nothing that made life easier for them. It didn't surprise anyone that Rachel Sims might have run off with a man who could give her a better life. In fact, some people expected it of her."

Finley was holding the Bible Laura left for him when he stepped off the third-floor elevator and walked over to where Schlepler's wheelchair was once again parked next to the large window in the lobby. Schlepler was staring almost catatonically out the window at the prairie.

"So, Aurther," Finley said cheerfully, "how have things been for you today? Anything new happening? I've been pretty busy myself, but I wonder if you had any time to look at the materials in that envelope I left for you the last time we talked. As I said, a young woman who came to me is struggling to understand why she has apparently been living under a false identity for most of her life. She just lost her mother, who was her only living relative, so she is quite distressed by everything that is happening to her. She feels completely lost and alone, not even knowing who she really is."

Finley paused to see if there was any flicker of recognition in Schlepler's eyes. Seeing none, he placed the Bible on Schlepler's lap.

"I'm going to leave this with you, Aurther. It's the Bible that belonged to my patient's mother. She underlined many passages. She also commented next to the story of Rachel in the *Book of Genesis* that it was 'So many lies!' I was hoping maybe you could help us figure out what my patient's mother might have meant by that."

Finley patted Schlepler gently on the shoulder and walked over to the nurse's station.

"I left a Bible with Aurther," Finley explained to the nurse behind the desk. "It belongs to one of my patients. Please be sure to put it in the top drawer of his vanity when you wheel him back to his room."

"Did you ever figure out why the envelope I put in the top drawer wasn't there?" the nurse asked.

"No," Finley said, glancing over his shoulder at Schlepler. "But I have my suspicions."

# CHAPTER SEVEN

In the morning, Laura ate breakfast with Gunda on the front porch of the bed and breakfast. When Laura asked her what she remembered about Rachel Sims, Gunda said she had heard the name before, but knew very little about what happened on Hodges Island in 1952 because she had been working in Chicago at the time. She suggested that Laura talk to Pete Solvie because he would probably remember the incident. She added that he had worked in the quarries on Hodges Island for many years. Laura remembered Solvie as the elderly man who had introduced himself to her in the city park.

As they finished breakfast, Gunda reminisced about her childhood. "When I was very young," she said, "old timers in this area told us many stories about Hodges Island. They said the early Native Americans thought it was a supernatural place. They gave the island a name that meant 'The Island of Lost Spirits.' Old timers also told us the first white settlers in the area claimed they sometimes saw strange figures walking on the riverbank at night. They called them 'Heaven's Outcasts.' Still others thought it was a beautiful place because of the lilac bushes that fringed the riverbanks. They saw something almost artistic about it, especially in the spring. So, Hodges Island had a mysterious past long before Rachel Sims disappeared over there."

While they were talking, a late-model, white station wagon with rusty fenders drove slowly past, heading in a northerly direction. Gunda smiled and waved at the driver. "That's Reverend Sinclair," she explained.

"How many churches are there in Point Tyson?" Laura asked.

"None. They're all gone. Either moved to bigger cities or just folded up and disappeared. Reverend Sinclair was sent out here to revitalize the Unitarian Church of the Apostles. But it was too late. There was no congregation left. He ended up overseeing the auction of the church property. Pews, altar, and everything that wasn't bolted down were auctioned off. Only things that didn't sell were the church and rectory. He still lives in the rectory."

"Seems like kind of a strange thing to do," Laura speculated. "I would think he would become a pastor of another church somewhere."

"I think the whole national church folded. He probably didn't have any place else to go. He still ministers to the people in this area, though. Spends most of his time driving around the countryside in that beat up old station wagon delivering food and medicines to the poor people who can't get to town. Lots of rural poverty out this way." Gunda paused to look to the north where the station wagon had disappeared. "Reverend Sinclair has done a lot of good work for people around these parts. But that doesn't stop the rumor mill from talking about him."

"What do you mean?"

"Some people wonder what it was in his past that motivated him to stay in this isolated corner of the state after his church folded. Some thought maybe he was running away from something."

Laura glanced at her watch and realized it was getting late. She quickly excused herself, picked up her purse from the chair next to her, and walked out to her car. As she unlocked the car door, she noticed a piece of paper that was attached to the radio antenna on the other side of the vehicle. She walked around the car, slipped the paper off the antenna, and turned it over.

Someone had scribbled in bold, threatening penmanship, "Leave well enough alone!!!"

She looked in all directions, not certain what to make of the note, other than the fact that it was obviously a threat.

*Someone doesn't want me asking questions about Selma Madison or Rachel Sims! Or maybe both! Is whoever Mother and Father were hiding from still in this town?*

Laura pondered the significance of the note as she drove over to the city park. She was deeply concerned by the threat, but she was equally determined to find some answers to the many troubling questions she had asked herself since she found her mother's letter to Selma Madison.

*Someone apparently wants to keep some small town secrets buried in the past.*

Pete Solvie was sitting on the same bench he had been sitting on the day Laura arrived in town. He was an exceptionally short man, but his arms were long and his hands were calloused from years of hard work. He smiled at her as she approached the area where he was sitting.

"Decided to hang around for a while?" he asked.

"Yes. I'm staying at Gunda's Bed and Breakfast. In fact, she sent me over to talk to you. She said you might be able to help me."

"Well, I'll be glad to try. What is it you need?"

"Do you remember a Rachel Sims who disappeared over by Hodges Island in the early 1950s?"

"Yes. I didn't know her. But I do remember the story about how she disappeared."

"From what I can gather," Laura explained, "many of the people in Point Tyson thought she ran off with another man. Do you think that's what happened to her?"

"No, I don't," Pete replied emphatically. "I don't think that's what happened to her at all."

"What do you think happened?"

"Well, you have to remember that I worked for many years in those quarries on Hodges Island. I know a lot about what's out there. It's a very dangerous place."

"Why do you say that?"

"Because normally granite is mined in big open-pit quarries. But that's not always the way it was done on Hodges Island. There was some very high-grade granite on that island, the most expensive kind. But it wasn't found in huge deposits. It was scattered all over the island in smaller deposits. To get at it, we dug into every part of that island. Later, when the quarries were abandoned and the brush and weeds grew back over those holes, they were death traps. Anyone who wandered into those areas was taking their own life in their hands. Cows and even a couple of horses vanished over there, undoubtedly at the bottom of one of those old quarry holes."

"Do you think that's what happened to Rachel Sims?"

"Yes. I remember at the time someone saw her walking in that area. He claimed she went into the island. If so, one false step off the old quarry road, and that would be the last anyone ever saw of her."

Laura paused to contemplate what Pete had just told her. "Did anyone ever consider the possibility that maybe she was the victim of foul play?"

"Well, her husband considered that possibility, as I remember. And some people even suspected he was the one responsible for her disappearance. But that didn't seem likely. He put ads in the newspapers for months after his wife disappeared, begging anyone who knew what had happened to her to contact him. He even offered a reward, I believe. That's just not something a man who murdered his wife would do. Unless, of course, he was real smart and wanted to cover his tracks. But I don't think that was the case at all with Grant Sims."

"No," Laura agreed. "That sounds more like someone who loved his wife very much."

"Yes, it does."

"Yesterday, I talked to Charlie Flanigan out in the city cemetery. He said someone by the name of Jesse Willert came out there many times to visit the grave of Grant Sims. Do you remember Jesse Willert?"

"Course I do. He owned a granite quarry north of town. Made many of the cemetery stones you see in cemeteries throughout this part of the state."

"Is he still alive?"

"That I don't know. Haven't seen or heard about him in years. For a long time, he had a half-breed Indian laborer named Hank who did everything for him. Drove a battered old green pick-up truck to town to buy groceries, deliver cemetery stones, and do everything else for him. Willert was never very social. But many years ago, he just stopped having anything to do with the rest of the world."

"When did this happen?"

"Well, let's see. I guess it was . . . It was probably around the time this Rachel Sims disappeared, or not too long afterwards. You know, the person you might ask about Rachel Sims is Phil Swanson. He owns the grocery store right over there. He's got a sign on his door that says he's running some errands. But he should be back in a few hours."

"You think he might know what happened to her?"

"I don't know about that. I just remember that he mentioned her name a few times during some of our card games. He seemed to know something about her the rest of us didn't know."

&#10799;&#10799;&#10799;&#10799;

Before leaving the park, Laura asked Pete Solvie for directions to Jesse Willert's home. Outside of town, she noticed a rusty windmill that was peppered with holes and leaning against a small, windowless shack. A ghostly gray, abandoned farmhouse and barn were located next to a small grove of trees a few hundred yards farther north.

She had pretty much concluded that Grant Sims probably didn't have anything to do with his wife's disappearance. His apparently sincere and genuine attempts to find her, together with his dying requests, were not the acts of a man who had murdered his wife.

*The other possibilities seemed more plausible. Perhaps Rachel Sims had run off with another man, or perhaps she did fall into one of the old quarry holes on Hodges Island.*

But Laura sensed that even the more plausible possibilities did not explain what had happened the day Rachel Sims disappeared. She sensed it was something else, something that ran much deeper and was more ominous. She sensed that it probably involved the mysterious Jesse Willert who visited the cemetery so often and seemed so curious about what Charlie Flanigan had seen on Hodges Island.

She was also convinced that the disappearance of Rachel Sims was connected in some way to her own family's mysterious past. She felt a strange, subliminal connection to the farm wife who had disappeared on Hodges Island in May of 1952.

*I feel like I know her. But how can that be?*

A few miles outside of Point Tyson, Laura saw a white truck approaching from the opposite direction. When she was about thirty or forty yards from the truck, she could see the sunlight reflecting off the driver's dark sunglasses. She could also see clumps of mud that were being tossed into the air by the truck's huge tires.

Suddenly, and without warning, the truck veered across the center dividing line and directly into the path of her car. She instinctively turned the steering wheel sharply to the right and slammed on the brakes, barely avoiding the truck as it rumbled past the driver's side of her car. The car came to rest on the gravel shoulder of the highway.

As the dust swirled across the windows, she paused for a moment to catch her breath. Her hands were shaking uncontrollably

*That was no accident! That was deliberate!*

She opened the door and stepped onto the highway. In the distance, she could see the white truck disappear behind a small foothill.

*That was the same truck that was parked by the gasoline pumps yesterday! The one with the busted fender and bloody streaks across the hood!*

She waited for a few minutes, trying to compose herself. Then she got back in the car and drove north. She was now convinced that the note on her car was more than a simple warning. It was a serious threat. Someone was determined to stop her from learning the answers to the questions she had been asking about Selma Madison and Rachel Sims.

*How far would that person go to stop me from finding out what-ever secrets this small town was hiding?*

Laura spotted the entrance to Jesse Willert's property as Pete Solvie had described it, and she turned onto a dirt road that curled around a foothill. Below her, an elongated quarry sprawled along the base of some rock-covered hills. The reddish-purple walls of the granite quarry were covered with weeds and thick clumps of grass that grew out of cracks that spider-webbed across the rough stone surfaces. Large, angular boulders, apparently shattered by dynamite, lay in heaps along the bottom of the quarry.

On the other side of the road, near the top of a foothill, several large gables from a huge stone house with a wooden roof towered above the oak and elm trees that covered the hillside. Three of the upper windows, set deeply in the stone walls, were visible through the leaves and tree branches. A large weathervane in the shape of a hawk adorned the uppermost peak of the house. The hawk, which had its wings extended backwards and upwards, looked as though it were about to leap off the roof of the house and soar into the sky.

She parked the car next to a metal gate that was bolted into the stone fence that surrounded the house. She pushed hard on the gate, and it groaned on its huge, rusty hinges, but it would not swing open. Looking down, she noticed a padlock that was attached to a chain wrapped around the bottom of the gate. She realized she would have to find another way to get inside.

Walking along the base of the fence, she came to an area where the annual frosts had spilled the granite blocks into a shallow ditch, creating an opening in the stone wall. She stepped through the opening and walked up a long gravel road to the top of the hill.

As she approached the house, she saw that it was decorated with stained-glass windows that glowed brilliantly in the sunlight. The granite walls were dark brown or bright, reddish-purple, depending upon the angle of the sunlight striking the rough stone surfaces. The ornamental woodwork on the windows and gables had turned a pale gray.

The home was unlike any she had ever seen before. If it reflected the character and personality of its owner, she decided Jesse Willert must be a true eccentric.

A late-model, green pickup truck was parked near one corner of the house. From that direction, she could hear the steady sound of metal scraping against metal. As she walked past the pickup truck, she noticed that the bed was lined with a thick layer of straw, and a double-barreled shotgun leaned against the passenger side of the front seat.

On the other side of the house, she saw a smaller, less conspicuous house that was partly concealed in thick bushes and tall trees at the far end of the back yard. The house, which looked like it might have once provided temporary lodging for the men who worked in the quarry, had no gables or stained-glass windows, but it was constructed out of the same reddish-purple granite blocks that had been used to build the larger home.

In the middle of the back yard, a tall man with long white hair was sitting on a granite rock that protruded out of the ground. A bright blue handkerchief was tied tightly around his forehead to keep the sweat from falling into his eyes as he scraped a metal file across the long curved blade of a scythe. Some recently cut weeds lay on the ground nearby, next to several gravestones that apparently marked the location of a small family cemetery.

When the man looked up, his white hair glistened in the bright sunlight, and his brown eyes seemed to stare straight through her. From his muscular arms and chest, Laura surmised that he was not as old as she had first thought. He seemed, instead, to be someone whose hair had turned prematurely white.

"I'm sorry to bother you," she said awkwardly. The eyes that looked up at her were expressionless. "I was hoping to speak to Jesse Willert. Are you Jesse Willert?"

The man continued to sit on the rock, his eyes betraying no emotion. "You're trespassing. Did you know that?" he finally said.

"I'm very sorry," Laura apologized. "I wouldn't have bothered you. But I'm trying to gather some information on two of the people who are buried in the Point Tyson City Cemetery. Actually, one of them is buried there. The other one disappeared, but there's a gravestone in the cemetery with her name on it."

A strangely puzzled expression flickered across the man's face. "What two people?" he asked.

"Grant and Rachel Sims," Laura replied. "I was told that Jesse Willert might have known them."

"Jesse Willert died ten years ago. I'm just the caretaker here."

"Are you Hank?"

The man nodded slightly, but he did not speak.

"Before Jesse Willert died, did he ever mention anything to you about Grant or Rachel Sims?"

"Jesse Willert died almost ten years ago," he repeated. "And you're trespassing. I must ask you to leave."

"Please . . ."

"I don't want to have to forcibly remove you from this property," he said in a menacing tone of voice as he stood up. He held the scythe in a threatening manner that made it appear he was fully prepared to use it as a weapon. "But I must ask you once again to leave."

Recognizing that there was apparently nothing she could do to convince him to help her, and realizing the imposing figure in front of her seemed willing to follow through on his threat, Laura reluctantly turned and walked back down the driveway. As she approached the gate, she heard the ancient weather vane turn and groan on the roof of the Willert home.

Laura glanced periodically at the granite quarry as she drove back to the main road. She stopped the car when she spotted some structures at the bottom of the quarry. Several wooden buildings surrounded a small pond in the middle of the quarry. Next to the buildings, three rusty conveyor systems slumped against a large pile of granite boulders.

Another aging wooden structure that looked very much like Sibley Fields's Antiques Warehouse was located closer to the road on the rim overlooking the quarry. As she gazed at that building, she thought she saw a face suddenly appear and disappear in one of the dusty windows.

*Maybe he will be more helpful than the man I just talked to on the Willert property.*

She quickly drove over to the building and walked up to the front door. Inside the building, sunlight streaked through several holes in the roof, and a large rope pulley system dangled loosely from wooden beams high overhead. Several wagons in various stages of disrepair were scattered around the outer walls, and dusty, unpolished granite blocks were stacked on thick wooden planks that covered the floor. A small, flatbed truck was parked in the middle of the building.

"Is anybody here?" she yelled. She waited a few seconds and yelled again, "Is anybody here?"

There was no answer or sound anywhere in the building.

She walked to the rear of the building to see if anyone was out back, but there was nothing except some piles of stone rubble and the chassis of an abandoned truck.

*Maybe I was seeing things.*

Convinced that she had been mistaken about the face in the window, she walked back to the front entrance. As she did so, she noticed a large poster that had been tacked to one of the walls. Several smaller posters were organized on both sides of the larger poster.

The larger poster was obviously very old, for many sections were riddled with holes from silverfish. It was an advertisement for an auction of equipment and furniture for the Willert Granite Quarry when it went out of business sometime in the 1950s. Silverfish had eaten away the last number, so she could not tell what year the auction had been held.

While Laura studied the information on the poster, she heard a loud rasping noise overhead. As she glanced at the dust that was drifting across the rays of sunlight that poured in through the holes in the roof, she suddenly heard wood shattering and metal grinding against metal.

She leaped under a huge wooden crossbeam as a large stone suddenly plummeted out of the shadows near the exposed rafters. The stone plunged across the beams of light that filtered through the roof and crashed onto the wooden floor a few feet behind the flatbed truck. The stone shattered the floor and sent dust and fragments of wood flying into the air. Overhead, several birds that were nesting in the rafters flew frantically out of the holes in the roof.

She waited a few seconds for the dust to clear. Then she walked over to where the stone was partially buried in the wooden floor. It was an unpolished granite cemetery stone. Looking directly overhead, she realized the stone had been suspended by one of the pulley systems, apparently to be loaded onto the truck.

Walking over to a huge iron plate that had been bolted into a wooden post that supported the overhead beams, she saw that the rusty bolts had pulled loose, causing the stone to plummet to the ground.

*Did someone deliberately loosen these bolts?*

When Laura entered Point Tyson's city limits, she turned left and parked next to a small store on Main Street. The sign above the store indicated that it was "Phil's Groceries." When she stepped into the store, she saw that the owner had somehow managed to organize every item in meticulous, detailed rows and displays. Nothing seemed to be out of place. Although every other store on Main Street was either abandoned or barely functional, the owner of the grocery store had somehow managed to create a moderately successful business enterprise amid so much failure.

A head suddenly popped out from behind one of the displays in the middle of the store, and a bald, bearded middle-aged man who was barely four-foot tall greeted her in a booming voice. "Can I help you?" he asked cheerfully.

As he walked behind the counter, he appeared to grow increasingly taller.

Laura realized he must have a ramp that enabled him to reach the items on the shelves attached to the rear wall.

"Are you the lady who's doing that research project on the old quarries?" he asked.

"Yes, I am," she admitted.

"Pete Solvie told me about you. Name's Phil Swanson," he said, reaching a chubby hand across the counter. "Pete told me you were interested in that Rachel Sims who disappeared on Hodges Island back in the 1950s."

"Yes. I read about that incident in an old copy of the *Point Tyson Chronicle*, and I was wondering what might have happened to her."

"Well, you're not the first person who wondered about that. There were all kinds of rumors about how she might have disappeared."

"What do you think happened to her?"

"Well, I don't know," he sighed. "I didn't really have an opinion. But Alfred Kron did."

"Who's he?"

"A friend of mine who owned a shoe and bike repair shop down the street. He did quite a bit of research into it. Just the way you're doing. He apparently had some strong opinions about what happened over on that island, but he kept most of what he learned to himself. He just said things weren't what people thought they were. That's all. I knew Alfred fairly well, and I was certain he knew more. He just didn't want to talk about it."

"Is he still alive?"

"Oh, my, no, he's been dead for some time. He was killed in a bike accident."

"Bike accident?"

"Alfred didn't drive a car. He rode a bike everywhere he went. He was killed on that road out there, about five miles north of Point Tyson. Hit-and-run."

"Did they ever figure out who was responsible?"

"Nope. Probably someone from out of town who just decided to hightail it out of the area rather than hang around to face the music. People drive crazy on that stretch of highway. I don't know why. It must be an optical illusion or something. Makes them think they're going slower than they really are. Car probably came over one of those hills too fast and couldn't stop. They found Alfred's bike all smashed to pieces on the side of the road. Alfred was lying in some tall grass at the bottom of the ditch."

"So, Aurther," Finley said as he sat down in a chair next to the window where Schlepler's wheelchair was parked, "were you able to learn anything from the Bible I left you yesterday? Anything at all that might help my patient?"

Schlepler continued to stare out the window without acknowledging Finley's presence.

"It's pretty important to my patient," Finley continued. "It may be the one clue that will help her find wherever it is that she belongs in this world. I asked the nurse to put the Bible in the top drawer of your vanity. When you're feeling up to it, maybe you can look it over for us. It might tell us a lot about the world my patient came from, the one she can no longer remember." Finley slowly stood up and prepared to leave. "I know these things matter to you, Aurther. I know that's why you have retreated from the world. I know you have seen too much pain and cruelty in your lifetime. But maybe you could find it in yourself to help one last person who might be a victim of a terrible crime."

Finley turned and started to walk down the hallway. He thought about stopping by Schlepler's room to see if the Bible was in the top drawer of the vanity as he had requested. Almost immediately, he heard a rustling sound behind him and quickly turned around.

"Come back tomorrow, Ned," Schlepler said, his back still turned toward Finley.

"What did you just say?" Finley asked.

"I said come back tomorrow. We will discuss your patient then."

# CHAPTER EIGHT

"I talked to Phil Swanson yesterday," Laura said as she walked over to where Sibley Fields was working on an old kitchen table in the rear of his antique store. "He told me Alfred Kron was very interested in Rachel Sims. Kron was apparently convinced that there was something more sinister behind her disappearance. Did you know him?"

"Yes, I knew Alfred," Sibley replied, looking up. "He was a good man, but he was a bit paranoid. He saw cynical motives behind everything. I'm not sure how much stock you could place in anything he said about Rachel Sims."

"Think his death was an accident?"

"Well, it was a hit-and-run," Sibley admitted. "But many people warned him about riding his bike on that highway. Too many rolling hills and blind spots. He ignored those warnings, and, well, you know what happened."

"Phil said they never did find the person responsible for the hit-and-run."

"Yes, that's true."

Sibley reached for a bottle of dark furniture polish and used a cotton ball to lightly dab some scratches on the kitchen table. He leaned down and studied the scratches from several different angles.

"Did you also know a Jesse Willert who lived north of here?" Laura asked.

"I didn't really know him," Sibley replied, "but I attended the auction when he sold off most of his business equipment."

"Did anyone ever speculate that he might have been involved in the disappearance of Rachel Sims?"

"Not that I can remember," Sibley replied. "Why do you ask?"

"Charlie Flanigan told me he visited Grant Sims's grave quite often. I was wondering what the connection might be."

"I don't know anything about that."

"Do you know why he decided to go out of business?"

Sibley threw the cotton ball in a trashcan and glanced off in the distance. "That was a long time ago," he reminisced. "All I know is that he auctioned off everything except for the smaller scale equipment that he used to make cemetery stones. After the auction, I don't think anyone saw much more of him. He lives closer to Pelican Lake, the county seat. He had more to do with that town than this one. My uncle told me he served with him in the Korean War, but that's all I know about him."

"The caretaker on his property told me Willert died ten years ago."

"That could be true. He always kept to himself. So, it wouldn't be surprising that he died and no one over here has mentioned it. You know, if you're interested in Jesse Willert, there is something you might want to see." Sibley scratched his chin and glanced at a far corner of the warehouse. "When he auctioned off his business property, I didn't bid on the heavy industrial equipment. But I did buy a lot of office furniture and things like that because many of those pieces were very old. Dealers from the big cities snapped them up right away after I brought them over here to the warehouse. But I also picked up some odds and ends that the auctioneer virtually gave away at the end of the auction. Over the years, I've learned that you never know what little treasures you might find hidden among things other people consider junk."

"What kind of things?" Laura asked.

"Come over here and I'll show you." He led her over to a far corner of the warehouse where several old wooden boxes were piled high with dusty ledger books and small business equipment. "I wasn't able to sell any of this stuff, so I just dumped it here. It all came out of the Willert quarry buildings. You're welcome to look through these boxes, although I doubt that you'll find anything important. It looks like it's mostly just records of business transactions. An old timer told me Jesse Willert did his own accounting after he took over the business from his father, except for the time that he was in Korea. So, whatever is in those books, he probably wrote himself."

Laura pulled a chair over to the wooden boxes and began indiscriminately paging through the business ledgers. As Sibley said, they were records of various Willert Granite Quarry sales and purchases dating back to the early years of the twentieth century. She decided to concentrate on the ledgers from the late 1940s and early 1950s. If there was anything in the ledgers that connected Jesse Willert and Rachel Sims to a business transaction, she decided those would be the most plausible dates. Perhaps she might also stumble across some reference to Selma Madison or her own parents.

There was nothing unusual about the business records from the late 1940s. They were meticulously detailed, carefully calculated summaries of sales and purchases. Occasionally, there would be a brief note in the margins describing something unusual about a failed or highly successful transaction. Sometimes there were brief personal notes or reminders. For a time in the early 1950s, someone else was obviously making the entries because the handwriting was significantly different.

A little later, the person who had made the entries in the 1940s started making the entries again. But this time there was a noticeable shift in tone and style. There was less careful attention to detail, and the marginal comments often increased in length and emotional intensity.

The marginal comments were becoming more disconnected from business transactions, and more personal, philosophical, and at times deeply cynical. Willert was clearly going through an emotional crisis, probably brought on by what he had experienced in the Korean War. Those experiences apparently made it impossible for him to concentrate on the routine activities of running a business. Instead, he scribbled some of his innermost thoughts, like brief journal entries, in the margins and across some of the pages of the business ledgers:

JUNE 6, 1952
The war was absolute hell! I cannot leave it behind! But nothing is more agonizing than this uncertainty! I struggle every day to care about this business. The business of life is all that matters—and that business is not going well.

JUNE 17, 1952
I stand by my window and gaze for hours at a lone tree on the distant quarry rim. It is all that I have. It reminds me of everything I have lost.

AUGUST 13, 1952
I make my living mostly through the sale of cemetery stones, the appropriateness of which seldom escapes me. A man who cares nothing for the business of life is forced to earn his living selling symbols of death.

JANUARY 3, 1953

It was a good year in the business sense. Many people died and I have scarcely a single cemetery stone left to sell. As for life, it crawls along as usual.

APRIL 14, 1953

I have decided to restore the weathervane that adorns the uppermost peak of the house, so that it can more easily chase the sun across the sky. Oh, that one could set the hands of the clock to move at a faster speed and put this thing called life more quickly out of its misery.

MAY 15, 1953

Sometimes, when I sit in the cemetery and stare across the river at Hodges Island, I feel Rachel's presence as strongly as when we were together. It has been one entire year since she disappeared, and still I cannot find it in my heart to admit that she is gone. The death of someone we love is difficult enough. But when someone we love simply vanishes, it unleashes a pain that gnaws at the soul and refuses to diminish with time.

JUNE 14, 1953

I have decorated the interior of the house in a way that suits my fancy. In there, I shall live out my days as best I can. And so, perhaps the years that remain will pass by more quickly. Seldom has a soul practiced such self-deception upon itself.

JUNE 23, 1953

Before he died, Grant Sims's requested that a stone with Rachel's name be placed next to his grave, should she ever return and consent to be buried next to him. Now that it is clear to me that Rachel is gone for good, I shall have to be content with an eternity spent below ground with the grieving husband. For I have purchased the cemetery plot on the other side of the grave reserved for *our* Rachel.

JULY 9, 1953

Becky finally succumbed to the madness that was eating away at her soul. I kept her home as long as possible, but I can do so no longer. I have finally committed her to a mental institution.

JULY 13, 1953
When I visited Becky today, her eyes were fixed on other worlds. She was no longer one of us.

JULY 25, 1953
When I drove over to Hodges Island, near the area where Rachel was last seen, it seemed to have changed very little. The Island of Lost Spirits remains an eternal mystery. What diabolical force insisted that Rachel's spirit was doomed to become trapped on that island with all the other lost souls who are rumored to have become imprisoned there?

OCTOBER 10, 1953
An epidemic came through our area, and yet it passed me by. The disease and I have become business partners, for one prospers in direct proportion to the other. Never have I sold so many cemetery stones in such a short period of time. I have become the new "Profit of Death."

OCTOBER 23, 1953
Perhaps I spoke too soon. The fever that signals the onslaught of the disease has crept into my bedroom and has taken refuge in my lungs. I lie here, trying to attend to the mundane affairs of my business, but my mind strays constantly to other matters. I have changed my mind about how I am to be buried. I have decided to have my remains cremated so there will be nothing left of me to remind anyone that I ever lived on this cruel planet.

OCTOBER 24, 1953
I have informed Hank that if I die, he is to dump my ashes wherever it is convenient and without any public ceremony. I look forward to making a hasty departure from this world and everything in it.

OCTOBER 26, 1953
I grow weaker.

OCTOBER 30, 1953
I long only to die and pass out of this world, and yet I have somehow defeated the horrible disease that has killed so many others! What monstrous fate has taken control of my destiny?

><><><

Laura sat by the wooden boxes in the antiques warehouse long after she had read through the last of the business ledgers. She realized that the handwriting from the first to the last entry was larger and more indecipherable, as though Willert was becoming increasingly mentally unstable. She also realized that she had just exposed another possible motive for the mysterious disappearance of Rachel Sims. Yet, she was dumbfounded by what she had discovered.

*Rachel Sims was apparently deeply involved with two men, her husband and Jesse Willert. Yet, neither man was apparently involved in her disappearance, although any police detective would have made them the prime suspects.*

It was clear from Willert's comments that he loved Rachel Sims deeply and was devastated when she disappeared. It was equally clear that Grant Sims was so devoted to his wife that he grieved for her long after she vanished, and even had her name inscribed on a gravestone next to his own. It was a classic lovers' triangle, one that had motivated many a jealous husband or lover to commit murder. Yet, that did not seem to be the case with Grant Sims, Rachel Sims, and Jesse Willert.

*Maybe Rachel Sims did leave Point Tyson with a man who was driving a car with Iowa license plates. If she was having an affair with one man outside of her marriage, wouldn't she be capable of leaving her husband for another man who could offer her a better life?*

Laura knew so little about Rachel Sims that she could not exclude that possibility completely. But from what she did know about the mysterious woman who vanished in 1952, she did not believe Rachel Sims was a common adulterer. Something inside of her did not want to believe that was the case.

She felt like she had stumbled into a complicated series of interconnected passageways and corridors. Rather than finding any light at the end of the labyrinth, she seemed to find only more darkness and confusion. Still, one possibility seemed more ominous than all the others.

*Am I connected to this love triangle in any way?*

Laura decided not to make any calls from the telephone Gunda provided for her guests in the lobby of what had once been a living room. She wanted more privacy. She had checked out the telephone booth next to the mailbox on Main Street and, as she suspected, saw that the phone had been removed and was not in service. On one of the side streets near the newspaper office, she found what appeared to be the only functional telephone booth in Point Tyson. She quickly called Annie to update her on how she was doing. Her next call was to Farmington. The receptionist immediately put her through to Dr. Finley.

"Dr. Finley," Laura explained. "I'm calling from a coin-operated telephone booth, so I only have a few minutes before my time is up."

"I can call you back from my office if that would be helpful," Finley replied.

"That won't be necessary. I just wanted to give you a quick summary of what I have learned in Point Tyson. Then I would like to meet with you later in the week to fill you in on the details. Is that possible?"

"Of course. I can fit you in just about any time that works for you."

"How about 3 o'clock this Friday?"

"I'll pencil you in."

"Good. What I want to talk to you about involves something that happened in Point Tyson back in the spring of 1952. A young woman by the name of Rachel Sims disappeared near a place called Hodges Island, just outside of town. I've located a newspaper article that describes the details of her disappearance. I've also talked to several residents who still remember her. They have many different opinions about what might have happened to her. One of them, a cemetery caretaker, claims he still sees her walking the riverbanks on dark spring evenings. The townspeople say he's a little crazy. I don't know why he would make up that story. But he is very convincing. I also found entries in some discarded business journals that suggest this Rachel Sims might have been involved in a love triangle."

"Do you think this might be the Rachel your mother was commenting on in her Bible?"

"It's a possibility. She might have been involved in some way in my parents' decision to assume new identities and go into hiding. At least I would like to explore that possibility with you."

"How might I be able to help you?"

"We could try regressive hypnosis. I know you said there are dangers involved. But I really need to know who I am and where I came from. That's much more important to me."

"And you think this Rachel Sims might be the key to unlocking those hidden doors?"

"I don't know. But I feel like I've been in this town before. I can't explain those feelings. They're just there. I feel the same way about Rachel Sims. I only learned about her a couple of days ago. Yet, I feel her story very deeply. I don't think I've ever felt that way about someone I've only known through stories other people have told me, but have never even met."

"So, Aurther," Finley said as he sat down in a chair next to the third-floor window, "have you decided to join humanity again?"

When Schlepler ignored him, Finley positioned his chair between Schlepler's wheelchair and the window overlooking the prairie. He sat down and looked directly into Schlepler's eyes. "Last night, as I was leaving, you said you would discuss my patient with me today. Are you ready to have that discussion?"

When Schlepler continued to stare straight ahead, Finley leaned forward and placed the Bible on his lap. "I found this in the second drawer of your vanity," Finley said, "although the nurse insisted she placed it in the top drawer. The same thing happened with the envelope I left for you earlier. I know you've been looking at them. I just want your opinion on what all of this might mean. That's all I'm asking of you."

Schlepler lowered his head and his fingers moved slowly across the surface of the Bible. Without looking up, he said softly, "Why is this so important to you, Ned?"

"The patient who gave me these things recently learned she has been living under a false identity created by her parents when she was very young. She is struggling to find out who she really is. She has no explanation for what is happening to her. Some of her memories seem to come from experiences that are not a part of her own life. She doesn't know what to make of those memories."

"You told me that earlier," Schlepler replied.

"So, you were listening to me the other day when you were staring out this same window," Finley gently chided his old friend.

"Didn't you have another case like this a few years back?" Schlepler asked, ignoring Finley and looking out the window.

"Yes, I did. A couple of them actually."

"Think this is another one?"

"I don't know. I know so little about this young woman. But from everything she has told me, and the contents of the envelope and the marginal comment in this Bible—well, it's very strange to say the least."

Schlepler sighed deeply. "Do you know what I've been doing these past few years?"

"All I know is you've spent most of your time looking out this window."

"No, Ned, that's where you're wrong. I haven't been looking out *this* window. I've been looking out another window. A window that only those who disengage completely from the world can see. The things on the other side of that window are really quite fantastic. They flit past the window so quickly it is impossible to tell who or what they are. Most of them have lost all interest in us. A few linger in front of the window before fleeing back into the darkness. Only one or two stop long enough to look through the window in our direction. They seem to be the ones who are not sure where they are, or on what side of the window they belong."

"Did you . . ."

"Ned, while I looked out that window, I was reminded of one irrefutable fact about life."

"What's that?"

"Scientific explanations can take us part of the way to that elusive thing we know as 'the truth'. But something else has to help us complete the journey."

"And what is that?"

"Art."

"Art?"

"Yes. But it is not how we normally think of art. It is not a poem or a painting or a musical composition. Yes, they are forms of art, and every person who has ever tried to create one of these artistic works has struggled desperately to look through the window I have just described for you. None of them has succeeded because life itself is the ultimate artistic endeavor. It is the purest expression of the creative force that pulsates through the universe, the force that we know as 'God'. Very few people achieve that kind of creative life. So, there are very few true artists among us."

"What does this have to do with my patient?"

"I know very little about her. The letter and the other materials you left for me, especially the Bible, say more about her mother. She was a very unhappy woman. She did not like living a lie, but she had no choice. She felt she had to do it to protect someone else."

"Was Laura's life in danger?"

"All of their lives were in danger."

"Who were they hiding from?"

"I don't know," Schlepler replied. He opened the Bible to the story of Rachel. "It had something to do with this Bible. There is wisdom in this Bible, but there are also people who have distorted its messages and used it for personal gain. They have stifled and destroyed the truly creative souls whose very lives are meant to be examples for the rest of us. It was never meant to be that way."

"Is Laura related to any of those people?"

"Why do you ask?"

"Because I spoke with her today on the telephone. She told me the story of a Rachel Sims who vanished outside of a small town called Point Tyson, not too far from here. My patient thinks she's connected to her in some way."

Schlepler ran his fingertips across the page of the Bible where Laura's mother had written her marginal comment. "I can only tell you that the person who wrote this comment was not referring to the biblical Rachel. She was referring to another Rachel. Perhaps the one who disappeared outside of that small town you just described. There is a hidden voice somewhere in this Bible, a very powerful voice. Perhaps that Rachel is still tapping on the other side of the window. Perhaps she hopes someday someone will hear her."

Laura ate supper that night in Max's Café, the only restaurant on Main Street. It was a small diner with several booths along one wall and a row of metal stools next to a linoleum-covered counter. A doorway had been punched into a wall of one of the abandoned stores next door, and three tables were scattered across the room. In one corner, a television set and radio had been placed on a fireplace hearth next to a jukebox. A card game was in progress on a table in the middle of the room.

While the radio blared out the latest news concerning live-stock and grain prices, Pete Solvie, Phil Swanson, and two farmers played euchre. Phil sat on a wooden box that had been placed on one of the chairs. The four men exchanged good-natured verbal insults as they slapped card after card on the table.

"Damn your hide, Pete," one of the farmers exclaimed, "you suckered me inta that one! I shoulda known you were too stingy to give anything away."

"That's just the way ya play the game," Pete replied cheerfully, scooping up the cards and reshuffling the deck.

"Maybe in your day it was," another farmer chortled. "But those days are gone. Today, we call it cheatin'."

When Laura was through eating, she walked into the next room to study some of the photographs and newspaper clippings that were preserved behind thick coats of varnish that had been applied to the walls. One of the photographs was a picture of Point Tyson's Main Street as it looked much earlier in the century, when a group of smiling, well-dressed businessmen gathered around the historical marker in the park to celebrate some chamber of commerce achievement. In the background, huge elm trees towered above the men.

Some of the articles preserved behind the thick, brown coats of varnish were newspaper clippings and photographs of men from various wars. In one of the photographs, several Korean War soldiers were smiling broadly while they rode on convertibles and waved to the people gathered along Main Street.

On the same wall, Laura noticed a newspaper photograph of former Senator Joe McCarthy. Other photographs preserved behind the thick coat of varnish were of various political figures who had held office in Archer County. She gathered from accompanying newspaper articles that there had been some bitter political campaigns earlier in the century. She remembered Norbert J. Samuelson, one of the politicians involved in those campaigns, as the state senator who had drowned in the Lonely Willow River a few weeks before Rachel Sims disappeared.

Noticing that the card game was over and Pete Solvie was playing solitaire, Laura walked over to where he was sitting. "Pete," she said, sitting down on a chair next to him. "Have you ever heard of a Becky Willert? I believe she was Jesse Willert's sister."

"I'm not the one you should ask about the Willerts. I just don't know a lot about them. Why are you interested in her?"

"I read something about her today," Laura replied. "It said she was committed to a mental institution."

"I wouldn't know anything about that."

"Did anyone ever try to connect Jesse Willert or his sister to the disappearance of Rachel Sims?"

"Not that I know of," Pete said. He paused and scratched the stubble on his chin with one of the cards. "You know, until you started talking about that incident over on Hodges Island, I hadn't thought about it in a long time." He suddenly turned and addressed one of the farmers who was sitting on a stool next to the counter. "Wally, do you remember that Harlowe Meyers who lived over by Hodges Island twenty, thirty years ago?"

"Ya, I remember him," the farmer said, turning slightly and speaking over his shoulder. "What do you want to know about him?"

"Whatever happened to him?"

"He was from the south. He got in trouble with the law. I think he went back home to Alabama."

Pete turned and looked at Laura, "The reason I asked about Harlowe Meyers is because, as I remember, there were some people who thought he might be mixed up in the disappearance of that Rachel Sims you've been asking about. But no one could connect him to it. Some folks around this area were pretty scared of him. I do remember that."

"*Why* were they scared of him?"

"He had a reputation for getting into fights. Apparently, he was pretty violent."

"But you don't remember a Becky Willert?"

"No. But that doesn't mean anything. The person you should ask is Charlie Flanigan. He had more contact with Jesse Willert than anyone else in this town. Willert made many of those gravestones in that cemetery."

Later that evening, as Laura drove back to the bed and breakfast, she impulsively made a U-turn and drove out of town in the opposite direction. She turned east onto the gravel road that led to the Point Tyson City Cemetery. As she approached the front gate, her headlights reflected off the larger gravestones on the other side of the crumbling stone fence that enclosed the cemetery.

When she stepped out of her car, the moon was full and bright stars were spread across the night sky. She heard the rustling sounds of some birds nesting in one of the tall trees that towered above the cemetery. The moonlight illuminated the path as she walked down to Charlie Flanigan's small cabin by the river.

She knocked three times on the screen door. When there was no answer, she peered into one of the windows. Inside the cabin, she could see a kerosene lantern glowing on a shelf above a small wooden table.

Seeing no one in the cabin, she turned and stared at the fog that was gathering along the riverbank. She could hear the river's current sloshing gently against the branches of the uprooted tree.

Reluctantly, she started walking back up the hill to her car. As she passed the area where the path branched off in two different directions, she decided to follow the path that would take her past the graves of Grant and Rachel Sims.

Guided by the moonlight, she found the pile of dead vegetation Charlie had brushed away from the two gravestones. Freshly picked lilac flowers had been placed in the middle of both graves.

Suddenly, a beam of light flashed through the fog that was gathering at the base of the riverbank. Seconds later, Charlie stepped out of the fog and walked over to where Laura was standing. "Did ya see 'er up here?" he asked excitedly.

"See who?" Laura replied.

She was startled by Charlie's sudden appearance on top of the hill.

"The Lilac Lady," Charlie explained, pointing first at the flowers on the two graves and then at the fog that had accumulated along the riverbank. "Earlier this evenin', I caught sight of her over there on Hodges Island. She's the one who put these flowers here. Jus' the way she always does."

Finley sat at his desk that night, paging through the Bible and looking for any other marginal comments Laura's mother might have written. He found nothing more, only the one comment about the biblical Rachel. He was about to turn off his desk lamp and retreat to his cot, when he noticed a slight discrepancy between the front and back covers. The inside front cover seemed to be a slightly different color and texture than the inside back cover. As he held the book up to the light from his desk lamp, he realized someone had glued the first blank page of the Bible to the inside cover.

Intrigued, Finley searched for an envelope opener in his desk and gently inserted it between the blank page and the inside cover. He carefully ran the thin blade across the top of the page until he had separated it from the cover. He did the same with the bottom and outer edges of the page. When he had separated the first blank page from the original inside cover, he exposed the handwritten inscription, "To Esther, on her very special day. Love Rachel."

*Laura's mother apparently wanted to keep this inscription hidden. However, she didn't want it destroyed because only the outer edges, not the entire page, were glued to the cover. Why was she so determined to preserve something she was hiding?*

Charlie Flanigan was too excited and agitated for Laura to get anything coherent out of him. After a long, rambling discourse about the Lilac Lady, he walked into the fog with his flashlight, and Laura drove back to Point Tyson. As she approached the city park, she decided to get out of the car and sit for a few minutes on one of the benches by the bandstand. Her encounter with Charlie in the cemetery had left her befuddled and perplexed. She decided she needed some time to collect her thoughts before she returned to the bed and breakfast.

The stars and a full moon were still silhouetted against the darkness that hovered over the small town. The moonlight illuminated the branches of the dead elm trees and washed gently across the pitted concrete surface of the dance floor. A single light glowed in one of the windows above the abandoned stores on Main Street.

As Laura sat on the park bench, she thought about what she had experienced in the cemetery. She could only think of three possible explanations for the flowers on the graves of Grant and Rachel Sims. Either Charlie was involved in some bizarre, on-going prank that meant nothing to anyone anymore, except himself. Or someone else had slipped into the cemetery and placed the lilacs on the graves. Or there was some mysterious, supernatural presence that wandered through the cemetery at night, placing lilacs on the graves.

Charlie had been so sincere about what he thought he had seen that it was difficult not to believe him. Still, Laura was extremely skeptical about his explanation. She was convinced that either he was continuing a bizarre prank he had started many years ago for reasons only he understood, or someone else had come out to the cemetery and placed the flowers on the graves under the cover of darkness.

*But who would have done that? And why?*

She pondered what, if anything, it had to do with the curious note her mother had scribbled next to the biblical Rachel.

*Was that note a comment on the Rachel Sims who disappeared in 1952? Were the "lies" Mother referred to in the note a reference to the gossip that followed in the aftermath of her disappearance?*

Then another possibility suddenly occurred to her.

*Could Rachel Sims have faked her own disappearance? Was it possible that she lived somewhere else and returned to the cemetery under the cover of darkness to place flowers on her husband's grave? Was it a remorseful response for having left him for another man?*

Laura awoke that night in a panic. She struggled to remember what it was that had frightened her so terribly.

*It's the dream again!*

She tried to remember the details of the dream. It was always vague, always tantalizingly close, yet always distant and unreachable.

*There was the darkness again, with flashes of light, movement, and strange faces. This time there was a human figure gliding through the darkness. It was a woman, and she was holding something. But she appeared and disappeared so quickly as to be unrecognizable. Then the darkness covered everything, and the fear and sense of loss were overwhelming.*

# CHAPTER NINE

At breakfast the next morning, Gunda told Laura about a small historical society in a former church school east of town. She said they had some records of the Sentinels of God Church stored in the basement. Since Rachel Sims apparently belonged to that church, Laura decided to drive out there to see if she could find anything that might connect the missing farm wife to her parents. The note, "So many lies," her mother had scribbled in the margin next to the story of the biblical Rachel seemed even more ominous in the context of what she had learned about the disappearance of Rachel Sims in 1952.

Her emotional response to the mysterious Rachel Sims was becoming even more deeply subliminal and powerful. She did not know why. She only knew that it was becoming an obsession. After thinking about it for much of the night, she was convinced there was a connection between the disappearance of Rachel Sims and her parents' decision to go into hiding.

*I just need to dig deeper into this small town's history to find that connection. It must be there someplace.*

She still did not know what to make of Charlie Flanigan's bizarre behavior in the cemetery the previous evening. None of the possible explanations for what had happened out there made any sense. Rather than speculate any more, Laura decided to concentrate on trying to establish a link between Rachel Sims and her parents—if one existed.

*If I can make that connection, then perhaps a lot of other things that seemed unexplainable might start to make more sense.*

On the way out of town, she drove past several three-story, post-Victorian homes with huge, circular porches and steep gables. Some of the homes were boarded up and abandoned. Others had late-model automobiles parked in pitted driveways next to weed-infested yards. All the homes spoke of an earlier time when Point Tyson had a moneyed upper class that lived in considerable luxury.

She drove east for several hundred yards on a county road that ran parallel to the northern channel of the Lonely Willow River. Then she lost sight of the river when it disappeared behind a thicket of trees. Overhead, the sky was partly cloudy, and in the south rain clouds were forming on the horizon.

As she drove into a dirt parking lot and stepped out of the car, she saw that the school was constructed out of gray granite blocks cemented together with a lighter colored gray mortar. A simple cross, created out of a darker colored stone, was positioned prominently above the front door. There were no other decorations or biblical ornamentations anywhere on the stone structure.

As she walked into the school, she saw that the interior was similarly plain. The desks and chairs had been removed to make room for three wooden tables and six chairs. Various documents and books were stored in unfinished wooden bookcases around all four walls. Another plain wooden cross hung above a blackboard at the front of the room.

An elderly woman's head suddenly appeared from the open doorway of a closet next to the blackboard. Her white hair was pulled back in a ponytail, and she was holding cleaning rags in both hands. She gave the immediate impression that she was a one-person historical society, and she was trying to fulfill all her roles simultaneously.

"Can I help you?" she asked, smiling politely.

"I was just hoping to look around," Laura replied. "Gunda Arneson told me you have the old records for the Sentinels of God Church stored here."

"Well, we have some of them. But certainly not all of them. Is there something specific you were looking for?"

"I'm trying to find some information on a Rachel Sims who disappeared near Hodges Island in the early 1950s. I was told she was a member of this church."

"I've heard of that incident," the woman replied. "Mostly second hand, I'm afraid. I've only lived in Archer County for nine years. Olga Peterson's the name, incidentally."

"Laura Fielding," Laura said.

"What exactly are you trying to find out about this Rachel Sims?"

"Well, I really don't know. I guess maybe something about the people she was related to. Things like that."

"We don't have the birth records, of course. They're at the County Recorder's Office in Pelican Lake. We have some of the old baptismal and confirmation records. The rest are stored in the basement of the new church in Pelican Lake."

"New church?"

"Younger members of the church split with the original members back in the 1950s. There are only a couple of the earlier members of the original church who are still alive."

"Why did they split?"

"The original Sentinels of God Church was deeply opposed to all types of modernization. They kept their lives simple and their numbers limited. The younger members were more ambitious. They wanted to take advantage of television, radio, and all the other newer technologies to spread the Gospel to a much larger audience. They moved to Pelican Lake and started their own church. They call themselves the New Sentinels of God Church."

"Who owns this building now?"

"County bought this school about ten years ago from the last of the original members of the church. Turned it into a rural historical society. We have no connections to the New Sentinels of God Church. We inherited many of the records of the original church, but we also have other records pertaining to rural Archer County history that have nothing to do with the church. The problem is that most of what we have has never been catalogued or indexed. I don't get much help, I'm afraid."

Laura glanced around the room at the wooden bookcases. "I was told the church leaders would not allow members to be photographed. Is that true?"

"Well, it's partially true. They were not allowed family pictures, or pictures of themselves outside of church events. That kind of photography was considered an act of vanity. All photographs had to be authorized by church leaders. Usually, they were formal pictures taken during church events. The photographs and baptismal records we have are in the basement. That's probably where you should start looking for the things you've described to me."

Olga led Laura over to another doorway on the opposite end of the blackboard, and they descended a wooden staircase into a basement that was illuminated by a single overhead light. The four walls were constructed out of stone that had been plastered over and whitewashed. Several plank bookcases and numerous wooden filing cabinets were organized around the outer walls. A table and two chairs were in the middle of the basement. At the top of each wall, a single window was set deeply into the stone blocks.

"I wish I could tell you where to start looking," Olga said, shaking her head slowly. "Maybe in that filing cabinet over there. Another volunteer started to organize these records, but she got real sick and died about three years ago. That's when I took over."

Olga excused herself and quickly walked back up the staircase. Laura heard the door slam shut, and then she walked over to the filing cabinet. She pulled the top drawer out of the cabinet, placed it on top of the table, and started going through its contents. After several hours of wading through old church documents, she did not discover anything about her parents or Rachel Sims. She did, however, gain some insights into the Sentinels of God Church.

From the documents she read, Laura gathered that the Sentinels of God were absolutely convinced that Satan was a real entity in the world, and the church itself was involved in an on-going war with the forces of evil. She also sensed that church leaders believed they had to harden themselves and return to a strictly fundamentalist interpretation of the Bible if they were to be victorious in the war against the powers of darkness. Sexual transgressions were clearly the focus of their morality. There did not seem to be any room in their thinking for independent spirits who refused to toe the line and accept church policies or teachings.

When she finished with the first drawer, she placed it back in the filing cabinet and quickly opened and surveyed the contents of the three remaining drawers. The bottom drawer, which contained prayer books and other religious materials, did not seem very promising until she noticed a leather-bound Bible buried beneath some confirmation documents. The Bible reminded Laura of her mother's Bible.

*It has the same cover! The same print type! The same cardboard inserts!*

Laura placed the drawer on the table and slowly sorted through its contents. Near the bottom, she found a handful of formal photographs that were taken at various church functions. In one of the black and white photographs, the congregation had assembled on the front lawn of the church. There was no date, but someone had meticulously drawn arrows to several of the people who were identified as Isaiah Thompson, Thaddeus Morton, Zechariah Morton, Nathaniel Klinger, Ruth Klinger, Theodore Turner, Sarah Turner, and Mathew Franklin. All the men were bearded, and they had stern, emotionless expressions on their faces, while their wives posed stiffly and obediently by their sides. There were no children in the photograph.

The clothing they wore seemed to come from an earlier century, as though the years between did not exist. All the clothing, whether worn by the men or the women, appeared to be variations of the same drab colors and designs. There was clearly no room for individual expressions in either their attire or religious culture.

Two of the written notations were smudged and almost indecipherable, but as Laura held the photograph up to the light, she could make out the names Grant Sims and Rachel Sims. Grant Sims was posed much like the other men in the photograph, except that there was a glow of kindness in his eyes that was not evident in the eyes of the other bearded men. Nor did Rachel Sims pose as stiffly and obediently as the other women. Instead, she had an almost imperceptible half smile on her face as she looked warmly into the camera.

Studying the other faces in the photograph, Laura noticed something else. An unidentified couple standing near Grant and Rachel Sims reminded her of two people she knew very well.

*Mother! Father! They are very young, but this must be them!*

Trying to control her excitement, she rushed up the staircase. But when she reached the top step and pushed hard on the basement door, it would not open. Frantically, she turned the metal knob back and forth. Still the door would not open.

"Is anyone out there?" she yelled. When no one answered, she knocked on the door and yelled again, "Is anyone there?"

After several more minutes of struggling with the locked door, she walked back down to the basement. She picked up a chair and carried it over to one of the windows located high in the stone walls. As she stood on her tiptoes and stared out the window, she saw a black spider pressed against the other side of the glass pane.

A short distance beyond the green lawn that grew up to the very edge of the school's foundation, she saw a horse-drawn carriage moving slowly down the gravel road. A tiny spiraling cloud of dust swirled out from behind the carriage wheels and dissipated over a nearby field.

As the carriage drew nearer, she could hear the muffled rattle of leather against leather and the creaking of the carriage frame. Moments later, the carriage passed the school and disappeared.

"I can see that you've pretty much destroyed my old room, Ned," Schlepler said as a male orderly pushed his wheelchair into Finley's office and over to the desk. The orderly quickly left the room. "You must believe in chaos theory," Schlepler continued. "I, at least, developed some semblance of order when I lived here. You have none."

"An uncluttered mind is a shallow mind," Finley replied good-naturedly.

"Perhaps," Schlepler countered. "However, the first rule for utilizing space is to leave enough room for people to sit and walk. You have ignored that fundamental principle."

"Whatever you might think of my slovenly ways," Finley replied, reaching for the Bible on his desk, "I'm glad you are getting around again and decided to stop by. Remember when you said you sensed a 'hidden voice' in this Bible. Well, there *was* a hidden voice. A handwritten inscription actually. I found it last night. It was hidden behind a blank page that was glued over the inside cover."

Finley placed the Bible on Schlepler's lap and settled back into his chair. He watched as Schlepler slowly ran his fingertips across the inscription.

"Yes, I believe this is the voice I heard," Schlepler speculated softly.

"Do you think it's the same 'Rachel' who disappeared over by Point Tyson in the 1950s?"

"Most likely."

"What about . . ."

"Ned, this Bible was held by many people. It retains something from all of those who have touched it. Some more than others."

"Who is the 'Esther' referred to in the inscription?" Finley inquired.

"Obviously whoever was given the Bible as a gift," Schlepler replied somewhat impatiently.

"Laura's mother?"

"Probably. Unless she was not the original owner."

"Why would anyone go to such extremes to glue a blank page over the inner cover of a Bible to conceal an inscription?"

"There are many possibilities."

"Such as?"

"If the person who glued the blank page was the second or third owner, she might have concealed the inscription to create the impression that it was a new Bible before passing it on as a gift to someone else."

"Wouldn't she have glued the entire page and not just the edges, so no one could ever separate it from the cover as I did?"

"I would think so."

"What are the other possibilities?"

"If the person who received this changed her name later in life, she might not have wanted anyone to ask why she owned a Bible that was a gift to someone named Esther. Or she might not have wanted her daughter to see it and ask who Esther was. Or she might have been concealing her relationship to Rachel, while keeping a gift that meant a great deal to her."

"So, which is it?" Finley asked.

"The person who held and read this Bible more than all others cherished the inscription and always wanted to know it was there, but she was terrified of something that involved the Rachel who gave her the Bible. The fear is evident in every page she read or touched."

"And that person had to be Laura's mother, the Esther in the inscription?"

"I think so, yes. The other voice is even stronger, although it is confined mostly to the few short words that were concealed behind the blank page."

"Rachel?"

"Yes. In that inscription, and on other pages where she touched this Bible even briefly, she is trying to get our attention, her daughter's attention, and anyone else who will hear her."

"Her *daughter*?"

"I believe Laura is Rachel's daughter," Schlepler said softly. "I believe she was raised by Esther for reasons that are unclear. Your patient is testing her own early memories of her mother. But she is probably also responding to a voice she hears from somewhere in her past—or perhaps from a voice she hears behind the window where strange forms flit back and forth in the night, and sometimes one of them stops and tries to communicate with her."

>◇◇◇◇<

"Is anyone out there?" Laura yelled as she stood once again on the top step of the basement staircase. "Please, is anyone out there?"

Suddenly, she heard footsteps and the door burst open. "I'm so sorry," Olga apologized. "I should never have shut that door when you were down there. The lock is broken and it sometimes sticks. I had to run a few errands. I'm very sorry."

"I found this," Laura exclaimed. She was still excited about the photograph she had found in the filing cabinet, even though she had been locked in the basement for almost an hour. "It's a picture of the church congregation, apparently taken sometime in the early 1950s. Grant and Rachel Sims are in this picture."

"So, you found what you were looking for?"

"Yes, and much more," Laura said. She was apprehensive about telling Olga that her parents were also in the photograph. She felt it was more prudent to keep that information to herself until she knew where her parents fit into the mystery that surrounded the disappearance of Rachel Sims. "Is it possible to get a copy of this photograph?"

"We haven't been able to afford a copy machine," Olga explained. "But I could take it home with me and have a copy made in Pelican Lake. You could pick it up tomorrow."

"I would appreciate that. Tell me something else. I was told the Sentinels of God Church has its own cemetery. Where is it located?"

"About one mile east of here? You can't miss it. It's right next to the church."

"Is the church open?"

"Not officially. The few remaining members of the old church only use it for funerals. But that doesn't happen very often, since they're almost all gone. Other than that, they do mostly home worship. Most of them are too sickly to go out very much."

"How do I get inside?"

"Just walk through the front door. Lock's been broken long as I've been here. Just push hard on the door. It'll open."

Laura thanked Olga for her help and quickly walked out to her car. She drove east another mile until she spotted a church surrounded by pine trees on the northern side of the road. She parked outside the gates and walked under a rusty archway with the words "Sentinels of God Church" intertwined in the metal frame.

At the uppermost part of the archway, three bearded figures holding staffs and Bibles peered into the distance. Undoubtedly, she decided, they were the "sentinels" who were responsible for protecting the church community from the forces of evil that were everywhere in the outside world.

*Even in death, the deceased members of the Sentinels of God Church were apparently not safe from the powers of darkness.*

The cemetery was located just inside the gates. As Laura passed the marble and granite gravestones, she recognized several of the names she had seen on church documents in the historical society basement. The stones, although varying in size, were as simple and plain as the school building. None had any decorations or ornamentations inscribed on them.

The church, also constructed out of gray granite blocks, was almost a replica of the school. She pushed hard on the front door, as Olga had instructed her to do. As it creaked and scrapped open, she could smell the dank, musty odor of mold and rotting wood. The interior of the church was dark and gloomy, and the woodwork was sharp and angular. The wooden pews and altar had darkened with age, making the interior seem even more gloomy and repressive.

She sat down in one of the pews and pondered what she had just learned at the historical society. Now that she had found a photograph of her parents standing next to Grant and Rachel Sims, there was no question that they were all connected in some way.

*But what precisely was the connection, other than the fact that they obviously belonged to the same church?*

She tried to imagine what her parents might have looked like sitting in the Sentinels of God Church during a Sunday service. It was difficult to imagine their lives as members of a church congregation that seemed to belong to an earlier century. She struggled to see them in that setting, dressed in the same drab clothing that seemed almost to be a uniform appropriate for Sunday services.

Then she tried to imagine what Grant and Rachel Sims might have looked like, sitting in one of the pews next to her parents. From the church photograph, it was obvious they were more relaxed and less concerned with decorum than others in the congregation.

*They were probably smiling gently during the sermon, while the other members of the congregation sat erect, their faces betraying no emotion.*

As the sun slowly shifted and entered the church windows from a more horizontal angle, she felt an omnipresent sense of guilt lingering in the air. It seemed as though the sins of many generations who had worshipped in the Sentinels of God Church had remained behind, while their bodies were buried out back in the cemetery. It was an unsettling feeling, one that was reinforced by the pervasive odor of mold and decaying wood that filled the church.

*It seems like a grim, unforgiving place.*

As she continued to study the interior of the church, she had another feeling. At first it was subtle, almost imperceptible, but it soon became more intense. It was intangible, unconnected to any thought or sensation, yet as real as the dark, gloomy pews, altar, and other woodwork that surrounded her.

*This is not the first time I've been in this church! I've been here before!*

When she finally stood up to leave, she noticed a framed document hanging on the back wall, just inside the doorway. The undated document, which was clearly very old, was titled "Honor Role of the Sentinels of God Church." Below the title, some of the names she had seen on the gravestones and church documents were listed among the honorees.

One name that she had not seen before was also listed on the honor role: Selma Sims.

*Selma Sims! Selma Madison? Was she related to Grant Sims?*

By the time Laura walked outside, the storm clouds that had been gathering in the south had moved off in a different direction. The sky overhead was clear and blue. A slight breeze was gently massaging the pine trees that surrounded the cemetery.

She walked back and forth among the rows of cemetery stones, studying each one to determine if it was the grave of the Selma Sims she had just seen on the list of honorees posted in the back of the church. It was a small cemetery that contained no more than two hundred graves.

The gravestones were organized in a hierarchical pattern, with the larger stones in the middle, and the less pretentious, ground-level stones on the perimeters.

*Even in death the church hierarchy remains supreme.*

The largest gravestone in the cemetery was inscribed with the names Theodore Isaac Turner and Sarah Marie Turner. Nearby, a much smaller gravestone was inscribed Phoebe Ruth Turner. Many of the white marble and reddish-brown granite surfaces of the gravestones had darkened and discolored with age. It took her less than an hour to walk the rows of cemetery stones. Although she found the last name Sims on two of the older stones, there was no Selma Sims buried anywhere in the church cemetery.

There was one recently dug grave on the northern end of the cemetery, next to two spades that had been thrust into a pile of black soil. As Laura walked past the grave, she wondered if perhaps a trip back to Baxter, Wisconsin, might be in order. Maybe she should visit Selma Madison's home again to see if anything there connected the elderly woman to Grant Sims. Or perhaps the name Selma Sims might call forth some faint recollection from Selma Madison, even in the fog of her dementia. If so, she would know the elderly woman was related to Grant Sims, probably his sister.

*I now know that Mother and Father knew Rachel Sims, and they were all members of the Sentinels of God Church. But the role of Selma Madison in their lives is still murky and unclear. She seems to be the key to where I fit into this deeply troubling, impossibly complex relationship. What were the motives that brought them all together and unified them in a mutual bond of secrecy and false identities they maintained for the next two decades?*

As Laura drove west, she saw a horse-drawn wagon moving slowly in her direction. Moments later, she realized it was two horse-drawn wagons. An elderly, bearded man, who wore a black coat and round-brimmed black hat, drove the first wagon, which carried a plain wooden casket. An elderly couple followed behind the casket in the other wagon. The man in the second wagon was also dressed in a black coat and hat, and the woman wore a black dress and bonnet.

Laura glanced in her rear-view mirror as the horse-drawn wagons turned into the church cemetery and disappeared behind the pine trees.

# CHAPTER TEN

Before driving to Farmington to meet with Dr. Finley, Laura stopped at Point Tyson's only functional phone booth and made a call to the Lake View Retirement Home in Baxter, Wisconsin. The receptionist who had been working behind the desk when Laura visited Selma Madison answered the phone.

"I'm Laura Fielding," Laura explained. "I stopped by last week to see Selma Madison."

"Yes, I remember you."

"I was thinking about driving over to visit her again this weekend. I thought I would check first to see if she is able to have company."

"I'm so sorry," the receptionist said gently. "Obviously you didn't get the news about Selma. She died in her sleep three days ago. It was very peaceful, and not unexpected."

"I'm . . . I'm sorry to hear that," Laura stammered.

"Selma checked the box on her admission papers that indicated she wished to be cremated, should she die while she was under our care. The county carried out her wishes yesterday. There was no one at the funeral service, although a man did call and ask about her."

"Who was he?"

"He never identified himself. He hung up as soon as I told him Selma had passed on."

Laura paused to consider the implications of what she had just learned. "What was the cause of death?" she asked.

"Oh, she had so many things wrong with her. It could have been almost anything. Most of us were surprised she held on as long as she did."

"I've been doing more research into my family history," Laura explained. "I think I might be related to Selma in some way, but I'm not exactly sure how. Do you know if there was anything in her records that indicates her name might once have been Selma Sims?"

"Funny you should ask about that. I was packing up Selma's things to give to charity when I noticed the initials on her old suitcase were 'SS'. I figured it was probably the only suitcase she ever owned, and those were her initials before she got married."

"Was she ever married?"

"I don't know," the receptionist replied sympathetically. "Poor Selma. Her ashes hadn't even been scattered when someone broke into her home and vandalized it. Apparently took some of the few things she had left in this world. Some people even prey on the recently deceased, I guess."

"Do they know who did it?"

"No. The funny thing is they didn't take anything valuable. Just some of her personal belongings and apparently some of the photographs that were still hanging on her walls. That's why the authorities think it might be someone who was close to Selma. At least that's what they told us when they came out here to see what we knew about her."

"What did they want to know?" Laura asked.

"They wanted to know if Selma had any visitors lately, and I showed them your name in our guest register. I told them you were the only one who ever came out to see her as far as I knew."

"Who were these 'authorities'?"

"Just some detectives from Madison. At least that's what they told me. They were dressed in plain clothes and showed me their badges. I assumed that's who they were."

Laura thought about the implications of her conversation with the receptionist as she drove to Farmington to see Dr. Ned Finley. She didn't know if the visit the authorities made to the Lake View Retirement Home was a routine follow-up to a home break-in, or whether it had more sinister implications. She didn't even know if the "authorities," as the reception described them, were working for law enforcement or were posing as detectives to gather evidence about the people who might have visited Selma Madison before she died. She also wondered if perhaps their visit had something to do with the questions she had been asking the people in Point Tyson. Perhaps it had something to do with the disappearance of Rachel Sims and the reasons her parents had gone into hiding for all those years.

*Whoever it was now has my name, and they know I was inter-ested enough in Selma Madison to visit her at the retirement home.*

An even more troubling possibility suddenly occurred to her.

*What if the home break-in and follow-up visit to the retirement home were connected to the threatening note and white truck that almost ran me off the road? If so, the break-in and visit to the retire-ment home had far more sinister, deeply threatening implications.*

As she parked in Farmington's spacious lot, she decided to put those questions out of her mind, at least temporarily. She had other pressing concerns she wanted to discuss with Dr. Finley. She walked quickly past the mental patients sitting on benches that lined the hallway near Finley's office. Finley was sitting be-hind his desk when she entered the room.

"From your last telephone call, I take it you have something important to share with me," he said, looking up and gesturing for her to sit in the chair on the other side of the desk.

"Yes. I've learned a lot since I last talked to you," Laura ex-plained. "I found a photograph of my parents standing next to Grant and Rachel Sims at a church function. When the Archer County Recorder's Office opens next Monday, I'm going to check to see if they have birth certificates for any children born to Grant and Rachel Sims. I think I might be their daughter."

"Why do you think that?" Finley asked.

"I *feel* it more than anything else. I just *feel* it."

"I discovered something that might validate those feelings," Finley said, reaching for the Bible and handing it to Laura. "I was looking through your mother's Bible the other night when I realized something didn't seem right about the inside front cover. The first blank page was glued to the cover, apparently to conceal an inscription."

Laura opened the Bible to the inside cover and read the inscription out loud. "To Esther, on her very special day. Love Rachel."

"Aurther Schlepler thinks Esther might be your mother's name before she changed her identity and went into hiding," Fin-ley explained.

"I thought you said he hadn't talked to anyone in years."

"He didn't. But he's developed an interest in your case. I primed the pump a bit."

Laura read the inscription again. "This would certainly ex-plain why I saw all of them standing next to one another in the church photograph."

"Yes, it would," Finley agreed. "Aurther also thinks you might be Rachel's daughter. I don't know how he came to that conclusion, but usually he's pretty perceptive about those kinds of things."

Laura looked briefly out the window and then back at Finley. "Remember that dream I told you about, the one I had many times when I was young?"

"The one where you're surrounded by darkness and unrecognizable faces?"

"Yes. It's back. And every time there are more details. Now there's a young woman gliding through the darkness, and some of the figures are becoming more real. Like they've been inside me all my life, and yet I've never known them. I don't know if I'm subconsciously adding things to the dream from what I learned in Point Tyson, or if they're real memories. But they seem real."

"Maybe you're recalling your earliest childhood memories."

"Maybe."

"There is one way to find out. We can try regressive hypnosis. It might yield up some of the answers we're looking for. But there are risks. As I explained earlier, it can open up memories that are perhaps better off left in the past, unexposed."

"It's worth the risks," Laura replied emphatically. "I need to find out how my parents and I fit into this bizarre puzzle, and why my whole life up to this point has apparently been one big lie. If Rachel Sims is my mother, then I need to know why she disappeared and why I was raised by another couple."

"Okay, then," Finley said, "let me explain how regressive hypnosis works. It's not exactly the way they portray it in movies, although there are some similarities. I will be developing a mental image that I want you to concentrate on completely. I am going to describe it in some detail, so it will take time. Then I am going to change that mental image and reverse the chronological progression of your life so we take you backwards in time until we hopefully unlock the subconscious memories from your earliest childhood."

"What do you mean by 'mental image'?" Laura asked.

"Something concrete. Something that can age and die and be replenished again. Something organic like a plant or tree works well."

"I've always loved the blossoming lilac bushes," Laura said softly. "My mother said even as a young girl I would pick the purple flowers off the bushes in our back yard and bring them inside for her to put in a vase. And now I've learned from the townspeople in Point Tyson and the cemetery caretaker that the person who may be my mother is also associated with lilacs. Maybe we could use a lilac bush in the regressive process."

"I was thinking of that as a possibility, but I wanted you to make the choice." Finley walked over to a black reclining chair and removed the books that were stacked on it. "Please come over here and sit down. I want you to relax completely while we take you back in time to your earliest childhood memories."

As Laura sat down in the reclining chair, Finley placed another chair next to it. He started a tape recorder on an adjacent table. "I will be recording this session," he explained. "That way I can replay it to determine if there is anything I have overlooked. Anything that might help us understand what is locked inside your subconscious mind. Is all of this clear to you?"

"Yes, I understand what we're doing."

"Good. Now I want you to concentrate on developing a picture in your mind of a single blossoming lilac bush in the spring. The bush is filled with beautiful purple flowers, and it stands alone in a field without anything else around it. The flowers are waving in the breeze. Can you see the beautiful purple flowers, Laura?"

"Yes, I can see them."

"Good. Now concentrate on those purple flowers as we go backwards in time. The purple flowers slowly shrink back into the branches of the lilac bush and disappear completely. Now it is winter and the lilac bush is barren of leaves and flowers. It stands alone in the middle of a field while snow drifts across the landscape. Then it is fall and dead leaves are all that remain of the foliage on the lilac bush. Summer brings back the lilac flowers, only they are ghostly gray in color. Then it is spring again, and the purple flowers reappear once again on the lilac bush. Laura, can you see the changes in the lilac bush as the seasonal cycle is reversed?"

"Yes, I see it," she whispered sleepily. "I see it . . ."

"Now we are going to speed up the cycle and make those changes happen so fast the colors become a blur. It is spring and the purple flowers appear on the lilac bush. Then winter arrives and they disappear. Then it is fall and all that remains are the dead leaves. Then it is summer and the ghostly gray petals appear. The cycle of time keeps turning faster and faster, and the purples and grays become a blur that slowly surrounds and pulls you into a swirling vortex of time . . ."

><><><

For over half an hour, Finley directed Laura more deeply into the hypnotic trance. He continued to use the image of the lilac bush as it changed in a reversed seasonal pattern to gradually expose earlier and earlier memories. At one point, Laura started to cry softly. When Finley probed to find out why she was so sad, she responded, "I feel alone. I sit in my room and cry because I feel so alone."

Finley sensed that she was describing her emotions in the home she shared with the people she thought were her parents. He decided to take her even deeper into her childhood memories. "Laura," he said gently, "concentrate on the beautiful purple flowers of the lilac bush as they shrink back into the branches, only to disappear completely, then reappear again. I want you to reverse that seasonal cycle until it becomes a blur of purple and gray."

Finley paused for several seconds and then asked, "Laura, where are you now?"

Her lips moved almost imperceptibly.

"Where are you?" Finley asked again.

"A swing . . ." she said happily.

"Are you on a swing? Is someone with you?"

*Her mother's voice was soft, gentle. Then, suddenly, she was gone.*

"Gone . . ."

"Is someone with you by the swing?" Finley asked.

"Gone! Gone! Gone!" Laura whispered.

"Who is with you?" Finley asked. "Is it your mother?"

Laura started to cry softly, like a little girl who was overcome with sadness.

"Are you missing your mother? Is that why you are crying?"

"Mommy. . . Mommy . . ."

"Was Rachel Sims your mother?" Finley asked.

*She had waited by the swing, crying for her mother to return. Every morning she waited. The man with the beard and kind eyes would hold her and try to comfort her, but she could not stop crying.*

"No! No! Don't want to go!"

"Now what is happening?" Finley asked.

"Don't want to . . ."

"Is someone trying to take you away?" Finley asked. "Who is trying to take you away?"

*She stretched to look out the car window. The man with the beard and kind eyes kept waving at her until she could see him no more. Then she started to cry. She cried until she fell asleep. She dreamt about her mother and the swing.*

"What happened to you?" Finley asked emphatically. "Do you remember anything at all about the way your mother disappeared? Were you there? Did someone do something terrible to your mother?"

"Men! Angry men . . ."

"Who were these men?"

*Her mother was afraid. She could feel it. She too became afraid. Then there was another sound. Another angry sound. Her mother was running. Running away from the angry voices.*

"Run! Run! Run!" Laura screamed as she started thrashing around on the reclining chair.

"It's okay," Finley said firmly, but gently. "I'm going to take you out of the hypnotic trance now. I want you to reverse the pattern of the seasonal cycles and follow the changing colors of the lilac flowers as the years pass. When it is May of 1974, I want you to open your eyes."

Laura's eyes slowly blinked open. "What happened?" she asked.

"We visited some of your childhood memories," Finley explained. "Do you remember anything at all about what you just experienced?"

"I remember feeling terribly sad and alone. Then I was very afraid."

"You talked about your mother. Do you remember her?"

"Only that I missed her."

"You did miss her. You missed her terribly."

"Was she Rachel Sims?"

"I believe so. I believe you were a very young child during the events that led up to her disappearance. You were so young that they are only vague memories. Yet, somehow in those memories there are clues as to what happened to your mother, and who was responsible for her disappearance."

"There's something else, Dr. Finley," Laura said. "I've never been on Hodges Island, where she disappeared, and yet I just had the strangest sensation that I had been there before. It wasn't one of those quick flashbacks that appear and disappear, but mean nothing. I still feel it."

"Maybe you *were* there before," Finley speculated. "Have you ever heard of 'emotional memories'?"

"No. I participated in a psychology experiment once on memory. I was told I had an unusual memory, one that remembered everything in very vivid pictures. But no one used that term."

"They're memories we have of things we have experienced at such a young age that we don't remember them at the conscious level," Finley explained. "They are, however, very real at some deeper subconscious level. They come to the surface occasionally, then disappear again. Often, when early childhood experiences are deeply traumatic, they create huge emotional voids that we try all our lives to fill. They affect us into our adult years in ways we don't understand because we don't even know they are there."

"What kind of traumatic experiences would do that?"

"Many childhood experiences can create emotional memories," Finley explained. "A very common reason is a child's separation from its mother. That would constitute a classic example of an emotional memory. The child would try all her life to fill that void, and would probably never understand how that loss had affected decisions she made as an adult. It could easily create an attachment or bonding disorder that followed her through life. Before you leave today, I'll write down the title of a book on the subject. It should be available in almost any university library. You should read it."

"Sounds like my life story," Laura said. "It might explain the problems I've had with relationships and the strange dream I've had at different times in my life. Maybe it's based on something that happened to me when I was very young, even before I could remember things at a more conscious level."

"If Rachel Sims is your mother, and you were with her in the months before she disappeared, you would have bonded with her. In the years that followed, you would have been surrounded by the emotional memories of her presence in your life. Later, you would probably have remembered her at some deep, subconscious level—albeit those emotional memories would be colored with great sadness and loss."

"Maybe there's another explanation. Maybe they are her memories," Laura speculated. "Sometimes it feels like she has passed them on to me. Lately, every time I fall asleep, I feel her presence inside of me. I'm planning to go out to Hodges Island. That's where the newspaper article said she was last seen. I'm hoping that might provide some answers."

"You sure it's a good idea for you to go out there?" Finley asked.

"It's something I have to do," Laura replied firmly.

Finley reached into his desk drawer and pulled out a camera. "If you do go," he said, handing the camera to her, "could you take some pictures for me? I did some amateur photography a few years back, and I can develop the film in the basement of this building."

"What do you plan to do with the pictures?"

"Aurther used to visit crime scenes when he worked for police departments. He's too old to visit Hodges Island, but I've seen him do some incredible things with photographs."

"I suppose there's one other thing I should tell you," Laura said as she placed the camera in her purse.

"What's that?"

"I've received a series of warnings. A threatening note on my car, a truck that tried to run me off the road—things like that. There have also been other mysterious deaths in Point Tyson. One of them, a man named Alfred Kron, was killed in a hit-and-run accident. I was told that he was also trying to figure out what happened to Rachel Sims. Apparently, he didn't accept the gossiped version that she left the area with another man."

"Sounds like someone is still trying to discourage people from learning the truth about her disappearance."

"That appears to be the case."

"You need to be very careful," Finley said emphatically.

"I know," Laura replied. "But no one needs to know the truth about her disappearance more than I do. From what I just felt under hypnosis, I am now convinced she is my mother. I need to know what happened to her, and why I was taken away from her."

It was late evening when Laura arrived back in Point Tyson. A thick, dark cloud cover hovered above the small town, concealing the moon and stars. As she drove down Main Street, a bright streak of lightning suddenly flashed across the night sky, illuminating the dying elm trees in the city park. The only store that had any lights on was the café. Another light glowed dimly in one of the apartments above an abandoned hardware store. Gunda was sitting on the front porch when she drove up to the bed and breakfast.

"Looks like we could get some heavy rains tonight or tomorrow," Gunda speculated. "Thought I'd wait up for you out here. I like to use this front porch as much as possible, even when it's raining. Another two or three weeks, and there'll be too many mosquitoes. I'll have to use the enclosed porch on the other side of the house."

"If it's not raining tomorrow," Laura said, sitting down on one of the wooden chairs, "I'm going over to Hodges Island to look around. What's the quickest way to get over there?"

"Still trying to figure out what happened to Rachel Sims?"

"Yes, I am."

"Well, you need to be careful. I wouldn't go out there without first checking with Pete Solvie. He can tell you what to watch out for."

Another streak of lightning spread across the night sky, illuminating the Lonely Willow River. In the distance, a single farmhouse glowed like a tiny pin prick of light on an otherwise dark prairie.

Gunda glanced to her left at Point Tyson's Main Street. "You know," she said, "I've been sitting here, looking at those lights and thinking how everyone starts acting differently when a town is dying."

"In what way?"

"They stop connecting with one another," Gunda speculated softly. "They disappear into their own private worlds to protect themselves. Whatever it was that held people together and kept them going during the tough times—that's all gone. About the only good thing you can say about it is that people stop gossiping about one another. Other than that, it leaves you wondering why people ever put so much effort into building a town there in the first place."

Another streak of bright lighting suddenly flashed across the sky, illuminating a lone human figure walking across a pasture next to the Lonely Willow River.

"You'd think Sheldon would come inside once it starts raining," Gunda said sadly. "But he just keeps walking."

"Shouldn't someone go out and get him?" Laura asked.

"He won't come inside. He just keeps walking and walking until he's good and ready to stop. Then he goes back to his place in the alley behind the old drugstore."

Laura awoke again that night and stared into the darkness. She was fearful, apprehensive, not knowing where she was or how she had gotten there. Slowly, she realized she was in the upstairs bedroom of Gunda's Bed and Breakfast. She also remembered what had pulled her out of a deep sleep.

*It was the dream! Only this time there were even more details!*

Always before, the dream had been shrouded in darkness. This time there was more light, and some of the faces that flashed across the darkness were recognizable.

The men were bearded and had stern, grim expressions, except for one of them. He had a glow of kindness in his eyes. The woman standing next to him smiled almost imperceptibly as the light moved across her face. Slowly, the dark-haired woman raised her hand and held out a bouquet of lilac flowers. She nodded slightly in Laura's direction, as though offering her the flowers as a gift.

*She is reaching out to me! She knows who I am!*

# CHAPTER ELEVEN

Pete dumped a heaping tablespoon of sugar into his coffee and stirred it slowly. "If it was me," he said, "I wouldn't go out there."

"I need to see it," Laura insisted as she sat across from him in a booth in Max's Café

"Well, if you're that determined to go out to Hodges Island, then here's what you have to do. Look for the biggest granite boulder on the opposite riverbank. Stay to the right of it. As soon as you walk past that boulder, you'll be on a dirt road. Whatever you do, don't get off that road. Stay on it, and you should be okay. But I still wouldn't go out there if I were you."

"Where will the road take me?"

"It runs clear across the island. When the quarry was functioning, stone was hauled in both directions to loading docks on the river."

Laura remembered the dam she had seen when she drove out to the Point Tyson City Cemetery. "Why was the one channel closed?" she asked.

"Water levels were too low later in the summer. It wasn't cost effective to send stone down the river on barges that were only half full. The dam raised the water level in the southern channel, and fully loaded barges could go downriver until the winter freezes set in. Course even the dam didn't save the quarries. But it certainly solved some problems for a few years. It's one of the times a government project really did what it was supposed to do. We were lucky. We had a good state senator working for us."

"The one who drowned in the Lonely Willow River?"

"Yup. It was a real tragedy for this area. Let me finish telling you what you need to watch out for on Hodges Island," Pete insisted. "Right in the middle of the island, you'll see the abandoned buildings where some of the workers lived and the stone was cut. I haven't been out there in years, but I've heard they're in pretty bad shape. But again, don't get off the road and go over there to look at them. Those old buildings are deathtraps. I don't even go out there myself anymore."

"I was reading in an old *Point Tyson Chronicle* newspaper article that a farmer, I believe his name was Albert Felstuhl, saw Rachel Sims walking across the riverbed. Think she would have taken the same road you've described for me."

"If she was smart, she would have. It's the only real road on the island . . . You know, you could ask Albert what he saw that day."

"He's still alive?"

"Oh, yes. He still farms out that way. You might even talk him into walking with you over to the riverbed. He could describe exactly what he saw the day Rachel Sims disappeared."

After Pete excused himself to join his friends in the park, Laura wandered around the adjacent room, studying the newspaper clippings and photographs that were varnished to the walls. As she turned to leave, she glanced out the front window and saw the white truck that had almost run her off the road cruise slowly through town on the other side of the park. Laura watched as the truck disappeared behind some trees on the northern end of town.

*He must pass through this area several times a week!*

Finley and Schlepler listened attentively to the tape recording of Laura's regressive hypnosis session. Outside the office window, dark rain clouds were moving slowly, steadily toward Farmington. Finley gently tapped the eraser end of a pencil on his desk as he concentrated on Laura's responses to his prompts. When the session was over, he dropped the pencil on the desk and leaned over to turn off the tape recorder.

"So, what do you think?" he asked.

"There is much sadness in that young woman," Schlepler replied softly. "Deep and overwhelming sadness. There is something else, too. Something that is much more difficult to understand."

"What is it?"

"It's Laura's voice we're hearing," Schlepler attempted to explain. "At least it's her voice when she was a very young child. But as I listened to that tape, I also sensed the presence of her mother."

"Rachel Sims?"

"I'm not so sure she died on that island."

"You mean she's still alive," Finley asked, surprised by Schlepler's comment.

"Not in the way we normally think of someone being alive. No, I don't think that is the case. But she may be alive in some other way."

"Are you suggesting that the cemetery caretaker who sees her walking on the riverbanks is telling the truth? Do you believe he actually sees her on that island?"

"It's a strange universe we live in, Ned. It's possible that he's hallucinating or has some other motive for creating that story. But he may also be the one person who sees all of this more clearly than anyone else."

"Wait a minute!" Laura gasped. She paused in the middle of a muddy pasture to catch her breath.

"What's the matter?" Albert Felstuhl asked, glancing over his shoulder. Felstuhl was an older man in his early seventies, but he was lean and muscular. His long strides had carried him almost effortlessly across the pasture, while Laura struggled to keep up with him.

"Let me catch my breath," she said. "It's hard work walking through all this mud."

"It's spring," Felstuhl replied matter-of-factly. "When you walk across a cow pasture in spring, you gotta expect you're gonna run into some mud."

Laura looked across the pasture in the direction of Hodges Island. "Do you think you can show me the precise path Rachel Sims took the day she disappeared?"

"I think so, yes. But I'm not aimin' to spend any time over there on Hodges Island. I never liked going anywhere near that place."

"What were you doing over there the day you saw Rachel Sims?"

"I had this one old cow that kept gettin' outta this pasture. So, I had to go over there an' fetch her back. Got to where I hated that animal. I kept thinkin' 'bout just leavin' her over there until her tits filled up with milk an' she exploded. But, no, fool that I am, I went down into that old riverbed to fetch her back."

They continued to plod across the muddy pasture, while a cool breeze whipped through the grass and weeds. In the south, dark clouds were once again forming on the horizon. As they approached the riverbed, the steady chatter of the birds on Hodges Island grew louder.

"You know, if that storm that's brewin' in the south starts moving in our direction, you're going to get drenched," Felstuhl said somewhat apprehensively. "Maybe you should wait for another day."

"I'll be okay," Laura insisted.

At the end of the pasture, Felstuhl stretched open two rusty strands of a barbed wire fence, creating a space large enough for them to crawl through. They walked across a gravel road and stood on an embankment overlooking a riverbed.

"That's it, right over there," he said, pointing across the riverbed. "Hodges Island." Moments later, the birds on the island became strangely quiet. "Guess those birds know a storm's coming," he observed. He pointed at some rocks and boulders on the riverbed. "That Rachel Sims you were asking about, she was walking right down there. Looked like she had been there before too, 'cause she found all the dryer places to walk."

Laura stared across the riverbed, which was now a marshland covered with dead vegetation, tall weeds, and granite rocks. Large puddles of water had also formed in the riverbed, and thick bushes and a few trees had taken root in the muddy soil.

To the west, she could see the dam that had been built to close one channel of the Lonely Willow River. The island itself appeared to be an elongated piece of land that was covered with thick trees. The opposite riverbank was fringed with tall trees and thick bushes, many of which were covered with purple lilac flowers.

"How big is Hodges Island?" she asked.

"About a mile long, half a mile wide. It's not really an island in the sense that we usually think of them. Just a long piece of land that was isolated by the two channels of the Lonely Willow River."

"How did those lilac bushes get over there? Did someone plant them?"

"Story I heard many years ago is that some quarry worker decided Hodges Island was just too ugly a place to work on. He planted those lilac bushes to brighten the place up a bit. They spread little by little all across the island. They're just a pretty weed, you know."

"Can you show me where you last saw Rachel Sims?"

Felstuhl pointed across the riverbed. "Right over there, next to that big granite rock. She walked into an opening in those bushes, and that's the last I saw of her. Apparently, it was the last anyone else ever saw of her, too."

"I was told that someone by the name of Harlowe Meyers was one of the suspects in her disappearance. What do you know about him?"

Felstuhl shook his head emphatically. "I can't believe Harlowe had anything to do with it. He did get into some trouble with the law, and he did live about a mile east of here. But I just don't think it was him."

"Why are you so sure?"

"He made home brew and sold it illegally. That's how he got in trouble with the law. I can't believe he would harm a woman. He was actually very shy around women. I saw him in town once when a woman said hello to him. His face grew beet red, and he couldn't even speak. No, I can't believe he had anything to do with whatever happened to Rachel Sims."

"I read that some people thought she left town with a man who drove a car with an Iowa license plates."

"Ah, that just sounds like more gossip to me. Some people just like to think the worst of someone who made a mistake."

"Mistake?"

"I think she wandered off the main road and fell into one of the holes that pockmark that entire island. I suspect her body is still down there."

"You didn't notice anyone else around here that day, did you?"

"Nope. Just me an' that cow. Spent over an hour chasin' that dumb animal 'round the riverbed. Later that morning, Grant came out here looking for his wife, and I told him where I last saw her. He went over to Hodges Island to try to find her. He said he went all the way to the abandoned quarry buildings, where he found a ribbon that belonged to his wife. He said it was wrapped around some flowers she must've picked before she disappeared."

Laura pulled the camera Finley had given her out of her coat pocket and snapped a picture of the riverbed. Then she continued to study the area. Something about the riverbed seemed strangely, faintly familiar, although she did not know why. "Looks like someone could also get to Hodges Island on the walkway above the dam," she said as she gestured at the dam on the western end of the riverbed.

"They could," Felstuhl agreed. "But they would still have to walk along the riverbank to get to the dirt road that starts just to the right of that granite boulder. I suppose if they knew the island well enough, they might know of another way to get to the interior. But that would be awfully dangerous."

"Could someone get to the interior from the other side of the island?"

"Yes. If they knew what they were looking for, they could pull a boat up to the docking area on that side of the island and walk along the main road to the interior. But that docking area's awfully hard to find. Been overgrown with brush and trees for years."

"I think I'll go over there and get a closer look," Laura said. She started walking down the embankment to the riverbed. "Thanks for your help."

"Please be careful," Felstuhl warned her. "I don't want to be the last one to see another person who disappeared on Hodges Island. People will begin to suspect that maybe I'm involved in some way."

"I'll be careful," Laura promised.

She carefully selected a path through the brush, stones, and boulders that littered the riverbed. On the opposite riverbank, she paused to run her hand along the rough surface of the large granite boulder. She had a vague, inaccessible memory that connected her to this very spot.

*I've been here before! But when?*

She took a picture of the boulder before plunging into an opening between two bushes. She immediately found herself walking on a narrow, weed-infested dirt road. She heard the muffled chortle of birds nesting in the branches of tall trees that were waving slowly in the wind, creating an undulating canopy of green leaves high overhead. The dark clouds drifting in from the south blocked out much of the sunlight, making it seem more like early evening.

As she walked deeper into the interior of the island, she heard the steady rumble of thunder in the dark cloud formations. She also heard small animals rustling through the underbrush. On both sides of the dirt road, moss-covered tree trunks stood in the middle of tangled layers of climbing vines. In the wetter areas, lizards and snakes slithered across the path and disappeared into the thick foliage.

*What would she be doing in a place like this? Did it have something to do with Jesse Willert, the other man in her life? Or was she meeting someone else here?*

She stopped, startled by the sight of a dead rabbit in the middle of the dirt road. The rabbit had been gutted, and flies hovered around its entrails and bloody carcass.

*No predator ever guts a rabbit and leaves it lying in the middle of a dirt road! It must be another warning!*

Laura was frightened, but she decided to take a picture of the gutted rabbit and the surrounding area. Then she kept walking toward the interior of the island. Twice, she saw two narrow paths that branched out from the main road. In a tree next to one of the paths, she heard a loud, angry buzzing sound. Looking up, she saw a massive hornets nest attached to one of the lower branches. The hornets were flying furiously around the nest, seemingly ready to defend it against any intruder.

Moments later, she became aware of a strange silence that seemed to envelope the entire island. Even the winds had died. Nothing was moving. As though directed by some invisible force, every living thing had apparently ceased doing whatever it had been doing moments earlier. She had the distinct impression that she was the only living thing on the island that had not disappeared into some shelter or burrow.

Suddenly, a strong gust of wind roared down from the treetops and flattened the tall weeds and grass. She struggled to maintain her balance as she heard a loud snapping sound high overhead. A large tree branch crashed on the ground a few feet to the right of where she was standing. Glancing at an opening in the thick canopy of leaves, she saw a black tornado funnel twisting sinisterly across the sky.

She raced down the path in the opposite direction as trees and bushes tossed violently in the increasingly ferocious winds. Overhead, she heard more tree branches snapping and crashing to the ground as rain poured out of the sky.

She dove for cover behind a fallen tree trunk. Tree branches continued to crash all around her. She kept her face pressed to the ground, while she listened to the tornado roar and screech like an out of control freight train racing across the sky.

Outside Finley's office window, a heavy rain poured ceaselessly out of the dark clouds, and strong winds whipped the tree branches into a frenzy of motion. A young male orderly suddenly stepped into the open doorway and announced, "Radio just said a tornado touched down east of here, near the Wisconsin border. Sounds like it tore up some cornfields. We should be okay, though. It's moving away from us." The orderly quickly disappeared from the doorway. The sound of his voice continued to filter into the room as he made the same announcement to someone else further down the hallway.

Finley turned to face Schlepler, who sat nearby in his wheelchair. "What do you think of the new materials Dr. Herschler sent to me?" Finley asked, gesturing at several documents that were strewn across his desk.

"He was certainly very thorough," Schlepler replied. "He even included the title and a summary of your patient's proposed doctoral thesis."

"Yes, I noticed that too," Finley admitted. "Herschler has always been somewhat obsessive about keeping a complete record of everything he discusses with his patients."

"The thesis is very illuminating," Schlepler mused.

"In what way?"

"If you weren't such a philistine, Ned, maybe you would be more open to what Laura has revealed in this summary of her thesis. You need to shed the narrow tunnel vision of a clinical psychiatrist and broaden your insights to include other areas of human knowledge that existed long before Jung and Freud came on the scene."

"What exactly did she reveal in her doctoral thesis?"

"That there are real life allegories that play themselves out over and over again throughout the centuries. The masks change, but the things behind the mask remain the same. They are the same things that have manipulated people since the beginning of time."

"What does that have to do with what Laura is going through right now?" Finley asked somewhat impatiently.

"Maybe something. Maybe nothing."

Finley decided to change the subject. "She's going out to Hodges Island today," he said. "She'll be taking some photographs of the area where Rachel Sims was last seen. Presumably that's the crime scene—if a crime took place. Think you'll be up to looking at those photographs with me."

"Yes, I'll look at them," Schlepler replied with little enthusiasm.

"You seem hesitant to get involved, Aurther?"

"I've worked many crime scenes. I've seen people who were strangled, shot, stabbed, disemboweled, tortured, cut into pieces, beaten until they were unrecognizable as human beings, buried alive, tied to a fifty-pound concrete block and thrown in a lake. I've seen people hacked to death, torn apart by dogs, drowned in bathtubs. I've seen just about every awful, depraved thing one human being can do to another human being. I never look forward to visiting a crime scene. I was hoping I was done with those privileged glimpses into the darkest side of the human soul. But I will do it. I owe your patient that courtesy."

"Do you think Rachel Sims was a victim of those kind of crimes?"

"I don't know. Her spirit, or at least what she has revealed of herself so far, seemed unusually pure and good, while the forces aligned against her seemed unusually depraved and malignant. She needs someone to help her. I'm willing to play that role, along with her daughter and you, until we find some resolution to this strange case and expose the terrible forces behind this latest version of an ancient allegory."

"Oh, my, what happened to you?" Gunda asked as Laura trudged up to the front porch of the bed and breakfast.

"I got caught out in the rain," Laura replied. Her clothes were soaked and muddy, and her black hair was plastered against her head. Somehow, she had managed to protect the camera, and it was undamaged. She placed it on a wooden porch table and took off her coat.

"I was worried to death about you," Gunda lamented. "I went into the basement, along with everyone else in town, I'm sure. But I kept thinking that maybe you were out on Hodges Island when the tornado came through."

"Did it touch down anywhere in this area?"

"Nope. It leaped right over us. Radio said it did some damage further east. But look, child, come inside and I'll get you one of my robes."

"I'm all wet and muddy," Laura said.

"Don't worry about it, dear," Gunda insisted. "I'll clean the floors later. First thing we need to do is get you into some dry clothes so you don't catch your death of pneumonia."

After Laura had dried off and put on one of Gunda's robes, the two women sat in front of a wood-burning fireplace, drinking hot chocolate.

"Did you find what you were looking for on Hodges Island?" Gunda asked.

"I'm not sure. I just kept wondering what a young woman like Rachel Sims would be doing out there alone. It isn't exactly the kind of place where someone would just go for a leisurely walk."

"Maybe she was planning to meet someone?"

"Maybe," Laura agreed. "But it's a very strange place for a meeting."

"Not if you wanted to be alone," Gunda said, seemingly reminiscing. "Then it would be the perfect place. You wouldn't have to worry about anyone coming along and interrupting whatever it was you were doing out there."

"Did you ever go out to Hodges Island to meet someone?"

"No. But I was young once. I have never forgotten how that feels. I wish I could go back and do it all over again. Especially those times when you felt like love was the only thing that mattered in life. I'd give anything to feel that way again."

"Think that's what Rachel Sims was feeling the day she disappeared?"

"I don't know. But it's better to think that than to think she just decided to take an early morning stroll on Hodges Island and fell into a quarry hole. I prefer the more romantic version, even if she was married."

Before falling asleep that night, Laura sat in her room in front of the window that had a view of the Lonely Willow River. Lightning crackled occasionally across the sky, but the dark cloud cover gradually lifted, revealing bright stars overhead.

She wasn't sure what she had learned on Hodges Island. Certainly, it hadn't put her any closer to solving the mysterious puzzle that was the life and apparent death of the woman she was now convinced was her mother.

*Maybe when the weather clears, I can take another trip to the interior of the island and get some more answers.*

Something else continued to bother her as she stared out the window. She hadn't thought too much about it at first. It just seemed like something that drifted across her thoughts before retreating into a more subconscious level of her mind. But as she approached the large granite boulder on the riverbank, and especially when she ran her hand over its rough surface, she again had the overpowering feeling that it was not the first time she had visited Hodges Island.

*Did my mother take me over there before she disappeared?*

There were others in Point Tyson who stayed up late that night, staring out their windows, fearful that an even more dangerous storm might be preparing to pounce on the small prairie town. Sibley Fields was one of them. As the threat diminished and the skies cleared, he turned away from the warehouse window and walked past the area where he kept the antiques he had salvaged from the stores on Main Street. No one noticed, but he had placed the furniture and other antiques on the warehouse floor in the precise sequence of the stores that had once housed them on Main Street.

For a moment, he wondered if what he had done to preserve those memories was really worth it. Then he walked upstairs to his apartment on the second floor. At the top of the staircase, he paused and slowly dimmed the lights illuminating the antiques on the warehouse floor. The talks he had with the young woman who was trying to solve the disappearance of Rachel Sims brought back too many memories of the small town he remembered from his youth. As the lights slowly dimmed on the warehouse floor, leaving the antiques covered in darkness, he knew it would be a long night. Sometimes it was difficult to live with the memories of what might have been.

# CHAPTER TWELVE

The next morning Laura decided to return to Hodges Island, but as she drove east she saw that dark clouds were forming once again in the south. She decided instead to drive over to the school to pick up the photograph of the church congregation and to go through some more of the church records in the basement. As she drove, she continued to ponder what it was about Hodges Island that had made her think she had been there before. She could remember nothing from her past that would have provided a similar experience.

*It seemed to come from early memories that were struggling to come to the surface, guided by an unseen force. Or maybe from someplace even more remote and inaccessible.*

Olga greeted her at the school, gave her a copy of the photograph, and escorted her down to the basement. Laura wandered among the filing cabinets, finally deciding on one that contained the Sentinels of God Church records from the late1940s and early 1950s. Two of the drawers were filled with old hymnals and other church publications that appeared to have been printed locally. A third drawer contained various handwritten church records.

One of the documents listed the governing body of the Sentinels of God Church in 1947. The three Elders in the church were Theodore Turner, Thaddeus Morton, and Mathew Franklin. In addition to being an Elder in the church, Theodore Turner was listed as the "Reverend of the Sentinels of God Church." All three of the Elders were on the Church Council, as were Isaiah Thompson, Mathew Franklin, Martin Lachish, and Nathaniel Klinger. Zechariah Morton was listed as the Church Treasurer. There were no women listed at any of the various levels of the church's governing hierarchy.

Another document revealed a familiar name: Selma Sims was listed as an "Assistant to the Church Treasurer" for a short time in the late 1940s and early 1950s. Later, her name disappeared from all church documents, replaced by a new Assistant Church

Treasurer, a man named Samuel Isaacson. Other documents revealed that the church went through a financial crisis in the early
1950s, although the exact cause of that crisis was never stated in
the church records. It was only implied in several brief commen-
taries and budgetary items that were cut or eliminated entirely.

Laura looked up at the light streaming through the windows
located high in the basement walls. Another possible scenario
slowly took shape in her mind as she contemplated what she had
just read in the church documents.

*Did Selma Sims flee with the church money? Is that why she as-
sumed a false identity? What about Mother and Father? Were they
part of some elaborate scheme to embezzle money from the church?
Was Rachel Sims also involved? Is that why she disappeared?*

Laura put the drawer containing the church documents back
in the filing cabinet and walked upstairs. Olga was sitting at her
desk next to the blackboard.

"Tell me something," Laura said. "From some of the church
records I just read, it appeared that the Sentinels of God Church
had a financial crisis back in the early 1950s. Do you know anything about that?"

Olga shook her head. "No, I'm afraid I don't."

"Did anyone ever talk about it?"

"No. You have to understand that the Sentinels of God Church
was a very closed community. They kept to themselves. They had
their own bank, their own food co-op. They even had their own
court that sentenced and punished those who violated church
rules. Church members who contributed money to the church
knew only what the Church Council would tell them. They were
dependent on the church for everything. If there was a financial
crisis, only the Church Council would have known about it."

"They sound like the Puritans who settled in New England,"
Laura speculated.

"They were very much like them. The Sentinels were intolerant, but very devout. Incidentally, I was thinking that perhaps
you should talk to Nathaniel Klinger. Maybe he could help you
find what you're looking for."

Laura remembered Nathaniel Klinger as one of the men who
was listed on the 1947 Church Council. "Is he still alive?" she
asked.

"Oh, yes. And so is his wife, although she's in very bad health.
They're the last of the original Sentinels. The others are all gone."

"Think he would talk to me?"

"He might. People have said he's been more open in recent years about the church's past. Maybe he's unloading a bit as he prepares to meet his Maker. One thing is for sure, though. He knows most of the church's secrets. Will he share them with you? That I don't know."

Nathaniel Klinger's farmhouse was buried in a thick grove of trees and bushes about two miles north of the Sentinels of God Church. As Laura approached the driveway, she saw that the surrounding fields were overgrown with mustard plants, dandelions, and other weeds. The fields had clearly not been planted and harvested for some time.

The farmhouse, a small one-story structure, was wedged so deeply into the grove of trees and bushes that only the front porch was visible from the driveway. A black carriage with cracked leather upholstery was parked in front of the house, and the rusted chassis of another carriage protruded above the thick grass and weeds in the front yard.

Laura knocked on the screen door and waited. Moments later, Nathaniel Klinger appeared on the front porch. Klinger, who appeared to be in his late eighties, had white hair and an equally white beard that covered a long lean face. He wore a gray shirt and black pants that were attached to black suspenders that curled over his shoulders. His entire demeanor still reflected the power and authority he had once commanded in the Sentinels of God Church.

Laura recognized him as the driver of the horse-drawn wagon that had followed closely behind the wagon carrying a wooden coffin on the road next to the cemetery. "I'm Laura Fielding," she said somewhat awkwardly, not knowing quite how to introduce herself to the intimidating figure standing in front of her. "Olga Peterson sent me over. Are you Nathaniel Klinger?"

"Yes, I am," he replied. Although he appeared to be outwardly cordial, Klinger's blue eyes reflected a wary, deeply suspicious temperament. "What can I do for you?"

"I was hoping to ask you some questions about the church records that are stored in the historical society basement."

"It was not my decision to give up those records," Klinger replied defensively. "Others saw fit to do so."

"I'm trying to learn more about some people who were members of the Sentinels of God Church back in the late 1940s and early 1950s. I was hoping you could help me."

"What people?" he replied even more suspiciously.

"Grant and Rachel Sims. Do you remember them?"

Klinger stared at Laura for several seconds. "Yes, I remember them," he said tersely.

"Then you must remember that Rachel Sims disappeared in May of 1952. And apparently no one has ever figured out what happened to her."

"Yes, I remember that incident. I believe she left her husband for another man. Someone from another state, if I am correct."

Suddenly, Laura heard a weak feminine voice calling from the interior of the house. "Who's out there, Nathaniel?"

"We have a visitor," he replied, turning and yelling over his shoulder.

"Why don't you . . . have him come inside?" the voice drifted out to the front porch again.

"I have to go," Klinger said firmly. "My wife needs me. She's not well."

"Would you mind if I came in for a few minutes?" Laura asked. "I really need to ask you some questions about Grant and Rachel Sims."

"Why are they important to you?" he replied, the suspicion in his voice bordering on hostility.

"I believe my parents knew them. But I'm not sure what their relationship was. My mother just died, and I'm trying to figure out how she was related to Rachel Sims."

Klinger continued to stare suspiciously at Laura. "Come inside, then," he said. "I only have a few minutes. Then I will have to attend to my wife's needs."

As Laura stepped into the kitchen, she saw that the table and chairs were constructed out of unfinished lumber. There were no light switches or electrical appliances anywhere in the room. An ancient wooden icebox was crammed into one corner next to a sink with a hand-cranked water pump. Several hand-carved wooden dishes, spoons, and other eating utensils were neatly organized on a nearby wooden countertop.

As they passed through the living room, an elderly woman with short white hair was sitting in a wheelchair that was constructed entirely out of wood and leather. Even the spokes were made of dark polished wood that was tapered at both ends and inserted into holes in the hubs and wooden wheels.

"Oh, I thought you said . . . we had a male visitor," Ruth Klinger stammered softly. "I thought maybe . . . someone from the church . . . came by to see us."

"No, Ruth," Klinger replied gently, but sternly. He adjusted a pillow on the back of the wheelchair. "Now you try to get some rest. I won't be long."

He led Laura into a room in the rear of the house that apparently served as both a study and a prayer room. The embers from a small fire glowed in a stone fireplace in one corner of the room. While Laura sat down on a plain wooden chair, Klinger pulled out a pipe with a long handle and curved bowl from a leather pouch. He stuffed the pipe with tobacco and lit it with an ember from the fireplace. Then he sat down on another wooden chair.

"Now, what is it you want to know about Rachel Sims?" he asked.

Laura debated whether to be subtle or direct. She decided on the latter approach. "What do you think happened to her the day she disappeared?"

"It was pretty common knowledge in our church community that she left her husband for another man," Klinger replied, the smoke from his pipe drifting toward the ceiling. "Those things happen, you know, even in a religious community like ours. It wasn't completely unexpected."

"Why do you say that?"

"The sin of Eve makes all women susceptible to sins of the flesh. Rachel Sims was more susceptible than most."

Laura shook her head. "I still don't understand."

"She had the reputation of being an immoral woman," Klinger explained. "No one was terribly shocked that she left her husband for another man. She was a temptress. Even from beyond the grave, she apparently continues to tempt us with her seductive charms."

"How do you know she's dead?" Laura asked quickly. "You just said most people thought she left her husband for another man."

"I was only speculating."

"Is it possible that someone in the Sentinels of God Church might have been responsible for her disappearance?"

Klinger looked deeply and genuinely puzzled. "Why do you think that?"

"Because of her reputation in the church community. It sounds like she might have had enemies. Someone who had a reason for wanting her dead."

"We are not murderers," Klinger replied sternly. "We have been engaged in a long battle with the powers of darkness, but we are not murderers. Murderers, like all sinners, will face their own Judgment Day. If you have studied your Bible, you know that the *Book of Revelations* states that Christ will someday return to slay the serpent and to judge those who have been the serpent's willing accomplices in this world."

"Was Rachel Sims one of the serpent's accomplices in this world?"

"When she disappeared, we believed so, yes. But it was not for us to render final judgment on her soul. That was for God, and only God, to decide. Still, what she did was despicable beyond words. She not only abandoned her husband to whom she was joined in a Christian marriage, but she also abandoned her young child who was conceived out of that marriage."

Laura tried to remain calm, but she was barely able to control her emotions. "Rachel Sims had a child?" she asked, her voice becoming noticeably louder.

"Yes, a young daughter."

"What happened to her?"

"Grant gave her up when he learned that he was a dying man."

"Who did he give her to?"

"No one knew. Grant took that secret with him to the grave. You have to admit that only a despicable woman would abandon both her husband and her young child."

Laura reached for the photocopy of the church congregation in her purse and handed it to Klinger. "Those two people standing next to Rachel Sims. Did you know them?"

Klinger studied the photocopy, and then handed it back to Laura. "Yes, I knew them," he admitted softly.

"What can you tell me about them?"

"Nothing."

"What do you mean?"

"They were excommunicated. When church members are excommunicated, we never speak their names again. They cease to exist as far as we are concerned."

"Was Rachel Sims also excommunicated?"

"Not officially."

Laura heard a creaking noise out in the hallway, and she turned as Ruth Klinger's wheelchair rolled into the open doorway. She had a strangely puzzled expression on her face, and her white hair glistened in the light that filtered through a window behind her. "I heard you . . . talking about . . . Rachel," she said. Her eyes looked up at the ceiling, and her thin fingers curled and uncurled on her lap. "I think . . . I remember."

"No, Ruth," Klinger insisted. He stood and walked over to where his wife was sitting in the open doorway. He turned the wheelchair around and pushed it back into the hallway. "It's better that you don't remember."

As Laura drove back to the county road, she continued to be puzzled by what Klinger had told her about Grant and Rachel Sims. He seemed openly hostile to them and others who had apparently defied church teachings. But he insisted that no one in the church could possibly have been responsible for Rachel Sims's disappearance. When Laura showed him the photocopy of the church congregation, his reaction was equally puzzling, even disturbing.

*Why had Mother and Father been excommunicated? Was it connected to the financial crisis the church went through in the early 1950s? Or was it associated in some way with whatever happened to Rachel Sims? Or perhaps her disappearance was also connected to the financial crisis in some way?*

As Laura thought about what she had learned from Klinger, a white station wagon slowly approached from the south. When she pulled over to the shoulder of the road to allow it to pass, she saw that it was the same station wagon with rusted fenders Gunda had identified as belonging to Reverend Sinclair.

The driver of the station wagon, a thin, bearded man, kept his eyes on the road as he passed Laura's car. The back of the station wagon was filled with boxes and bags of groceries. Glancing in her rear-view mirror, Laura watched as the station wagon drove slowly down the county road and turned into Klinger's driveway.

><><><

After supper, Charlie Flanigan walked outside into the darkness and sat down in a wooden lawn chair he had reconstructed after finding it lying in a ditch near the cemetery. The chair creaked and groaned as he settled into it. He looked up and down the river for any dark cloud formations that might be covering the stars. Satisfied that it was going to be a peaceful evening, unlike the previous day when he had watched the tornado twisting and hovering above Hodges Island, he leaned back in the chair and watched the moonlight shimmer on the water near the fallen tree. Shadows and darkness covered the opposite riverbank.

Unlike the townspeople who refused to come out to the cemetery at night, it never bothered him to live and sleep among the dead, or even to intermingle with them on the darkest evenings. He felt more protected in the cemetery than he did in any town. He reasoned that the living could still hurt you: the dead were no longer capable of inflicting their anger and vengeance on anyone else.

After a few more minutes of gazing across the river into the darkness, he stood to leave. Suddenly, he heard something unusual on the opposite riverbank. It was a scrapping noise, like the sound a boat makes when it pulls up to or leaves a pebble-covered shoreline.

He quickly rushed into the cabin, grabbed an ancient set of binoculars off one of the kitchen shelves, and strode down to the edge of the river. He trained the binoculars on the opposite riverbank and studied the shadows on the shoreline. The darkness made it impossible to see much through the binoculars. But in the distance, he saw a faint reddish glow of light, followed by a short pause, and then another reddish glow. Then he heard the scrapping sound again, and he watched the shadowy movement of what appeared to be a small boat moving away from the riverbank. It appeared briefly in the moonlight as it drifted slowly downstream. Moments later, the boat and whoever was smoking the cigarette were swallowed up in the darkness.

><><><

Laura stayed awake much of that night, thinking about what Nathaniel Klinger told her. Despite Klinger's suspicious, often hostile responses to her questions, he nonetheless provided her with one invaluable piece of information. He verified that Rachel Sims had a daughter her husband had given to another couple when he learned that he was dying of a terminal illness.

*I must be their daughter. That must be what Mother meant in the letter when she wrote, "Everyone has a right to know who they are." Is that why I felt like I had been on Hodges Island before? Is that why I feel such a close bond with Rachel Sims? If I am her daughter, how old would I have been when Grant Sims gave me up? Are those the memories that are still alive inside of me?*

Something woke her up shortly after she fell asleep. What it was, she did not know. But it sounded like it came from the gravel parking lot in front of the bed and breakfast. Then she heard the soft crunching sound of footsteps somewhere outside. She walked cautiously over to the window and stared into the darkness below.

At first, she could see nothing unusual. Then she saw what looked like a small, red ember glowing next to the trunk of an elm tree. A few seconds later, she saw the glowing red ember again— and she realized someone was standing in the darkness, smoking a cigarette just outside her bedroom window. The silhouette of a human figure slowly began to take shape in the darkness. The cigarette glowed again, and the figure suddenly vanished.

Laura slept fitfully for the rest of the night. The intruder smoking a cigarette outside her bedroom window made the earlier threats seem even more ominous. She was now convinced that someone still living in the area definitely did not want the disappearance of Rachael Sims to be solved.

*The threats are getting closer. So are the memories. The photograph of the Sentinels of God Church congregation, the trip to Hodges Island, and the regressive hypnosis session are unlocking old memories. Most of them seem to be memories of experiences from my childhood. Some seem to be breaking through the barriers from a previously unreachable world.*

# CHAPTER THIRTEEN

Laura awoke early and ate a quick breakfast. She immediately walked outside to her car and drove to Pelican Lake. She kept a wary eye on all on-coming traffic, making certain the white truck that almost ran her off the road was not approaching from the north.

The incident the previous evening, when she spotted someone smoking a cigarette just outside the window of her room, continued to trouble her. She had asked Gunda if anyone else was staying at the bed and breakfast, and Gunda said, "No, it's just the two of us." That made Laura's late-night visitor seem even more threatening. If he was not a hotel guest, he had picked a very strange place to smoke a cigarette in the middle of the night.

*Someone must be watching every move I make, apparently even when I'm asleep. Someone is obviously not happy about the questions I've been asking the people in this town.*

Pelican Lake was in plush, rolling farmlands in the northern part of Archer County. A mile outside of town, Laura saw several two- and three-story buildings silhouetted against billowing white clouds. On both sides of the road, high voltage power lines arched above the fields and pastures, converging on Pelican Lake from three different directions.

On Main Street, several shoppers were entering stores or peering into display windows. In the middle of town, a banner had been stretched across the street and attached to two metal streetlights. The banner announced an upcoming community festival that would include an appearance by Congressman Jerry "Jake" Harstad and several other political figures.

She spotted the Archer County Courthouse, a refurbished Victorian structure, at the very end of Main Street. The building, which was decorated with elaborate brown and white latticework that covered a brick exterior, was located on top of a small foothill, where it hovered over the other buildings on Main Street. A large clock was in a bell tower on top of the building, and two massive gables were positioned on both sides of the bell tower.

She parked the car and walked up two flights of stairs to the third floor, where a middle-aged, heavy-set woman with badly dyed, reddish-brown hair was working behind the counter of the County Recorder's Office. A nametag on her blouse identified the woman as "Sylvia Foster, Assistant County Recorder."

"What can I do for you?" she asked, smiling cheerfully.

"I'm trying to locate a birth certificate," Laura explained. "But I don't know the person's name. I only know who the parents were."

"If you know the parents' names, I should be able to locate the birth certificates for any of their children if they were born in this county."

Suddenly, an elderly woman who had just labored up the staircase staggered into the room. She set her purse on the counter and tried to catch her breath.

"Hi, Phyllis," Sylvia greeted the elderly woman. "What brings you over here today?"

"Oh, those Social Security people have messed up my husband's file again," the woman complained. "I need to send them birth certificates for both of us. They don't think we were ever born, I guess."

"Well, let me help this young lady with her request first, then I'll find those birth certificates for you." Sylvia turned to address Laura, "Now, what were the parents' names?"

"Grant Sims and Rachel Sims."

"I'll be right back."

She disappeared into a vault in the rear of the room and did not return for several minutes. When she finally walked back to the counter, she was holding a birth certificate.

"This might be it," she said, placing the document on the counter. "It's a birth certificate for an Anna Rachel Sims, born June 3, 1951. Parents are listed as Grant and Rachel Sims. Is that the person you're looking for?"

"Yes, I believe it is," Laura replied. She studied the information on the birth certificate. "What does this mean?" she asked, pointing at some words that had been scribbled in the box titled "Place of Birth."

"It means this child wasn't born in a hospital. She was delivered in a private home."

"Wasn't that unusual in the early 1950s?"

"Yes. By that time most babies were born in hospitals. Why this one wasn't, I can't say. Someone also checked the box that indicated this baby was premature. Perhaps the parents simply did not have time to make it to the hospital."

"I don't mean to pry," Phyllis said, "but I couldn't help over-hearing what you've been talking about. Actually, over in the Point Tyson area there were quite a few home deliveries, even in the 1950s. The people over there who belonged to that Sentinels of God Church, they didn't believe in hospitals. All the women in that church gave birth in their homes, usually with the help of a midwife. The midwife would fill in all the information, and the pastor would sign the birth certificate. That's Reverend Theodore Turner's signature right there," she said pointing at the birth certificate.

"How do you know so much about those church people?" Sylvia asked, gently teasing the elderly woman.

"Because my cousin, Bertha Mickelson, was the midwife who delivered many of those babies. They didn't trust outsiders, but for some reason they trusted Bertha. She had medical training most of those women did not have. She told me those church peo-ple believed bringing a child into this world should be painful, but they didn't want their wives and daughters to die in childbirth."

Laura suddenly had another thought. "Do you also have mar-riage certificates here?" she asked Sylvia.

"Oh, yes, we have them too."

"Could you see if you have a marriage certificate for Grant and Rachel Sims? And if you do, could I have copies of both the birth certificate for Anna Rachel Sims and the marriage certificate for her parents?"

"I'll be right back," Sylvia replied. Again, she disappeared into the vault. When she walked out, she was holding another legal document. "I have it right here. Let me make copies for you."

While Sylvia made copies of the documents, Laura turned to address the elderly woman standing next to her by the counter. "Did your cousin work as a midwife in Point Tyson in the early 1950s?"

"Oh my, yes," Phyllis replied. "For the longest time, she was the only midwife in Point Tyson. In fact, she is the only person still living in the second-story apartments on Main Street. I've tried for years to get her to move to someplace else where it's less depressing. She won't do it. She just sits most of the day and looks out her window at that dying small town."

"Dr. Finley," Laura said, speaking into a pay telephone on the first floor of the Archer County Courthouse, "I'm now convinced that I am Anna Rachel Sims, and my parents were Grant and Rachel Sims. It's the only explanation that makes any sense. But I'm still a little confused by the dates on the birth certificate and marriage license."

"What's the problem?"

"Even if Anna was conceived on the very night Grant and Rachel Sims were married, she would be seven weeks premature. I didn't know that babies who were seven weeks premature had any chance of surviving back in the 1950s."

"Is it possible that someone doctored the records?" Finley speculated. "Just to make the pregnancy look more respectable."

"That's what I was thinking. If that child was conceived *before* Grant and Rachel Sims were married, perhaps they felt they had to make it look more respectable for their church. From what I know of the Sentinels of God Church, they considered sex outside of marriage to be the worst of all possible sins."

"They would still need someone to doctor those records. Someone who was willing to lie for them."

"Yes, I know," Laura admitted. "Even in a home delivery, someone would have to verify that the child was premature. I'm going to try to talk to an elderly midwife who still lives in Point Tyson. Maybe she can explain this discrepancy."

"If you are Anna," Finley said, "how old would you have been when your mother disappeared?"

"Close to one year, if the birth certificate is correct."

"And how old would you have been when Grant Sims gave you up?"

"Probably close to two years old."

"When you were tested, didn't you learn that you have an unusual memory?"

"Yes. I was told that the way I remember things in pictures was exceptional."

"That would explain a lot," Finley replied. "When do you plan to come back to Farmington with the photographs of Hodges Island?"

"After I can get out there again," Laura explained. "I took a few photographs the first time I went out there, but a rainstorm drove me back before I could make it to the quarry buildings. I thought if I actually made it to the area where Grant Sims claims he found the ribbon, and where the crime probably occurred—if there was a crime—we might have more to work with."

"I hope you find what you're looking for," Finley said. "Be careful."

"I will."

"One other thing," Finley said. "Remember the first day we met when you told me you had one friend, another graduate student named Annie. You said almost all of your other friendships and relationships had failed."

"Yes, I do remember us talking about that."

"That birth certificate you located may explain why that friendship lasted, when others did not," Finley speculated. "The name 'Annie' would be similar to your own name 'Anna' during your early childhood, when you were seemingly happy and secure, and your mother was still alive. Your friend's name could have subconsciously evoked memories of that time and created a comfort level you did not feel in any other relationship."

Laura parked her car and walked past an abandoned hardware store on Point Tyson's Main Street. A faded stencil on the display windows indicated that the name of the failed business enterprise was "Prairie Hardware." As she peered through the dusty window, she saw that the store was empty except for some cardboard boxes and other discarded items that littered the floor.

Spotting an enclosed staircase attached to one side of the abandoned store, she walked up the wooden steps to the second floor of the building. On both sides of the staircase, strips of greenish-white wallpaper had peeled away from the walls, exposing a gray plaster undercoating. At the top of the staircase, a screen door hung loosely from two rusty hinges.

Laura knocked several times and waited as she heard footsteps shuffling across the floor. Moments later, an elderly woman's wrinkled face and thick eyeglasses appeared behind the screen door. The woman's white hair was neatly pulled back into a ponytail and secured with a rubber band. She wore a faded green cotton dress that had been fashionable much earlier in the century.

"Yes," Bertha Mickelson inquired, peering through the screen door at Laura. "Who is it?"

"My name is Laura Fielding. Your cousin Phyllis, I didn't get her last name, said you might be able to help me."

"Phyllis Ritter. Yes, we're related."

"I'm trying to gather some information on a Grant and Rachel Sims, and their daughter Anna. Your cousin told me you were a midwife in this area for many years. She said you might remember them."

"Are you related to them?"

"I might be," Laura replied evasively. "Would you mind if I came in for a few minutes to ask you some questions about them?"

Bertha swung the screen door open wider. "I suppose that would be alright," she replied. "But you will have to excuse my place. My eyesight does not allow me to do much in the way of fixing up this apartment."

Surveying the contents of the small apartment, Laura saw that every wall and cabinet had been painted the same drab, grayish-white color. A rocking chair had been placed next to the window overlooking Main Street. As Bertha sat down in it, she reached out one hand to pet a white cat that was slumbering on the windowsill. Laura sat down on a dark green couch that had faded to a much lighter green on the side facing the window.

"How may I help you?" Bertha asked, folding her wrinkled hands in her lap.

"I just left the Archer County Recorder's Office in Pelican Lake," Laura explained. "I was able to get copies of a birth certificate for Anna Rachel Sims and a marriage certificate for Grant and Rachel Sims. I had some questions about both documents."

"Why is this important to you?" Bertha inquired gently.

"Because I may be Anna Rachel Sims. I'm not completely sure. I was raised by another couple. I thought you might be able to help me find out if that's possible."

Bertha paused to look down at her wrinkled hands. "Isn't Rachel Sims the woman who disappeared over on Hodges Island back in the 1950s?"

"Yes, that was her."

"I remember that incident," Bertha replied, looking up.

"I was wondering if you were the midwife who assisted in Anna's birth. The birth certificate indicates that it was a home delivery."

"I delivered hundreds of babies in my time," Bertha sighed. "Many of them I have completely forgotten. But, yes, I do remember that delivery, probably because it was such a long and difficult labor. We almost lost that child. Then the mother simply vanished one year later. So that birth does stick in my mind."

"The thing I don't understand," Laura explained, "is that the birth certificate indicates Anna was seven weeks premature. I didn't know how that was possible back in the 1950s. Even today, it would be very difficult to save a baby that was seven weeks premature."

Bertha stared out the window at the city park. "I suppose it's long past the time when some old secrets should see the light of day," she reminisced. "Yes, that birth certificate doesn't tell the complete truth about the birth of Anna Sims."

"What is the complete truth?"

"I never violated my professional obligation to provide accurate and truthful information about the babies I delivered. I felt I owed it to them, so that when they were older their birth certificates would reflect an honest account of how they came into the world." Bertha paused and looked directly at Laura. "In the case of Anna Sims, I made an exception."

"Why?"

"She was a full-term baby. But the parents had not been married for a full nine months. They were very worried about how their church community would react to a child who had been conceived out of wedlock. They were worried about themselves, but even more worried about how the child would be treated throughout her life if the truth got out. They begged me to falsify the birth certificate, and I did. A year later, when Rachel disappeared, I wondered if maybe it had something to do with the birth of that child. I knew many of the people in that church very well. I helped deliver their babies. They were devout, but very intolerant of anything that smacked of sin, especially sex outside of marriage."

"Was there anyone in the church community who was capable of murder?" Laura asked.

"I just don't think so," Bertha replied, shaking her head slowly. "They were intolerant and self-righteous. But I don't think they were capable of murder."

"They had some very strange ideas about women."

"Strange to us, maybe, but not to them."

"What do you mean?"

"They believed every woman who labored in great pain to give birth was atoning for the sin of Eve. That's why they didn't use hospitals. They believed women brought sin into the world, and they had to atone for it through the pain of childbirth. So, yes, I understand why Grant and Rachel begged me to falsify the birth certificate."

"The *Point Tyson Chronicle* reported that some people thought Rachel left her husband for another man, someone who drove a car with Iowa license plates. Others I talked to still believe that's what happened to her."

Bertha shook her head more vigorously. "I never believed that story," she insisted.

"Why?"

"Because I saw how much Rachel loved that young daughter of hers. When I handed that child to her for the first time, all bloody and covered with afterbirth, she lit up in a way I had never seen before. All new mothers are thrilled with their babies. Rachel's joy filled the room. No, she would never have left that child."

"Think her husband was involved in any way in her disappearance?"

"No," Bertha replied emphatically. "I could tell they loved one another deeply. When he knelt next to his wife's bed as she held that baby for the first time, he was crying with joy. Rachel reached out a hand and brushed it gently across his bearded cheek. Those two people loved each other very much."

Laura took the photocopy of the church congregation out of her purse, unfolded it, and handed it to Bertha. "The two people standing next to Rachel. Did you know them?"

Bertha studied the photograph for a few seconds. "Could you hand me that magnifying glass on the table next to you?" she said. "This is kind of a blur to me." After Laura handed her the magnifying glass, Bertha moved it slowly around the photograph. "I'm sorry," she said. "I just can't see well enough to identify any of the people in this photograph. Maybe you could describe them to me."

"Well, the man is quite tall. The woman, apparently his wife, standing next to him is shorter, but still fairly tall for a woman. They both seem to be blonde and have fairer complexions than the other members of the church congregation."

"Did you say they were standing next to Rachel?"

"Yes."

"It sounds like you're describing the two people who were closest to Rachel, next to her husband of course. They came by shortly after Rachel's baby was born, and they were very happy for her. I remember the woman you described started to cry when she held that infant."

"What were their names?" Laura asked.

"Jonathan and Esther Anderson."

"Did they have any children?"

"No. They were childless. Esther had one miscarriage and one stillborn child. I assisted her both times. After that, she was not able to have children. I think that's why she became so emotional when she held Rachel's baby girl. She was happy for Rachel. But she wanted a baby of her own so badly that I think it hurt her to hold that child."

"Do you know what happened to them?"

"One day they just up and left the area."

"When did they leave?"

"It was, let me see . . . I believe it was a few months after Rachel disappeared. I think that was probably very difficult for them, and they just decided to have a new start at life somewhere else. I don't think anyone around here ever heard from them again. I could be wrong about that."

"When did . . ."

"Have you ever heard the term 'wreckage of passion'?" Bertha asked, interrupting Laura.

"No, I have never heard that term."

"I read those words somewhere when I was much younger. I think about them many times when I look out this window at our city park." Bertha reached out to pet the cat, and then she folded her wrinkled hands in her lap as she continued to stare out the window. "I understand our small town has fared rather poorly over the past few years. But when I look out this window, all I see is a beautiful small town that is full of hope and promise. So maybe it's a blessing that I'm going blind. Otherwise, I think my life would be much too depressing."

Laura parked her car on the shoulder of the road next to Albert Felstuhl's pasture. As she stepped outside, a gentle breeze was blowing through the tall grass. Overhead, several large birds rode the air currents over to Hodges Island, where they descended into nests they had built in tall trees.

As she looked across the riverbed, she thought about her conversation with Bertha Mickelson. She now knew the names of her parents before they changed their identities to Harold and Margaret Fielding. She also understood their relationship to Rachel Sims, and why Grant Sims would give up his daughter to the childless couple who were closest to his wife when he learned he was dying of a terminal illness. But that still didn't explain why the people she had thought were her parents had assumed new identities, and why they went into hiding for all those years.

Laura had heard of childless women and couples who kidnap babies and raise them as their own. Some even killed the mothers. Still, that was clearly not the case here. Grant Sims had apparently given up that child to Jonathan and Esther Anderson when he learned that he was dying. Furthermore, the local gossip that Rachel Sims left the area with another man seemed less and less plausible. It seemed more like a story someone had started to cover up the truth about what had happened the day she disappeared.

*Something else happened to her. Something much more insidious. Whatever it was, it was buried in the past beneath layers of conflicting rumors, gossip, and a few verifiable facts. The ultimate answer to what happened to her on that May morning in 1952 could only be found in one place: Hodges Island!*

Laura stared at the opposite riverbank. After her last disastrous visit to the area, she was apprehensive. But she was even more determined to learn why she had felt so strongly that she had been on Hodges Island before.

*There's only one way to find out!*

She walked slowly down the embankment and across the riverbed. She chose her path carefully, trying to avoid the wetter areas. She paused by the huge granite boulder and looked up and down the riverbank.

*I have been here before, a long time ago!*

She walked past the granite boulder and plunged into the opening between two of the bushes. The dirt road was littered with fallen branches that were torn loose by the ferocious winds that accompanied the tornado. She picked her way carefully through the branches, being careful not to stray too far from the dirt road.

Next to one recently toppled tree, she noticed ants pouring out of a large anthill so fast that they appeared to be small streams of lava flowing out of a miniature volcano. Occasionally, huge black garter snakes slithered across the path, disappearing into the underbrush or into the decaying logs that littered the area. Many of the snakes crawled along the ground in perfectly synchronized pairs, as their black, undulating bodies engaged in a rhythmic springtime mating ritual.

She paused apprehensively when she spotted the dismembered carcass of the rabbit in the middle of the dirt road. Ants and flies were swarming over the rotten meat and tissue in what remained of the rabbit's rib cage. As she walked slowly past the carcass, she pulled the camera out of her pocket to take more photographs while she journeyed deeper into the island.

She eventually arrived at what she assumed was the center of the island, for there were several toppled, decaying wooden and stone structures that were partially concealed in weeds, climbing vines, and huge overgrown bushes. She paused to survey the area on both sides of the road.

To her right, water erosion had exposed a rusty wheel, some iron spikes, and fragments of glass jars that had been buried in the black soil. An iron pot was also partially exposed in the soil next to the thick, gnarled roots of an elm tree.

Nearby, part of an embankment had given way and slipped into a gully, exposing some reddish-purple granite boulders. On top of the embankment, several granite blocks, apparently the remnants of a small cemetery, protruded from the earth. Laura was tempted to walk up the embankment to get a closer look at the gravestones, but she remembered Pete Solvie's warning to stay on the path.

To her left, a stone building was constructed into the side of an embankment. Behind the embankment, she could see the roofs of two more wooden structures that were partially concealed in brush and climbing vines.

From somewhere in the foliage that covered the old quarry buildings, she heard a strangely muffled sound. She could only compare it to the soft, swishing sound of tree branches rubbing against one another. But even that comparison did not describe what she was hearing.

*It could just be the wind!*

Near the entrance to the quarry buildings, there were four tin cans lying in the shadows next to some rotting pieces of lumber.

An enterprising spider had woven a web from one of the rusty cans to the branches of a bush. Two of the other cans were much newer. Their labels were intact, and ants were swarming over tiny food particles that still clung to the lids. A cigarette butt lay on the ground next to one of the cans.

*Someone has been out here recently!*

She glanced quickly in all directions. She was extremely apprehensive now that she had found evidence that someone else had visited the center of the island within the last few days.

Hearing the strangely muffled noise coming once again from behind the toppled stone and wooden structures, she walked very cautiously in that direction. She paused almost immediately when she felt the ground shift ever so slightly at her feet. Prodding into the underbrush with a stick, she realized she had almost stepped on the collapsed ceiling of what had once been an underground structure that was now concealed by weeds and brush.

*Pete was right! This place is a deathtrap!*

She walked quickly back to the main road and used up the remaining film in the camera. She took enough photographs of the quarry buildings and the surrounding trees and vegetation to create a three-hundred-and-sixty-degree view of the area once the pictures were developed.

Suddenly, the soft, swishing sound she had heard earlier built in intensity. Almost immediately, a thick, undulating blanket of black garter snakes poured out of the underbrush behind the toppled wooden and stone structures. Within seconds, the snakes were slithering past the area where she was standing.

As Laura walked back across the riverbed, she thought about what she had seen on Hodges Island. She wondered if Rachel Sims had made it to the center of the island, or whether something had happened to her before she got that far.

*Did someone intercept her before she made it to the center of the island, and then later drop the ribbon and .flowers near the quarry buildings to divert attention away from the real scene of the crime? Or did she make it to the quarry buildings and drop them during a struggle? Or did she inadvertently drop the flowers and the ribbon before she met with an unfortunate accident elsewhere on the island? Or did she drop the ribbon and flowers near the quarry buildings, walk all the way to the other end of the island, get into a boat, and fake her own disappearance to be with another man?*

After her conversation with Bertha Mickelson, Laura was convinced the latter possibility was the least likely scenario, albeit it was the one the townspeople believed. The way Bertha described Rachel Sim's relationship to her husband and young daughter made it virtually impossible to believe that she would leave them to assume a new life under a different identity.

*That leaves only two possibilities. Either she was the victim of an unfortunate accident after she dropped the flowers, or someone intercepted her on the island and she dropped the flowers during a struggle. But what was the motive, and why was someone still trying to cover up the crime—if it was a crime?*

The incident with the garter snakes had been unnerving, but she knew they were merely coming out of hibernation to mate. They were no threat to her or anyone else. The bigger threats were the tin cans and cigarette butt she found near the old quarry buildings. The food particles on the lids of the cans and the recently smoked cigarette were indisputable proof that someone had visited those abandoned buildings recently. Most likely, it was the same person who had gutted the rabbit and placed it in the middle of the dirt road as a warning.

*The only person who could possibly still be threatened by someone who was trying to learn what had happened to my mother was the person responsible for her disappearance. No one else would be threatened by the truth.*

The fact that she had almost stepped into one of the holes that littered the island was equally disconcerting. It made her realize that speculation regarding Rachel Sims's disappearance among those who believed she wandered into one of those deathtraps was understandable.

*She could easily have taken one more step than I did! And that would be the end! Still, that didn't explain the threats!*

Laura decided to check out something else. She had felt uneasy and apprehensive the first time she saw the dam that was built to close the northern channel of the Lonely Willow River. Those feelings were a complete mystery to her. She decided to park her car near the dam and walk across it to determine why she had felt that way.

The dam was constructed out of large granite blocks cemented together with concrete. A narrow walkway with metal handrails had been built across the top of the structure. As she started across the walkway, she saw that the water was almost three feet below where she was standing. The river's current was sluggish, almost imperceptible.

She paused in the middle of the walkway to look across the river. On the opposite riverbank, two fishermen were sitting on a fallen tree while they cast their lines out into the water. There were no boats or other fishermen anywhere in sight.

As she turned and looked at the dry riverbed on the other side of the dam, she felt her body stiffen. It was the same feeling she had experienced the first time she had seen the dam. Only it was much stronger.

Something about the dam brought back memories she could not remember or understand. She only knew that those memories, whatever they might be, caused her to tremble with fear.

*Something terrible happened on this dam!*

Before returning to her room at the bed and breakfast, Laura decided to pay a visit to the Pelican Lake Junior College Library. Her experiences on Hodges Island and the dam had reinforced her feelings that she had been there before, at a time in her life when she was too young to have coherent memories. She was also convinced that something terrible had happened there. Something that had shaped her life in ways she did not understand at all. She was determined to see if she could find the book Dr. Finley recommended. He had told her it was one of the best books written about the development of early childhood memories.

Night had settled over Pelican Lake, and the streets were nearly deserted as Laura passed a large sign in the middle of a spacious lawn. Two bright lights, one at the top of the sign and one below it, illuminated white letters against a black background. Laura pulled over to the curb when she saw the words "New Sentinels of God Church" in bold letters on the sign.

Several names on the sign were also illuminated by the lights, including the Very Reverend Samuel Morton, Phillip S. Johnson, Charles Simmons, and other church trustees. Behind the sign, a large opulent stone and wooden structure stretched into the night sky. Lights from inside the church illuminated large windows in three triangular-shaped gables. Spotlights on the church lawn illuminated the windows on the sides of the church. A large wooden cross hovered over the front entrance.

*The original Sentinels of God Church is clearly on the downward cycle of its existence. But this one seems to be doing just fine.*

When she arrived at the library, the reference librarian helped her locate the book Dr. Finley recommended. She sat down at one of the tables and scanned the index for the term "emotional memories." One Chapter of the book, which was titled "How Human Memories Develop," pretty much summarized everything Dr. Finley had already told her about emotional memories. Another Chapter described the various stages of human development, and the different ways memories form and influence adult behavior. One paragraph described the challenges people face when they try to recall the events that created their early emotional memories:

> Emotional memories occur at such an early age that the incidents that created them (child abuse, separation from a parent, physical trauma, etc.) probably cannot be recalled. However, if the person is given enough details about the event that created the emotional memory and revisits the place where the emotional memory was created, it can begin to seem like a real memory. The subconscious mind can even begin to provide some of the missing details. The memory will not be a real memory, but it can be a plausible substitute. However, people who try to recall the events that created emotional memories from what they have been told about their early childhoods should be warned that if they have been given false information, the subconscious mind can create a memory that seems real, but is fraudulent.

Laura looked up from the book and stared across the room. There were some twenty or thirty people browsing through the stacks or reading at different tables. From behind one of the bookcases, she saw a man who appeared to be staring in her direction. His face, below his nose, was concealed behind a row of books. He was acting very suspiciously as he stared across the room at her.

Laura walked cautiously over to that side of the library. As she walked around the corner of the bookcase, she saw that the man was struggling to remove a turtleneck sweater. Somehow, he had managed to pull his shirt up to his armpits, revealing his chest and stomach. Seeing Laura, he smiled sheepishly and said, "It's just too blasted warm in here."

She smiled and nodded in his direction. When she walked back to where she had been sitting, she looked down at the books she had left on the table. Two words had been written in bold capital letters across the top of one of the pages: "STOP NOW!"

><><><

Bertha Mickelson sat up that night, petting her cat and looking out her second-story apartment window at the city park, as she did so often when she could not sleep. This time, however, it was something different that kept her up late, gazing out at the dead elm trees that appeared to her dim eyes to be shadowy, motionless silhouettes barely visible in the darkness. This time she remembered something she had almost forgotten. Something that came back to her after her visit with the young woman who thought she might be Rachel Sims's daughter.

Bertha remembered one evening in the early 1950s, when she had attended a concert in the city park. She sat in one of the folding chairs near the back row. Bright lights illuminated the bandstand and the concrete dance floor. As she listened to the music, she glanced to her right and saw a young woman in a gray dress partially concealed behind one of the elm trees. Bertha recognized her as a member of the Sentinels of God Church, and she wondered what the young woman was doing at a concert. Bertha knew from her interactions with other women in the church community that they were not allowed to attend such events.

Bertha was momentarily distracted by something near the bandstand. When she looked back, the young woman was no longer standing by the elm tree. She had disappeared. A well-dressed man strode briskly across the same area and quickly disappeared behind the same tree.

At first, Bertha thought it was probably one of those meaningless things that became locked in her memory for no good reason other than the fact that the young woman in the gray dress looked so completely out of place at the concert. Later, after Rachel Sims disappeared, Bertha thought back to that evening. She was certain it was Rachel partially concealed behind the tree. But since the man's back was turned to her, she had no idea who he might be.

In the years that followed, especially after Rachel disappeared, Bertha wondered if perhaps the young woman was frightened of the well-dressed man, and that was why she left the concert so quickly.

✕✕✕✕✕

Laura spent most of the night sitting by the window, looking out at the parking lot to see if anyone was watching her room from the shadows. As she gazed into the darkness, she reviewed the many threats she had received since she started asking questions about Selma Madison and Rachel Sims. The most recent threat in the library seemed the most ominous.

*Whoever is behind the threats is becoming more desperate and seemingly more determined to keep me from learning what happened to my mother!*

She felt like there were two powerful voices inside of her, both trying to assert total control over her decisions. One voice was urging her to exercise extreme caution. That voice told her to leave Point Tyson before the person behind the threats could find some way to silence her permanently. That voice also told her she must be approaching the inner circle of the small town's darkest secrets, much as Alfred Kron had probably done in the days before he was killed by a hit-and-run driver.

The other voice was even stronger. It seemed to come out of the depths of the dream she had from the time she was a young child. That voice was becoming more invasive. It was now intruding into her waking hours. It was relentless. It was demanding a resolution.

She felt as though Rachel Sims, her mother, was alive inside of her, speaking to her, urging her to peel away at the darkness until there were answers, real answers, not the rumors and gossip that had started in 1952 and spread like some disease for the next twenty-two years. Through Laura's earliest memories, Rachel Sims was pointing her finger at whoever was responsible for her disappearance. Yet, whatever she was pointing at was elusive, unrecognizable. Still she kept urging her daughter on, whispering to her from the past, subtly leading her out of the maze of false clues, gossip, and deliberate misinformation.

*I will try, Mother! I will try!*

# CHAPTER FOURTEEN

Finley cleared his desktop, and Laura arranged the photographs of Hodges Island in the sequence she had taken them. "I'll organize these as though we were following the same path my mother took the day she disappeared," she explained. "That way you can more easily visualize what she experienced that day."

Schlepler sat nearby in his wheelchair, watching Laura create a trail of pictures that duplicated the sights on the dirt road leading to the center of Hodges Island. At the end of the trail, she created a circular arrangement of photographs to approximate the locations of the abandoned quarry buildings and foliage near the area where Grant Sims found the ribbon and flowers.

When Laura had placed the last photograph on the desk, she stepped back and reviewed the sequence. Satisfied that they were in the right order, she placed the photocopy of the church congregation in front of Finley and Schlepler. "This is the Sentinels of God Church congregation in the early 1950s," she explained. "That's Grant and Rachel Sims right there. The two people standing next to them are Jonathan and Esther Anderson. Esther was Rachel's best friend and the woman Grant gave me to shortly before he died." Laura placed the birth certificate for Anna Rachel Sims on the desk next to the photocopy of the church congregation. "This is my birth certificate and my name before the Andersons took me away to live with them."

Finley examined the birth certificate while Schlepler continued to study the photocopy. "This is pretty conclusive proof that Rachel Sims was your mother," Finley said.

"I also talked to the midwife who delivered me," Laura continued. "She provided many of the details of my birth and the events that followed it. Everything fits together once you realize that Rachel Sims is my mother. There is no other explanation for all of this."

"They did not like her," Schlepler interjected as he studied the photocopy.

"Who did not like her?" Laura asked, puzzled by his statement.

"There are some good people here. But many of the people in this church congregation did not like her."

"Why?"

"She was different than most of them. She was a truly creative spirit. Therefore, she was a threat to everything their church stood for. She had enemies."

"How do you know this?" Laura asked, a note of skepticism in her voice.

"I sense it in this photograph," Schlepler replied softly. "It is a very strong presence. Photographs reveal much more than people realize."

"The important question is what happened to your mother?" Finley said. "And why was it necessary for all of you to go into hiding?"

"That's why I came here today," Laura replied. "I still need your help." She pointed at the first photograph in the sequence. "This is the view of the dry riverbed my mother walked across the day she disappeared. The farmer who saw her that morning pointed out the very path she took over to Hodges Island. This second photograph is the large granite boulder that marks the entrance to the dirt road that runs the length of the island. The farmer told me he saw her walk past the boulder and start down the main road. So, we know she made it this far without anything happening to her."

"Did anyone question the farmer after she disappeared?" Finley asked.

"Yes, they did."

"Did they verify his story?"

"He's apparently told everyone the same story ever since she disappeared. Since he was the last person to see her, he seems sincerely concerned that others might suspect that he is involved in her disappearance." Laura pointed at the next photograph in the sequence and explained, "This is as far as I got the first day I was out there. Moments after I took this picture, a tornado came roaring through the area and I had to run for cover."

"What's this?" Schlepler asked, pointing at the carcass of the disemboweled rabbit in the middle of the dirt road.

"I assume someone left it there as a warning to me," Laura replied.

Schlepler picked up the photograph and examined it more closely. "You assumed right," he said, placing it back on the desk.

"The rest of the pictures show various rocks, trees, and wetter areas along the dirt road," Laura said. "At the very end, I have organized the pictures of the quarry buildings as you would see them when you reach the center of the island . . ."

"There's something missing here," Schlepler insisted.

"Where?" Laura asked.

"Right here," he said, pointing at a photograph of the area on the opposite side of the road from the quarry buildings. "Something over here, just out of sight. It is a place of death. Many deaths."

Laura looked more closely at the photograph and realized that Schlepler was referring to the cemetery. "There are some gravestones over there," she explained, "on an embankment just out of camera view."

"It's a place of death," he repeated. "A place where lonely men die and are forgotten."

The fact that Schlepler felt the presence of "many deaths" in a photograph that was taken near a cemetery he could not see quickly eliminated any reservations Laura had about his psychic abilities.

"You're right," she said. "It is a place of death."

"How do you know she made it this far?" Finley asked.

"The farmer who saw her said Grant Sims claimed he found one of his wife's hair ribbons wrapped around some lilac flowers near the quarry buildings. Either she made it this far, or else someone placed them there to divert attention away from the real crime scene."

"She made it this far," Schlepler insisted. "She didn't die here. But she made it this far."

"Why do you say that?" Finley asked.

Schlepler ignored Finley and pointed at another photograph of some overgrown vegetation near one of the quarry buildings. "There was something wrong here," he insisted. "Something was waiting . . . No, someone was watching . . . There was something wrong here."

Schlepler reached for the photocopy of the church congregation and began to examine it carefully. Then he looked off into the distance and remained silent.

"That's just about everything I know," Laura said after it became clear that Schlepler was deeply lost in his thoughts and was no longer responding to them. "But somewhere in this area is most likely where my mother met whoever or whatever it was that caused her to disappear."

"What about the story of her leaving with a man in a car with an out of state license plate?" Finley asked.

"I believe it was a cleverly planned rumor to discourage the authorities from engaging in a real search for her. Whoever was responsible for my mother's disappearance also used the rumor to divert any suspicion away from himself or herself."

"It's here," Schlepler suddenly interjected.

"Where?" Finley asked.

"In this photocopy of the church congregation."

"Are you saying someone in this photograph murdered Laura's mother?" Finley asked.

"I'm saying there is some evil presence here. It's very palpable. The same presence lingers in some of the photographs taken near the quarry buildings. I don't know who or what it is. But it's here . . ."

"What kind of evil presence?" Laura asked.

"They are obsessed with evil. So obsessed they do not see it in themselves. Only in . . ."

Schlepler paused in midsentence, and Finley and Laura exchanged puzzled glances. When Finley looked back at Schlepler, he recognized the look in his friend's eyes. He knew what it meant. The elderly psychic was once again staring out a far more distant window than the one that separated Finley's office from Farmington's spacious lawn.

The smell of cooked fish lingered in the air as Laura approached Charlie Flanigan's cabin. She knocked twice on the screen door. When there was no answer, she peered into one of the windows. On a small kitchen table, she could see a dirty plate piled high with fish bones. She could see no one in the cabin.

The current was sloshing gently against the uprooted tree as she walked down to the edge of the river. She glanced at some dead leaves that had piled up against one of the fallen branches. The leaves seemed almost to be trying to escape from the shoreline, but the current was too slow and sluggish for them to break free and float downstream.

She suddenly heard metal grating against metal farther downstream. Moments later, a small boat emerged from around a bend in the river. The steady sound of the oars grating in the oarlocks grew louder.

When the boat drew closer, she saw that it was Charlie Flanigan. His back was turned toward her as he carefully docked the boat next to the fallen tree. He deftly tossed a rope over one of the branches that was hanging out into the river. He secured the rope to the branch and sloshed through the shallows and over to the area where Laura was standing.

"Boat broke free and took off downstream," he complained, shaking his head in disgust. "I hadda run 'long the riverbank ta catch up with it. Thought I was gonna have ta chase it all the way ta the Miss'ippi." He took off his rubber boots and dropped them on the riverbank. "What brings ya out here today?"

"I have a few more questions I'd like to ask you," Laura explained.

"Have all the time in the world," Charlie replied. "But come on up ta the house. I'll make some tea an' we can talk up there."

Laura followed him over to the cabin. He politely opened the screen door and gestured for her to sit down in one of the two chairs next to the kitchen table.

"Let me heat up some water," Charlie said. He quickly removed the dirty dishes, a spoon, and a bent and misshapen fork from the table. "I'll be with ya in a minute."

Laura surveyed the contents of the one-room cabin. A narrow cot was partially hidden in the shadows, next to some unframed pictures that were nailed to exposed studs. A small, makeshift kitchen counter had been nailed into the wall next to the stove. Several planks had been nailed into the wall above the counter, creating shelves that were cluttered with canned goods, fishing lures, and various tools.

"Here, ya can have your own tea bag," Charlie said as he dropped an unopened tea bag on the table next to her. Then he carried the teapot full of steaming water and two stained porcelain cups over to the table. "Ya know, I'm not used ta havin' so much comp'ny."

"How long have you lived here?" Laura asked.

"I don't even remember. I've been livin' out here so long, I guess I jus' lost track a time. I don't know if I'd ever fit in any place else." His cheeks suddenly reddened, and he looked like he was eager to change the subject. "Ya know, for a time there, I didn't think I was gonna be able to fetch that boat back here. Every time I went out inta the river, current dragged it jus' a little farther downstream."

"The other day I walked out to the old quarry buildings on Hodges Island," Laura said. "Afterwards I went over to the dam. The water looks like it's about three feet below the top of the spillway. Is that normal for this time of year?"

"Oh, that all depends on how much snow we get. If it's snowed a lot, the river can be pretty full an' have a stronger current, 'specially farther downstream. Most of the time, though, it's a pretty sluggish river around these parts. That's why they put the dam over there. Needed to raise the water level."

"Charlie, I've been meaning to ask you something we talked about before. Do you have any idea at all why Grant Sims decided to be buried in this cemetery and not in his church's cemetery?"

Charlie shook his head slowly. "Nah, I really don't know. He's the only one a them church people not ta be buried in their own cem'tery. I always suspected he musta had some kinda fallin' out with the other people in that church. Maybe he jus' didn't like the things they was sayin' 'bout his wife after she dis'peared. An' ya have ta admit those rumors didn't make him look any too good either. Made it look like he had dis'pointed her as a husband."

"That Jesse Willert you told me about," Laura said, sipping her tea. "How often did you talk to him when he came out here?"

"Not very often. Us'ally, he and that helper of his set the new stones they brought out. But he'd almost always stop by that grave where Grant Sims is buried. Sometimes he came 'lone. Then he might talk ta me for a few minutes. But he wasn't a very social fella. An' neither am I. We didn't have much ta do with each other. I could tell he jus' wanted ta sit on the riverbank and look over there at Hodges Island. Many years ago, he stopped comin' out here with the stones. His helper came alone."

"Did Willert ever ask you about what you saw on Hodges Island?"

"Ya, he did."

"How'd he react?"

"He didn't. He just stared at me. I think he was tryin' ta see if I was tellin' the truth. He had kind of a menacin' look 'bout him. Ta be honest, I was a little scared a him."

"Why?"

"He jus' had that kind of look 'bout him, that's all. When I told him what I saw o'er there, well, he kinda made me feel like I shouldn't a said anythin' 'bout it."

Laura looked out the window at Hodges Island. "So, you're convinced that Rachel Sims walks along the riverbanks on Hodges Island on dark spring evenings?"

"Yup," he replied emphatically. "There's no question 'bout it in my mind. I'll go ta my grave believin' her spirit is trapped somewhere on that island, an' she walks the riverbanks at night pleadin' for sum'un ta help her out."

"What do you think she wants?"

"Maybe she wants ta be set free so she can get outta this world for good. Or maybe she jus' wants ta be over here on this side a the river . . . Or maybe we're not supposed ta know."

"I believe she's my mother, Charlie," Laura said gently. "That's why I need to find out what happened to her."

Charlie momentarily seemed unable to comprehend the significance of what Laura had just revealed to him. "Your mother?" he asked finally.

"Yes, I believe she's my mother. That's why I went out to Hodges Island. I need to know what happened to her."

"Well, ya'd better be careful," Charlie said sternly. "Couple a nights ago someone else was out there. I heard something over there an' got out my binoculars. Heard a boat pull 'way from the shore. Looked like he was smokin' a cigarette as he disappeared inta the darkness."

"What night was this?" Laura asked.

"Two nights ago."

"That's the same night I heard footsteps outside my room at the bed and breakfast. When I looked out the window, someone was standing in the shadows smoking a cigarette."

"Might be the same person," Charlie said. "Whoever it is, they're keepin' an eye on you. So be very careful."

Laura decided to spend the rest of the day going through Jesse Willert's business records in Sibley Fields's Antiques Warehouse. It was obvious that Willert was deeply involved with Rachel Sims. He was also the most elusively mysterious person Laura had encountered in her attempts to unravel the disappearance of the woman she was now convinced was her mother. The key to that mystery seemed to be Jesse Willert.

She found nothing of significance in three of the remaining wooden boxes Sibley had dumped in the back of the warehouse after the auction at the Willert Quarry. The last box contained various office mementoes and framed photographs that had apparently once been displayed in the business offices before the quarry closed. Most of the pictures were taken at different times in the quarry's history, as new structures were built and the business expanded. A few of the pictures were of quarry workers and office personnel posed in front of the buildings or in the quarry.

One photograph was of a young World War II or Korean War soldier in a battle helmet and uniform. The soldier cradled a rifle in his arms as he posed in front of a military barracks. The soldier's eyes stared out of the photograph in a way that was almost menacing. His head was turned slightly, and a small dimple parted his chin just below the lower lip.

The photograph reminded Laura of the statue of the World War I soldier she had seen in the Point Tyson City Cemetery. That statue, in its original conception, had apparently portrayed war as a highly glamorized, almost romanticized activity. However, as the World War I soldier gazed at the stump that was once his arm, his face seemed almost to reflect the horrors of war.

So, too, the World War II or Korean War soldier, whatever his original concept of war might have been, was now weary and hardened by the actual experience of combat. His eyes were tired and listless. There wasn't the trace of a smile on his lips. He was the very picture of disillusionment.

As Laura studied the photograph, she had another thought. She quickly walked to the front of the warehouse where Sibley Fields had been working earlier that morning. A sign on the front counter announced, "Out to Lunch. Back shortly."

She turned and looked back in the direction where she had been sorting through the items from the Willert Quarry. She placed the photograph on the counter and studied it carefully.

*I've seen this person before!*

Laura parked her car in a lot adjacent to the Archer County Courthouse in Pelican Lake. In a nearby park, a bandstand had been converted into a speaker's podium. Above the podium, a sign announced, "Reelect Congressman Jerry 'Jake' Harstad."

A tall, distinguished, gray-haired man in his mid-fifties was standing behind the podium. Nearby, a television camera and crew were filming the event. Below the bandstand, several hundred people were sitting in folding chairs that had been neatly arranged in rows across the green lawn. Many of the people held political signs expressing support for Congressman Harstad. As Harstad spoke, his supporters periodically pumped the signs up and down in the air.

As she walked past the political rally, Laura listened to Congressman Harstad address his supporters. "What is happening in Washington today is a travesty," Harstad said, his voice amplified by two huge speakers that had been placed at opposite ends of the bandstand. "Our country is in a cultural and spiritual crisis. We are in deep peril. We have lost our way. A nation that was once committed to Godly principles is adrift and faces an uncertain future. I ask you to pledge me your support so together we can protect our country from the insidious, Godless forces that are undermining the nation we love . . ."

Laura walked into the main lobby of the courthouse and up the two flights of stairs to the third floor, where Sylvia Foster, the assistant county recorder, was working behind the counter. "Back so soon," she said cheerfully.

"Yes," Laura replied. "I was hoping you might be able to locate a death certificate for me."

"What's the name?"

"Jesse Willert. He lived a few miles south of Pelican Lake. I was told he died ten years ago."

"Let me see what I can find for you," she said. She stood up and walked toward the vault. When she returned to the front counter, she shook her head. "Sorry, I have no death certificate back there for a Jesse Willert. Is it possible he died in another county?"

"He might have. Would that make a difference?"

"Well, it shouldn't. If he lived in this county, but died in another county, we should still have received a copy of the death certificate. It's been common practice for many years for counties to share those records. Are you absolutely certain he's dead?"

# CHAPTER FIFTEEN

Laura parked her car and walked through the opening in the stone fence that surrounded Jesse Willert's home. She started up the long gravel road to the top of the hill. On the roof of the house, the hawk-shaped weathervane groaned and grated in the breezes that swept across the hillside. The quartz crystals in the reddish-purple granite walls of the house glistened in the mid-afternoon sunlight. The sunlight illuminated the brighter colors in the stained-glass windows of the house.

She walked up to the front porch and knocked on the door. She waited patiently, then knocked again. When there was still no answer, she walked around to the back of the house. The late-model, green pick-up truck was parked on the side of the house where it had been parked during her previous visit, but the double-barreled shotgun was missing from the passenger side of the front seat.

Seeing no one in the back yard, she decided to take a closer look at the family cemetery she had noticed during her first visit to the Willert home. The knee-high granite gravestones that protruded out of the grass and weeds had three names on them: Josiah Willert, Amanda Willert, and Rebecca Willert. Some older stones were almost completely covered with weeds. As She was reading the inscriptions on the stones, she heard a loud, booming voice behind her.

"I thought I told you not to trespass on my property!"

Turning, she saw the tall man with the long white hair and muscular arms and chest standing near the corner of the house. As he walked over to where she was standing, his brown eyes glared angrily at her.

"Why did you come back?" he demanded to know.

"Because you lied to me the first time I came out here. You're Jesse Willert. I saw an old photograph of you, and I realized you were still alive."

"That's no reason to trespass on my property!" he replied sternly, angrily.

"I also came back because I know you were once in love with Rachel Sims. I thought you might be able to help me learn what happened to her."

"Why is Rachel important to you?" he demanded to know. "She's been gone for twenty-two years now."

"I have reason to believe she's my mother."

"Your *mother*? You're Anna!" he said, his tone of voice changing completely. "You're Rachel's daughter, Anna?"

"I believe so, yes. But I need to know for sure. I was hoping you could help me."

"Anna? I should have known. There is a resemblance." Suddenly, he glanced to his right. "It's okay, Hank," he said. "This young woman has come out here to talk to me."

Turning, Laura saw a small, wiry man with dark black hair standing next to a shed on the edge of the back yard. The man, who was cradling a double-barreled shotgun in his arms, wore a brown vest that was decorated with red beads. Around his neck he wore a blue stone that was attached to a thin strip of leather. He eyed Laura suspiciously, then disappeared around the corner of the shed.

"Why did you tell me you were Hank?" she asked, turning and addressing Willert.

"I haven't had a visitor in years," he explained. "I have never wanted any visitors. I just wanted to get rid of you. If I had known you were Rachel's daughter, I would never . . ."

"Will you help me?"

"Of course, Anna," he said warmly. "Of course. Let's go inside and we can talk."

He led Laura around to the other side of the house and through the front door. Inside the house, the stained-glass windows glowed even more brilliantly in the mid-afternoon sunlight, sending colorful shadows across the wooden floors. He led her into a master bedroom at the end of the hallway, and over to an adjacent room that served as an office.

As Laura walked through the bedroom, she noticed that the walls were covered with faded white wallpaper that was decorated with small blue flowers. At the other end of the room, a huge bed with dark maple poles was located next to a window. One of the pillows was soiled and compacted from years of use, whereas the other pillow seemed never to have been used. Similarly, one side of the bed had deep indentations, whereas the other side appeared never to have supported the weight of a human body.

Willert sat down in a stuffed chair in the office. He gestured for Laura to sit on a leather couch by the window. "How did you learn so much about me?" he asked.

"Charlie Flanigan told me about you."

"What did he tell you?"

"He said you always visited the graves of Grant and Rachel Sims whenever you brought a gravestone out to the cemetery. He said you seemed very troubled by her disappearance."

"I spent a good part of my life trying to figure that out," Willert reminisced sadly. "I finally had to let it go. It was too painful. I seldom leave this house, except to deliver an occasional cemetery stone to other parts of the county. This house is my refuge from a world that has proven to be much too painful. The war, the loss of those I loved. Many of them are in the cemetery behind this house. It all seemed so futile. I lost all hope and never wanted to have any again."

"What can you tell me about your relationship to my mother?"

"First, tell me why you believe Rachel is your mother."

"I was raised by two people who turned out not to be my parents. I didn't know that until the person I thought was my mother died. I found a letter she had written, but didn't mail. The letter said I was not who I thought I was. That letter led me to this town and the person I believe is my mother, Rachel Sims. That's why I need your help. I need to know who I am, and what happened to her. It's important to me."

"Do you know anything at all about your mother?"

"Very little. Only what I have heard second hand from the townspeople or read about in the *Point Tyson Chronicle*. Other than that, I know nothing at all."

"Don't listen to a word those people tell you!" Willert said, the anger returning to his voice. "They always wanted to think the worst of Rachel. When she vanished, it gave them reason to trot out all their cruel gossip and direct it at her again. None of it is true. None of it. Perhaps because I live here alone with my memories, I idealized her out of proportion to who she really was. Perhaps I am guilty of that. But my Rachel is closer to the real Rachel than the one the gossipmongers created in their vicious stereotypes of her as an unfaithful, adulterous wife. That's not the Rachel I knew. She was none of those things."

"What *can* you tell me about her?" Laura asked gently.

"Rachel had a difficult life," Willert reminisced slowly, sadly. "A very difficult life. Her parents died when she was a young teenager. From then on, she never had a home. She became a ward of the church. She worked as a hired girl for different families in her church community. Sometimes the church hired her out to other families in the area and kept whatever money she earned. When one family no longer needed her services, she moved on to another family, and another family after that. All the women in that church community worked hard. Rachel worked the hardest. I met her in the spring of 1950 . . ."

*Jesse Willert had just finished setting a gravestone in the Sentinels of God Church Cemetery, when he sensed that someone was standing behind him. He turned and saw a dark-haired young woman in a gray dress. Her long black hair was pinned to the top of her head, and she was staring sadly at the gravestone. In her right hand, she was holding a bouquet of flowers.*

*"I'm . . . I'm sorry," Jesse stammered as he stood up. "I didn't see you standing there. Someone you know?" he asked, gesturing at the gravestone.*

*The young woman nodded, but she seemed lost in her thoughts.*

*"A relative?" he asked gently.*

*"No. Just a person I knew."*

*"I'm Jesse Willert," he said awkwardly.*

*"Rachel Grote," she replied, smiling shyly. She slowly unpinned her long black hair and shook it loose. "I clean the church once a week. I always come out here first. My mother and father are buried right over there, next to the gravestone you were working on."*

*Jesse turned and looked down at a small cemetery stone that bore the names "Mathew Jonathan Grote" and "Anna Lenora Grote." The inscriptions on the gravestone indicated that they had died within days of one another.*

*"They died in the influenza epidemic that took the lives of so many others," Rachel said softly. She walked over to the cemetery stone and spread the flowers across both graves. She stood quietly for a time, staring at the ground. "When I was a young girl," she reminisced, "my mother taught me a poem about the flowers that grow on lilac bushes. The first lines are, 'If I should go, and you*

*should stay, remember me when the lilacs bloom, though I am far away'. The second stanza is, 'If I should go, and you should stay, I will blossom for you when next we meet, in a world so far away'."*

*"Who do you live with now?" Jesse asked.*

*"I'm a ward of the church. I work as a hired girl for many different families."*

*"I'm very sorry about what happened to your mother and father."*

*"I still feel my mother's presence every spring when the lilacs blossom," she replied. "Then I know she has not forgotten me. I don't dare recite that poem around the other members of our church, though."*

*"Why?"*

*"Our church teaches us from the time we are very young that beautiful things only masquerade Satan's evil presence in the world. My mother didn't believe in that. She said the beautiful things we hear in poetry, or see in nature, are the surest signs we have that God is present in the world and in our lives."*

*Jesse sensed that Rachel must be in her early twenties. Yet, she was so childlike and unworldly that she seemed to be much younger. Only the sadness and melancholy in her eyes made her seem older.*

*Suddenly, Jesse heard footsteps and a tall bearded man in a black, round-brimmed hat emerged from around the corner of the church. "Rachel," he admonished her sternly. "It is time for you to start cleaning the church."*

*"Yes, Reverend Turner," she replied quietly.*

*"Put the pins back in your hair," he reprimanded her. "You know it is not proper for you to wear your hair like that in public."*

*"Yes, Reverend. Turner," she replied nervously. As she walked over to join him, she pulled her hair back over the top of her head and pinned it into a neat bun. "I'm very sorry."*

*The next time Jesse saw Rachel was after he visited an acquaintance in Point Tyson. As he stopped to listen to a touring band that was playing a nighttime concert in the city park, he noticed a young woman who was partially concealed behind one of the elm trees. The girl seemed out of place in a gray dress, while the women and girls on the dance floor wore brightly colored, more formal dresses.*

*Jesse suddenly realized the girl standing behind the elm tree was the one he had met in the church cemetery only a few days earlier.*

*As he approached the area where Rachel was standing, she slipped behind the tree. Her head was tilted slightly upward, her eyes were closed, and her shoulders were swaying gently to the music that filled the night air. Except for the music, she was oblivious to everything else around her.*

*"Rachel?" he asked softly as he joined her behind the tree.*

*She looked startled and apprehensive as she opened her eyes and glanced all around the area where she was standing.*

*"What are you doing here?" Jesse asked.*

*Rachel quickly regained her composure. "My church hired me out to a family in town," she explained. "I was running an errand for them when I heard this . . ."*

*"You looked like you were enjoying it very much," Jesse laughed softly.*

*"We don't have music in our church," she explained. "We sing hymns, but there is no music. It is not allowed."*

*"Does your church . . .?"*

*"I have to go," she said suddenly. "They will wonder what is taking me so long."*

*"Wait," Jesse said. "How long will you be working in town?"*

*"Only a few days."*

*"When will you be cleaning the church again?"*

*"Next Tuesday."*

*"Can I come by to see you?"*

*Rachel paused before answering. "Yes," she said. "Stop by around noon. Reverend Turner should be gone by then."*

*Jesse watched as she slipped away into the darkness on the other side of the street.*

*Jesse saw Rachel many times over the next months. She told him which days and times she would be cleaning the church. He drove out to the cemetery on those days, telling his parents that he needed to check on some of the stones he had set. Rachel would come out of the church as soon as she saw him, and they would go for walks across the countryside.*

*Rachel became less apprehensive and more relaxed with each visit. For Jesse, she also became more charming and endearing.*

*She seemed to have missed out on everything the modern world had to offer. In return, something deep inside of her had developed a wisdom that somehow managed to avoid all distractions, while getting right to the very essence of life itself. She seemed thrilled by the smallest things: a baby bird nesting in a pine tree, every flower that blossomed on every bush and plant, the white, billowing clouds drifting leisurely across the sky. She noticed them all in a way Jesse had never experienced with anyone he had ever met before.*

*In his mind, Rachel's uncluttered life had given her a beauty that transcended physical beauty. She became for him the symbol of all those things her church saw as its enemies. She became the poem she had recited for him. She became the beautiful colors in every plant, tree, and bush she admired and caressed.*

*She also became the first woman, other than his mother and sister, he had ever really loved.*

*When she moved to yet another home, this one near where the Lonely Willow River flowed in a more southerly direction, it opened a whole new world for them to explore. One of their favorite places was a thicket of trees along the riverbank. An early frost had already turned many of the leaves to various shades of browns, reds, and yellows. They would sit for hours in the thicket, holding hands while they talked and admired the beautiful, colorful foliage that surrounded them.*

*One day, when Jesse joined Rachel in the thicket, she was despondent. He could tell that she had been crying. "What's wrong?" he asked, sitting down next to her and grasping her hand.*

*Her blue eyes filled with tears as she looked up at him and said, almost in a whisper, "I've been told the Church Council is looking for someone for me to marry. But I do not want them to make that decision for me."*

*"Can't you just refuse?" he asked.*

*"No. If I do, I will be required to work for others in the church for the rest of my life. I will never be allowed to marry. That is what happened to one of the women in the church many years ago. She still sits in the back of the church by herself. After church services, she goes to live with someone else. But she was never allowed to have a family of her own. I do not want that for myself."*

"Rachel," he asked gently, "did all of this start because of me? Did someone in your church see us together? Is that what happened?"

"I believe that is probably what happened. Reverend Turner has acted very strangely toward me since he saw us in the cemetery. I believe he knows I am seeing you."

"I'm sorry I got you in trouble," he said, stroking her forearm.

"It's not your fault," she replied tearfully, standing and preparing to leave. "It's the ways of my church."

"Does that mean I won't be seeing you anymore?"

"I don't know," she said, reaching out and touching his cheek. "I just don't know."

She gently stroked his cheek. Then she turned and walked briskly out of the thicket.

Jesse sat alone for some time, trying to sort out his feelings. Finally, he stood and walked over to the gravel road where he had parked his car. As he approached the road, he saw a horse and buggy approaching from the west. The buggy's wheels kicked up a small cloud of dust on the gravel road as it approached the area where his car was parked.

Jesse could see that the bearded man wearing a black, round-brimmed hat was Reverend Turner, the church elder who had admonished Rachel for not cleaning the church. Turner did not acknowledge Jesse as the horse and buggy drove past.

Jesse returned to the thicket the next week at the time he usually met Rachel. He waited for almost an hour, but she did not join him. As he was about to walk back to his car, he heard soft footsteps crunching through the autumn leaves. Rachel smiled warmly at him as she stepped into the small clearing and walked over to where he was standing.

There were a few seconds of awkward silence, and then Jesse said, "What did your Church Council decide?"

"They have put the decision off," she replied. "I didn't have to say no to them. I think they want me to work for them for a while longer, before I marry and have my own family."

Jesse reached out and pulled her close to him. She looked up and kissed him softly. As they clung to each other, he had the overwhelming feeling that the world was, at that very moment, full of *promise and hope. Anything and everything seemed possible. He clung to that hope while a soft autumn breeze swept gently through the clearing where Rachel was pressed against his body.*

><><><

*Jesse received his draft notice shortly after that meeting. The Korean War had just started, and he was given a few weeks to get his affairs in order before leaving by railroad to join the military. When he met Rachel in the thicket again, he explained what had happened and what they should do.*

*"We could get married before I leave," he said. "You could move into my home until I get back."*

*"I cannot do that," she said sadly. "I cannot just break completely with everything I am, and from everyone I have ever known. I cannot do that. I will wait for you until you return from the war. Then we will be married."*

*"And if your church says you must marry someone else? What will you say?"*

*"I will say, 'no', Jesse. I will meet you again someday, right here."*

><><><

*After basic training, Jesse was sent overseas. He was wounded six months later. He spent another three months convalescing in a military hospital. During the time he was in the hospital, he received news that both of his parents had died within weeks of one another. When he finally returned home, almost an entire year had passed since he had left Point Tyson.*

*He had not heard from Rachel during his entire time overseas. He knew she could not write to him because her church community did not use the postal service. He could not write to her for the same reason. Still, he clung to the hope that she felt as strongly about the promises they had made as he did.*

*He expected that maybe she would meet him when he and several other veterans arrived home. When she did not, he began to worry. The parade through Point Tyson's Main Street in their honor did nothing to rebuild his spirits. When he learned that she was married to Grant Sims of the church community, and they had a baby daughter, he was devastated.*

*He went into seclusion and did not talk to anyone. Even when the quarry business experienced severe setbacks, he remained secluded in his bedroom. By the time he finally owned up to the fact that Rachel was a married woman and mother, he was a pale, embittered shadow of his former self.*

*Still, he could not let go of his dreams. Several times each month, he drove over to the thicket where he had met her for the last time, and where she promised to meet him again some day. He sat among the autumn leaves, replaying that day repeatedly in his mind. With each slight noise that penetrated the thicket, he waited expectantly, hoping beyond hope that maybe this time it would be Rachel, returning once again as she had so often in the past. Each time he was disappointed. Each time he drove home alone, surrounded by the shattered hopes that had once made the world seem like a place where dreams were still possible, even if they were elusive and fleeting.*

*Finally, one day as he sat in the thicket, he heard a noise that sounded familiar. This time it was no illusion. His heart beat wildly as the footsteps approached the clearing. He stood as Rachel stepped out of the colorful autumn leaves. She was exactly as he remembered her. His heart continued to beat wildly with excitement as she unpinned her long black hair and let it fall to her shoulders.*

*She did not say anything. She just reached out her arms and pulled him close to her own body, as they both sobbed quietly. They stood there, clinging to one another, while the autumn leaves fell gently to the ground all around them.*

*"Why?" he asked, his voice trembling with emotion. "Why, Rachel?"*

*"Because I didn't fit into your world, Jesse," she sobbed. "I belong over here."*

"That day Rachel and I took up where we had left off," Jesse Willert reminisced as he stared out his office window at the abandoned buildings at the bottom of his quarry. "We would meet on Hodges Island. It was all very innocent. I just wanted to be with her. She wanted to help me adjust after I had lost everything I had ever cared about during the war. All we did was talk. Nothing more."

"Did her church decide that she had to marry Grant Sims?" Laura asked.

"I don't know," he admitted. "All she told me was that she was obligated to marry someone in her church community. She said it was expected of all young people in the church."

"Is that what *you* believed?"

"I was too confused, and too hurt, to know what to believe."

"Why did you start meeting her on Hodges Island?"

"The thicket was too far away from their farm. Hodges Island was within easy walking distance. Rachel could walk over there through the riverbed. I could go over by boat."

"By boat?"

"I had a fishing boat. I would dock it on the other side of the island and meet her by the old quarry buildings. That way, no one would ever figure out what we were doing."

"Were you planning to meet her over there the day she disappeared?"

"Yes," he replied. "But when I went out to my truck that morning, I had a flat tire. The spare also had a hole in it, and Becky was in town with the car meeting someone, although she said later that person never showed up. There was nothing else for me to drive. By the time I could patch the hole in the tire and put it on the truck, it was long past the time that I was to meet Rachel on Hodges Island."

"Did you tell anyone you were meeting her over there?"

"Only my sister Becky."

"What was her reaction?"

"She was very upset. She said until I stopped seeing a married woman, I really had no life and no future. Becky was very concerned about what it was doing to me."

"Did you ever consider the possibility that perhaps someone punched holes in those tires so you could not meet her that morning on Hodges Island?" Laura speculated. "Someone who knew you were going to meet her there, but wanted you out of the way?"

Willert looked puzzled, confused. "It would have to be someone who knew I was seeing Rachel out there. The only person who knew that was Becky."

"Your sister ended up in a mental institution in the 1950s. Why was she committed?"

"How did you know that?" he asked, looking very surprised.

"I read about it in your business ledgers."

"I had forgotten about them," he admitted.

"Why was your sister committed?"

"Ever since she was a child, she was prone to long periods of silence and depression. It's something we seem to have inherited. It became much worse as she got older. The times that she stayed behind a locked door in her bedroom became more and more frequent. Finally, she wouldn't talk to anyone or care for herself. I had no choice. I had to have her committed."

"Think she might have been responsible for my mother's disappearance?" Laura asked.

"No," Willert insisted, shaking his head vigorously. "I just can't believe Becky had anything to do with it."

"After my mother disappeared, did you go out to Hodges Island to look for her?"

"Of course I did. At first, I thought she had gone home when I didn't show up in time. When I learned that she had disappeared, I went out there many times to try to find her. It was impossible. That island is a maze of holes and quarries. She could be anywhere out there."

"Did you think it was possible that she might have left with a man driving a car with an Iowa license plates?"

"Absolutely not!" he replied angrily. "She would never have left you, Anna. I know how much she loved you. She told me you were her whole life."

"Do you know who might have started those rumors?"

"No, I don't," he said, shaking his head as tears welled up in his eyes. "I just remember what a hopeless, empty feeling I had inside of me in the days and weeks after Rachel disappeared. No one could possibly understand those feelings. When someone you love simply vanishes, a part of you becomes trapped forever in the past. You never see that person wither, fade, and die. While you watch yourself grow old every day in the mirror, you still see that person standing on some distant hill, forever young, forever radiant, forever alive. As much as you desperately want to join the person you love on that distant hill, you know that can never be. You watch yourself and everything around you grow old and die, while the thing you love the most grows more and more distant, while remaining tantalizing young and beautiful. The pain just never goes away. All I had left was a gravestone with her name on it next to her husband's grave. Yet, she was somewhere else, somewhere unreachable."

"Did you ever go out to the cemetery at night and place flowers on their graves?" Laura asked.

"No, I never did anything like that," Willert replied, slowly shaking his head. "I know Charlie Flanigan spread that story. But I don't know how the flowers got on those graves."

Jesse Willert stood by his bedroom window long after Laura had left. He gazed out at the quarry that sprawled across the bottom of the hill below his house. In the distance, a lone tree protruded above the rim of the quarry. As night fell, the sunlight spread slowly across the quarry walls and gradually faded.

Laura's visit had awakened some painful memories he had struggled all his life to put to rest. They had never completely disappeared. They were always there. But he had managed to erect a barrier between himself and the many disappointing turns his life had taken. It was a weak barrier, one that often collapsed with the slightest memory of a happier time. He had tried to avoid those thoughts and memories. He decided it was better to live without hope than to have that hope resurrected, only to disappear as quickly as the departing rays of sunlight on the distant granite wall.

When the young woman he had just talked to announced that she believed she was Rachel's daughter, he remembered in vivid detail the days and weeks before Rachel disappeared. She had seemed troubled, very troubled. He remembered that she seemed to want to tell him something, yet could not find the words to tell him. After she vanished, he wondered if her disappearance had anything to do with what was troubling her.

*What was it she was trying to tell him? Had someone threatened her? Or was it something else?*

He had never given the other possibility any real thought. It didn't seem possible, based on what Rachel had told him when they started meeting again after he returned from the war. Now he began to question if she had been hiding something from him, something she thought might be better for him not to know.

*Had she changed her mind? Was that the urgency he felt the last time they talked before she vanished? If so, what caused the urgency?*

As Willert continued to stare out his bedroom window, the lone tree in the distance began to tease and tantalize him as it had in the days and months after Rachel disappeared. As the sunlight faded in the depths of the quarry and lingered on the rim, the tree looked once again like a human figure beckoning to him from an impossible, irretrievable distance.

It brought back all the pain, all the vanished dreams. For a moment he wished he had never shared those memories with Rachel's daughter.

# CHAPTER SIXTEEN

"Yes," Bertha Mickelson said, peering through the screen door of her second-floor apartment. "Who is it?"

"I visited you earlier this week," Laura replied.

"Yes, I remember you."

"I was wondering if I could ask you a few more questions."

"I guess that would be alright, yes."

Bertha opened the screen door wider and led Laura into the living room. Laura sat down on the green couch, and Bertha sat in the rocking chair next to the white cat that was once again perched on the windowsill overlooking Main Street.

"The last time we talked," Laura explained, "you told me how Grant and Rachel Sims pleaded with you to change the birth certificate for their daughter."

"Yes, I remember telling you that story."

"You said they wanted you to state that the baby was premature, to protect both themselves and the child from others in their church."

"Yes, I remember that, too."

"I don't think you told me the whole story," Laura inquired firmly. "I think there's more to it."

"In what way?" Bertha replied somewhat hesitantly.

Laura decided to play a hunch regarding something that occurred to her during their first conversation. "I have reason to believe Grant Sims was probably not the father of that child," she said. "I believe there was another man involved. If so, and if I am Rachel's daughter—which I believe to be the case—then Grant Sims is not my father. My father was someone else, someone who might have been responsible for my mother's disappearance."

"I suppose enough time has passed now," Bertha sighed deeply as she reached out a wrinkled hand to pet the cat. "I suppose no one can be hurt by the truth anymore."

"What is the truth?"

"When Grant and Rachel asked me to change the birth certificate, I refused," Bertha replied slowly. "I told them I could not
do it. They pleaded with me, and still I refused. Finally, Grant
escorted me into the next room so his wife could not hear what
he was going to tell me. He told me he was not the father of that
child. He said his wife had gotten pregnant by another man, and
he had married her to protect both Rachel and the baby from the
wrath of their church."

"Did he tell you who the father was, or say anything that would
lead you to think my mother and me needed to be protected from
him?"

"No, he did not. I'm not even too sure Grant knew who the
father was. Rachel might have kept that to herself. I just don't
know."

"Is that why you suspected a possible connection between my
mother's pregnancy and her disappearance?"

Bertha slowly nodded. "Rachel worked as a hired girl, mostly
for the members of her church, but for other families as well. I
was concerned that she might have gotten pregnant by someone
who was a prominent member of the community, someone who
could have been ruined if she had exposed him as a common
adulterer and father of an illegitimate child."

"That's why you agreed to change the birth certificate?"

"Yes. What Grant told me convinced me that it was necessary
to protect the mother and the child. I thought it would legiti-
mize the birth to everyone, including the father. That's why I have
never revealed this secret before. I'm only telling you because you
have a right to know that Grant was not your biological father."

"Did you think about telling the authorities what you suspected after my mother disappeared?"

"Yes."

"Why didn't you?"

"I was only guessing. I had no proof." Bertha stared out the
window at the city park and sighed deeply. "The one thing you
must understand is that even though Grant and Rachel started
out their lives as a married couple in a most unusual way, they
became deeply committed to one another. That was evident to
me throughout the long childbirth. He was right there, helping
her every step of the way. Many months later, I remember Rachel
walking down that gravel road by the dam with her young daughter strapped to her back. She was the very picture of contentment.

Grant was happy, too. He loved you dearly and was a good father to you. I only saw him one time after he gave you up. I was driving past his farm, and I decided to see how he was doing. He was standing by your swing when I drove into the farmyard. I could see that he had been crying. He didn't have to tell me why. He lost everything when Rachel disappeared and again when he had to give you up. He had nothing left but the memories. Rachel and you gave him the family he needed, and he gave her the home she had always wanted."

"But neither of them ever said anything, anything at all that might have revealed the name of the person who was my biological father."

"No," Bertha replied, shaking her head slowly. "I just figured it was someone so important they had to keep that secret to themselves. If you are Rachel's daughter, you should also be very careful. Powerful people do not like to be exposed as moral hypocrites by their illegitimate children. Often their descendants are equally obsessed with defending the family name."

Laura stood in the sunbaked telephone booth near the *Point Tyson Chronicle* building. "Dr. Finley," she said, "I met yesterday with the other man in my mother's life."

"The one who drove a car with an Iowa license plates?" Finley asked.

"No. I don't think that person even exists. It was her first love, Jesse Willert."

"I thought he was dead."

"No. He's very much alive. He told me he was drafted and sent to Korea. During the time that he was gone, my mother met and married Grant Sims. Willert never stopped loving her. He told me as much."

"Think he might be involved in her disappearance?" Finley speculated. "Scorned lovers are always suspects."

"No, I don't. He seems as mystified as everyone else by what happened to her. He still found it painful to talk about her. The other news is that I met again with the midwife who delivered me. I sensed there was something wrong with the story she told me during our first visit. This time she admitted that Grant Sims told her he was not my father. He said my mother married him because she needed a father for her child. Apparently, my mother was fearful of how an illegitimate child might be treated by their church community."

"Did the midwife tell you who the father was?"

"She didn't know. She wasn't even sure if Grant knew. She suspected that since my mother worked as a hired girl in the homes of some of the area's most prominent citizens, one of them might be my father. She was fearful that whoever it was might have gotten rid of my mother to keep the scandal from ever becoming public."

"Is it possible that this Jesse Willert you mentioned was the father?" Finley asked.

"I nibbled around the edges of that question with him," Laura replied. "But I never asked it. I don't think he would have reacted well. He became noticeably angry when I mentioned those who questioned my mother's reputation after her disappearance. He seemed determined to protect her from that gossip. He just seemed to assume that the father was Grant Sims. However, that elderly midwife I talked to said it was someone else. Probably someone who had a lot to lose if he was exposed as the father of an illegitimate child. Willert had nothing left to lose. He said he had already lost everything that ever mattered to him."

"If your mother threatened to reveal the father's name to others in the community, especially a church community, that would be a very powerful motive for someone to silence her," Finley speculated.

"Yes, it would . . . Listen, I would like to meet with Aurther and you again tomorrow. I was hoping you might help me sort this out."

"You and I can meet, of course," Finley replied. "But I'm afraid Aurther won't be of much use to us for a while. He's slipped back into his own private world. Aurther doesn't have the same filtering system the rest of us have. He feels everything very deeply and often very painfully. I think he just reached the point where he was overwhelmed by all of this. When he tires of humanity and its cruelties, his natural defenses spirit him away to what he calls 'his window into the other world'. He sits and stares out that window for days, weeks, even longer."

><><><

Laura decided to visit Jesse Willert again to ask him what he knew of the families who had employed her mother as a hired girl. She also wanted to probe a little deeper to see if Willert knew more than he had revealed during their first conversation. After her second conversation with Bertha, Laura was convinced her mother might very well have been the victim of whoever fathered her illegitimate child. She was hoping Willert could help her identify that person.

*That would mean my own father was a murderer. But who was he, and was he still around? Did he or someone working for him leave the threatening notes, gut the rabbit on Hodges Island, and try to run my car off the road?*

When she walked up the driveway to Willert's home, the green pick-up truck was not in its customary parking place on the side of the house. When she knocked on the door, there was no answer. Although Willert said that he seldom left his property, this time he had apparently made an exception.

*What was so important that he needed to leave his home this time? Did it have anything to do with me*

Willert's absence made Laura question her earlier response to him. He had seemed so genuinely and deeply distraught, even twenty-two years after her mother disappeared, that it was impossible not to believe he was telling the truth. But she began to wonder if maybe he was just a very good actor, and he was throwing dirt over the trail of whoever was responsible for her mother's disappearance. Maybe that trail led to his own doorstep, and he was protecting himself—or his sister.

*He couldn't have had anything to do with my mother's disappearance, could he? His account of his relationship with her was tender, even touchingly sentimental. From what he wrote in his business ledgers, he seemed devastated by her disappearance. There would be no reason for him to fake those private expressions of grief. Still, there was something very strange about his whole life and withdrawal from people. Did he suspect his sister might have been involved in the disappearance of the woman he loved? She apparently strongly disapproved of her brother's relationship with a married woman. Was he covering up for her?*

On the way back to the main highway, Laura spotted a white truck in the distance. The truck passed the gravel road on which she was driving and continued north toward Pelican Lake.

*It's the truck that tried to run me off the road!*

She impulsively decided to follow the truck to see if it was possible to determine who owned it. She stayed several hundred yards behind the truck so the driver could not see her car in his rear-view mirror. Once they entered Pelican Lake, the truck made several turns before entering an alley. When she made the same turn, she saw the truck at the other end of the alley as it made a right turn onto another side street.

As she drove down the alley, a large furniture truck moved slowly away from a loading ramp, blocking her way. The driver backed the furniture truck cautiously into the alley, while another man stood at the rear to stop oncoming cars.

*Not now! Not Now!*

The furniture truck finally moved slowly down the alley and made a left turn at the cross street. Laura followed and made a right turn at the same cross street. She drove up and down the city streets for several minutes, looking for any sign of the white truck. She could see no trace of it anywhere.

She drove down a few more streets before pulling over to a curb next to a crowd that was gathered in front of the bandstand in the park near the courthouse. She rolled down the window and turned off the motor. The speaker behind the podium, apparently a preacher, was a stocky man in his mid-fifties. He had reddish-brown hair and a short, muscular neck. He perspired freely as he spoke into the microphone above the podium.

"The powers of darkness have gripped this nation as assuredly as they gripped the sinful cities in the Bible," the man's voice boomed out of the two speakers at opposite ends of the stage, while his hands and arms gestured dramatically to emphasize his points. "There are those among us who would turn this country into the new Sodom and Gomorrah. In biblical times, these cesspools of depravity and sin created a stench that reached heaven and offended God. This was only four hundred years after the flood. Four hundred years since God first saw fit to destroy the human race, allowing only Noah and his faithful, chosen few to survive. Four hundred years! That was all it took for humanity to return to its sinful ways at Sodom and Gomorrah. Now we find this same sinful chorus of non-believers, these same practitioners of ungodly, immoral lifestyles trying to spread their filth in our own country. As true believers, we must not allow this to happen. We are engaged in a war for the souls of the American people. This is a war that is being fought on many fronts. We must not, we cannot, lose this war . . ."

><><><

While she was in Pelican Lake, Laura decided to look at the records Olga had told her were stored in the New Sentinels of God Church. She surmised that maybe there was something there that would shed light on her own past and her mother's disappearance.

She drove over to the church and parked her car in a huge paved parking lot. She walked over to the front doors, stood in the open doorway, and studied the church's interior. The New Sentinels of God Church was simple in design, and yet it was built on a massive scale. There was little religious symbolism anywhere in the church's interior. The windows were clear glass, not the stained-glass windows in most churches. A single cross, suspended by two cables, was attached to huge wooden beams in the ceiling. The cross, which was constructed out of two pieces of highly polished wood, hovered over a large, circular wooden stage. Some television cameras and other equipment were parked off-stage. They were the only things in the church that did not conform to the otherwise grand symmetrical design that flowed outward in all directions from the circular stage.

*It's the same simplicity the builders of the original Sentinels of God Church worked into their architectural designs. But it has been duplicated on a massive scale, and at great expense, for the obvious purpose of appealing to a television audience. Without the cross, it would look more like a theater-in-the-round or a television stage set.*

She spotted a muscular, middle-aged man in blue denim work clothes pushing a dolly filled with television equipment through a door in the rear of the church. An older, more distinguished looking man in a dark business suit was pacing back and forth in the same area. He paused to inspect the television cameras. Then he stared overhead at several huge amplifiers suspended from the ceiling.

Laura walked down the aisle and over to where the man in the business suit was standing. "I've been told that some of the records from the original Sentinels of God Church are stored here," she said. "Who do I see about looking at those records?"

"Yes, we have some of those records," the man replied politely. "But I'm afraid they're not open to the public."

"Why?"

"It's church policy."

"But why?"

"The trustees made that decision many years ago."

The man quickly dismissed her and walked out the door in the rear of the church. She heard a muffled conversation somewhere just outside the door. Then the conversation faded as the two men walked farther away from the doorway.

*It looks like they have the same sense of secrecy as the church hierarchy that governed the original Sentinels of God Church. Only they're now known as "trustees." This could be a business—a very prosperous business—posing as a church.*

Laura decided to return to the historical society's basement to examine the church's records more closely. She was still working on the assumption that if her mother was involved with some prominent married man in Archer County, as Bertha Mickelson suspected, it might have been a member of the Sentinels of God Church. Her mother would have had more contact with them than other prominent people in Point Tyson. Furthermore, the position of an important member of the church would have been greatly jeopardized by the revelation that he had fathered an illegitimate child. Undoubtedly, that would have ended his career immediately.

*Perhaps he had been sufficiently threatened to make her disappear. Perhaps he still has considerable influence in Archer County. Or perhaps he is dead, and someone close to him is still trying to protect his reputation.*

Laura continued to be perplexed by the church's financial records. It was clear to her that the members of the church tithed virtually their entire salaries or farm profits to the Church Council, who then provided for their basic needs. What was not clear was how the rest of the money the Church Council collected was used.

*Much of it just seemed to disappear without any explanation.*

After struggling with the church's financial records for some time, Laura gave up and turned her attentions to the family records. There wasn't much to go on there either.

*The families were as secretive as the church leaders.*

Finally, she gave up and walked upstairs. Olga was studying some documents at her desk. She looked up and smiled as Laura approached. "Find what you were looking for?"

"Not really. But then I'm not too sure what I'm looking for. I guess that makes it doubly difficult."

"Something must have brought you back out here," Olga inquired.

"I'm considering the possibility that there might have been a scandal involving Rachel Sims and a prominent member of the Sentinels of God Church," Laura replied.

"What kind of scandal?"

"She might have gotten pregnant by a married man, maybe one of the church leaders, and she arranged a hasty marriage with Grant Sims to cover the whole thing up."

"Oh, my, that would have been a real scandal," Olga exclaimed. "The church considered those sins to be just about the worst things anyone could do."

"You haven't heard any such rumors, have you?"

"Well, the first year I worked here, one of the older volunteers told me the church wasn't at all what it seemed to be. She said they had to hush up a number of scandals."

"Did she mention anyone in particular?"

"Yes, she did. She said Nathaniel Klinger was rumored to have fathered a child outside of his marriage. She said Reverend Turner adopted the young girl and raised her as his own daughter until she died of some childhood disease. I believe her name was Phoebe. I didn't know what to make of it at the time, but the old woman insisted the rumor was true."

"Yes, what can I do for you?" Nathaniel Klinger asked Laura as he opened the screen door and joined her on the front porch of his home.

"I've been reading some of the old church records," she explained. "I have some questions about them."

"I would rather not be involved in that discussion," he replied, turning and walking back toward the door.

"Please," she pleaded. "I think a great wrong has been done to a former member of your church, and only you can help me."

"Rachel Sims?" he asked, turning and facing Laura.

"Yes, and maybe others as well."

"What do you need from me?"

"The records indicate that there was a financial crisis in the church in the early 1950s. What caused that crisis?"

"I cannot talk about those church affairs," he insisted. "They are reserved for the Church Council."

"The other members of the Church Council are all dead," Laura replied firmly. "Surely it can no longer matter if you reveal what you know about that financial crisis."

"That's all I am going to say about church business," Klinger said firmly. "I have already said too much."

"Then tell me something else. Do you know who started the rumor about Rachel Sims leaving town with a man driving a car with an Iowa license plates?"

"Many people in the church were talking about it," he replied. "I don't know who actually saw her leave in that car. I have told you repeatedly that I know nothing about the disappearance of Rachel Sims. Why do you continue to be so interested in all of this?"

"Because I believe I'm her daughter."

"You're Grant and Rachel's daughter?" Klinger replied, obviously surprised.

"Yes. I didn't know that the last time we talked. Now I do."

"I'm sorry about your mother," he said sympathetically, but firmly. "But I still can't help you. We all took oaths to keep church business confidential. I cannot violate that oath, even at this late stage in my life. The others would have done the same if they had outlived me."

Laura decided to play her trump card, the one she was certain would get Klinger's attention. "Perhaps you can tell me about another member of your church community . . ."

"I know nothing . . ."

"Phoebe Ruth Turner. What can you tell me about her?"

Klinger's hostility and anger quickly subsided. He became noticeably nervous and agitated. "What do you know about Phoebe?" he asked.

"I'll make a deal with you," she challenged him. "You tell me everything you know about my mother, and I'll tell you what I know about Phoebe Turner."

Klinger stared into Laura's eyes. Then he gestured for her to follow him inside. He led her to the study in the back of the house. She sat down on a homemade wooden chair, and he sat on another wooden chair near the fireplace. "I don't have much time," he said as he settled into the chair. "My wife is asleep now, but she will soon need me."

"This won't take long," Laura replied.

"Tell me what you know about Phoebe?"

"First, you answer some questions about my mother," Laura insisted. "An elderly woman told me she had always suspected my mother got involved with some prominent member of the community, and she became pregnant. That elderly woman suspected whoever was the father of that child may have been involved in her disappearance. Was there ever any talk in your church about such a possibility?"

"There were some rumors about the child, as I remember," Klinger reminisced. "There were questions about whether the child was conceived before or after the marriage. But I do not recall any talk of the type you just described to me."

"Was my mother especially close to any of the church leaders?"

"Well, she cleaned house for Reverend Turner and his wife. She even lived with them for a time. But it is inconceivable to me that he might be involved in an adulterous relationship outside of his marriage."

"Did he ever talk about my mother's disappearance to you?"

"Not any more than he talked about other people in the church."

"Why are you so convinced that he was not involved with her?"

"Reverend Turner and his wife were childless. He told me he had a childhood disease that had taken that ability away from him. What it left him in return was a higher resistance to temptation than the rest of us. He was not easily taken in by the things of this world."

"He was sterile?"

"That's your word for it," Klinger corrected her. "Please, I have answered your questions. Now, you owe me the same consideration. What do you know about Phoebe Turner?"

"I think you probably know what I have heard."

"I didn't realize it was common knowledge."

"It probably wasn't. Apparently, my mother was the victim of rumors and gossip within your church community, and so were you."

"All sins are difficult to accept," Klinger mused softly. "Some sins are harder to accept than others. Sins of the flesh are the hardest of all to accept. Even the most moral of men can fail, given the right circumstances. And Satan knows how to set those traps so they are barely visible. Only when they snap shut are we awakened to the reality of what we have done. By then it is too late."

"Maybe you are too hard on yourself," Laura replied. "Maybe it is human to fail, and to learn from those failures."

Klinger heard a soft cry from elsewhere in the house, and he stood to leave. "I must end our conversation now. My wife needs me. I will tell you that I think you are looking in the wrong place for the answers you seek. I believe what you are looking for is to be found elsewhere. You must know that there was another unusual death in Archer County in May of 1952."

"Norbert Samuelson?"

"I have said enough. If I were you, I would look a little deeper, try a little harder to see how things you might think are isolated and separated from one another, are connected at some deeper level by the powers that brought evil into this world and continue to perpetuate it in the lives of all men and women."

Laura immediately drove back to town and over to the antiques warehouse to ask Sibley Fields for the key to the *Point Tyson Chronicle* newspaper office. Then she drove over to the building that once housed the small town newspaper. Late afternoon shadows covered much of the interior of the abandoned building when she opened the door and stepped inside. She quickly walked over to the pile of yellowish-brown newspapers where she had left the May 6, 1952, edition of the *Point Tyson Chronicle*. She was hoping to reread the article that described the tragic death of State Senator Norbert Samuelson when his boat overturned on the Lonely Willow River. She saw immediately that someone had rummaged through the pile and scattered several of the newspapers across the floor. The May 6th edition was not where she had left it. She searched the adjacent piles of newspapers, but could find it nowhere.

*It's gone! Someone else has been here and apparently taken it! But why?*

She glanced apprehensively into the shadows. Then she walked quickly out the front door. She remembered that there were similar accounts of the incident involving Samuelson in the newspaper articles that were varnished to the walls of the card room adjacent to Max's Café.

As she walked across the park, she nodded at Pete Solvie, who was sitting on a bench under an elm tree. Two farmers were drinking coffee at the counter when she entered the cafe. In the rear, the television on the fireplace hearth was turned on, but the sound had been muted.

She found the newspaper articles varnished to the wall where she remembered seeing them earlier. The varnish obscured some of the texts of the newspaper accounts of Samuelson's death and related articles. Still, she could make out enough to determine that "Samuelson was fishing near the Hodges Island Dam when his boat overturned, and he drowned." She also read, "Frank Carver found the boat near the docking area for the southern entrance to Hodges Island." She was not able to read what appeared to be a description of precisely where Samuelson's body was discovered after the accident.

She walked quickly out of the café and over to where Pete was sitting in the park. "What do you remember about Norbert Samuelson drowning on the Lonely Willow River?" she asked.

"What is it you need to know?"

"The *Point Tyson Chronicle* indicated that Frank Carver found Samuelson's boat near Hodges Island. Who was Frank Carver?"

"He owned the quarry on the island. He was my boss."

"Is he still alive?"

"No, he died about twenty years ago. Committed suicide. But his wife Amanda still lives in Point Tyson."

"Do you remember how high the river was that year?"

"Oh, I'm not too sure. I don't think there was anything very unusual about that particular year. Didn't snow too much, or too little. So, the river was probably doing what it always does."

"It's not a very fast-moving current around the dam, is it?"

"No. That's one of the most sluggish sections of the Lonely Willow River."

"Did anyone wonder why Samuelson's boat overturned, and he drowned in a section of the river where the current was so slow?"

"If I remember correctly, he wasn't a very good swimmer," Pete explained. "I think that's why he drowned."

"How far downstream did they find his body?"

"About a mile."

"You know that area pretty well," Laura said. "Does it make any sense to you that the current would carry the body of someone who drowned near the dam that far downriver?"

Pete carefully considered the question. "That would depend completely on how far out in the river he was fishing. If he was in the middle of the river, the current could easily have carried his body that far downstream. If he was fishing closer to the dam, the more likely possibility would be that his body would have gotten trapped in the dead trees that litter the shallows near Hodges Island."

"If he was fishing in the middle of the river, wouldn't the boat also have been carried farther downstream?"

"Well, I don't know," Pete replied thoughtfully. "The currents out there can be tricky." He glanced at some of his card-playing buddies who were gesturing for him to join them in Max's Cafe. "Be right there," he yelled. Then he addressed Laura as he stood to leave. "I do remember one thing about that incident that always struck me as kind of peculiar."

"What's that?" Laura asked.

"This happened a few years back. I was sitting with some of my friends in Max's Café, and we were reminiscing about the old days. Reverend Sinclair was eating lunch at the counter. Eventually, we started reminiscing about Norbert Samuelson and all the good things he had done for Archer County. Bill Kreiser got to talking about the accident that had caused Norbert to drown in the Lonely Willow River, and we all agreed that it was a terrible thing. Well, about that time Reverend Sinclair was paying his bill, and he turned and said something very strange to us. He said in an angry tone of voice, 'That was no accident.' Then he turned and walked out of the café. The rest of us just sat there perplexed. None of us understood at all what he meant by that."

Finley walked over to where Aurther Schlepler was sitting next to one of Farmington's third-floor windows. He glanced out the window at a half moon that was hovering high in the night sky. In an upper corner of the window, the stars in Orion's belt glowed brightly, seemingly from the very edge of the universe. From somewhere in the darkness that covered the prairie, the sound of crickets chirping filtered into the room.

"Aurther," Finley said warmly, sitting down in an adjacent chair and turning to greet his friend, "Laura told me to thank you for everything you have done for her. She said she understands why you had to leave us. She said the insights you have given her have been invaluable. I thought you should know that."

Finley looked into Schlepler's eyes to see if there was any response, but there was none. "Look, old friend," he continued. "You have earned a rest. I'll be stopping by to see that you're well taken care of. I will miss our conversations, but I will not forget that you are here."

As Finley stood to leave, he paused by the wheelchair. Looking down, he saw a tablet with a drawing on Schlepler's lap. As he held the tablet up to the light, he realized it was a pencil drawing of a young woman walking on a riverbank, holding a bouquet of flowers, while a large black bird with huge arched wings hovered in the air a few feet above her head. The moon was partially concealed behind some clouds, and a river curled across the bottom of the drawing. The entire drawing was framed as though the scene was occurring behind a large window.

# CHAPTER SEVENTEEN

Finley and Laura studied Schlepler's drawing as they sat on one of the concrete benches on Farmington's lawn. An army of ants streamed across the sidewalk in front of them, carrying tiny pieces of an apple core someone had discarded near a gravel-filled flowerbed. One of the ants had apparently been too greedy, and it kept dropping a piece of the apple that was much too big for its tiny frame.

"I think Aurther is trying to tell us something in this drawing," Finley speculated as he handed the tablet to Laura.

"What do you think it means?" she asked.

"Well, the way this bird hovers above your mother, wings pointed downwards as though about to attack, I can only assume it is Aurther's vision of whoever or whatever it was that took her life the day she disappeared."

"Why did he draw that threat as a large black bird? Why not something else?"

Finley examined the drawing more closely. "It's too large for a blackbird or crow, although crows do get very big."

"It looks more like a raven," Laura speculated.

"What do you know about ravens?"

"Only what I've read," Laura admitted. "Some eastern religions and Native American cultures see the raven as a symbol of hope and renewal. But in Edgar Allan Poe's poem, the raven torments the speaker until he goes insane."

"So, it can be a symbol of good and evil, or hope and despair?"

"It can be either, or both. What do you think Aurther meant by it?"

"It could be a generic threat," Finley surmised. "Or it could be something more specific. Aurther's insights often come in very cryptic forms. Usually, he lets others come to their own conclusions. Still, I think he's trying to tell us that whoever or whatever took your mother's life has something in common with this bird as he draws it here."

Laura studied the details in the drawing and then set the tablet on the bench next to her purse. "Do you remember when Aurther looked at my photographs of Hodges Island and said my mother made it as far as the old quarry buildings?"

"Yes, I remember that," Finley replied.

"He also said 'someone was watching' her. What do you suppose he meant by that?"

"I don't know. His instincts are often uncanny. Maybe he meant someone was watching her from a concealed position before he attacked her. Or maybe he meant two people were involved in your mother's disappearance."

"Is it also possible that there was a witness that day? Someone who was not involved, but saw what happened?"

"I suppose that's also possible," Finley admitted.

"If that was the case," Laura speculated, "you would think that person would have told someone his or her story by now."

"Maybe he was silenced. Or maybe he went into hiding. Someone obviously doesn't want the truth to see the light of day. Maybe that someone is the raven Aurther drew here."

Laura studied the drawing again and then looked up. "Dr. Finley," she said, "there's something else I've been meaning to ask you."

"Yes. What is it?"

"Is it possible to leave a hypnotic suggestion implanted in someone's mind *after* they've gone through the regressive process?"

"Yes. There have been many experiments with post-hypnotic suggestions. It can be done. I just don't know what it would accomplish in this case. Why do you ask?"

"Because I plan to visit some more of the places where I might have been when I was very young and was still with my mother. I thought if I went there feeling the subconscious effects of the hypnotic suggestion that took me back to my childhood, it might help bring back some of the memories I haven't been able to penetrate at a more conscious level as an adult."

"We can try," Finley replied, "but there's also the possibility that it might incapacitate you and make it impossible for you to feel anything except more emotional pain and anguish."

"I'd still like to try it," Laura said emphatically.

"Then come back tomorrow, first thing in the morning. We'll give it a try."

><><><><><

When Laura returned to Point Tyson, she drove over to Sibley's antiques warehouse to return the key for the newspaper office and ask him if anyone else had used it recently. Sibley told her nobody had asked for the key except her. He added that it wouldn't surprise him if someone else had been in the newspaper office. He said other people in town had keys, including some of the people who once worked for the *Point Tyson Chronicle*. He said they sometimes went in there to reminisce about earlier times. That was why he put the table and chair in the back of the room. He was surprised, however, that someone would take a newspaper.

As soon as she left Sibley's antiques store, Laura drove over to a small church on the eastern end of town. A late-model, white station wagon was parked near the front entrance of the church. As she walked past the station wagon, she saw that the tailgate was open and the back end was half-filled with bags of used clothing and boxes of canned foods.

The church windows were boarded up, and the white paint on the siding was peeling. As she walked up the steps and into the front entrance, the interior of the church reminded her of a smaller version of Sibley's warehouse. The pews and altar had been removed, leaving a large room that was littered with piles of donated clothing, small furniture, and various grocery items.

A tall, thin, bearded man dressed in faded blue jeans and a matching shirt was sorting one of the piles of clothing into several smaller piles. He had a distinctly prominent chin, and his neatly trimmed beard was flecked with streaks of white.

"Here to make a donation?" Sinclair asked cheerfully, looking up at her from where he was kneeling next to the piles of clothing.

"No," she said. "I was hoping to ask you a few questions."

"What is it you need to know?"

"My name is Laura Fielding," she explained. "I've been doing some research on my family history. I was raised by another couple, but my mother was Rachel Sims, the woman who disappeared over by Hodges Island in the early 1950s. I was wondering if you ever talked to Nathaniel Klinger about that incident."

"Well, no, I haven't," Sinclair said, standing up slowly and stretching. "But then I don't think he would ever talk to me about something like that. We usually make a little small talk, and then I'm on my way."

"I've been out to his farm," Laura explained. "I asked him some questions about my mother. I think he knows much more than he was willing to tell me. I've also been looking into the death of State Senator Norbert Samuelson. I talked to Pete Solvie, and he told me you didn't think it was an accident."

"I don't remember saying anything like that," Sinclair replied tersely.

"Pete told me you were in Max's Café when the question of Samuelson's death came up. He insisted that you said it was no accident."

Sinclair stroked his beard. "Are you sure these are things you want to know?" he asked.

"Yes," she replied firmly. "I need to know what happened to my mother. I think some of the other deaths around here in the 1950s might be connected to what happened to her."

Suddenly, Sinclair's demeanor changed, revealing a significantly more explosive temperament than was evident when he first greeted her. "You have to understand," he said angrily as he proceeded to argue passionately against an unidentified adversary. "There are people among us who tap into some deep, dark side of human nature and shape it into a powerful force that transforms spirituality into some monstrosity that poses as virtue. They become a law onto themselves. They will silence anyone who tries to expose them."

"Who are these people?" Laura insisted.

"They pile up dead bodies everywhere," Sinclair continued. "They don't kill most of them. They destroy them in other ways. But if they must resort to murder, they probably will. Power is all that matters to them. People never see them coming because they camouflage their true intentions so skillfully."

"Who are they?" Laura insisted again.

Sinclair glanced at the open doorway and then back at her. "One of the first people I met when I moved to Point Tyson was Alfred Kron," he began cautiously, deliberately. "Alfred donated shoes, belts, clothing, and furniture to my ministry. He was unmarried and had no living relatives, so he also wrote into his will that his entire estate was to be donated to my church so I could distribute his life's possessions to the poor. When he was killed in that hit and run accident, I inherited everything, even things I did not want. Alfred also left behind some things he had written about his suspicions regarding those deaths over by Hodges

Island in the 1950s. He was convinced that Norbert Samuelson's death was not an accident. Alfred and Norbert were old friends. He indicated that Norbert had revealed some disturbing things to him shortly before the boating accident. Alfred was also convinced that Rachel Sims's disappearance was related to Samuelson's death in some way, although he did not know how . . ."

>◇◇◇◇<

"My husband was a despicable human being," Amanda Carver said matter-of-factly. "I know that might sound kind of harsh to you. But my life began the day he died. He treated my son and me the same way he treated the men who worked in the quarries. We were all disposable. None of us had any worth unless we served his purposes."

Laura stared across the dining room table at the tall, gray-haired matron who held her teacup with her thumb and right index finger, while her little finger extended outward from her hand. Frank Carver's widow was clearly someone who did not mince words. She was the least evasive person Laura had met in Point Tyson. Her entire demeanor reflected an elegant sense of refinement and good taste that contrasted with her blue dress, which was faded and threadbare around the elbows. She gave every impression that she had once been wealthy, but she had fallen on hard times. Still, she seemed comfortable, even relaxed with her status in life.

The Victorian-era house was itself the very symbol of fading elegance. The furniture in the dining room and adjacent living room was obviously very expensive. But the fabrics on the chairs and couch had faded, and some of the corners were torn, revealing white stuffing. On a long pole next to the couch, a bird chirped contentedly while it danced on top of a cage.

"An article I read in the *Point Tyson Chronicle* indicated that your husband was the one who found Norbert Samuelson's boat after he drowned on the Lonely Willow River," Laura said. "Did he ever talk to you about that?"

"No. He did not. My husband did not talk to many people the last years of his life, not even me. After the quarries closed, he was a broken man. He had a very difficult time dealing with that failure. Money and power were everything to him. Everything!"

"Did you or anyone else ever suspect that foul play might be involved in Samuelson's death?"

Amana seemed genuinely perplexed by the question. "Why do you ask that?"

"Well," Laura explained, "your husband found the boat near Hodges Island, but Samuelson's body was found much farther downstream. Didn't that seem a little strange?"

"I think people just thought it was an accident. Those things happen. Besides, Norbert didn't have any enemies that I know of."

Laura glanced at the bird that was walking playfully back and forth on top of the cage. "The quarries on Hodges Island were closed," she said. "What was your husband doing out there the day Samuelson drowned."

"He would go out there occasionally," Amanda reminisced. "He would visit his old office, or walk the length of the island on the old quarry road, probably just to relive a time when it was an active business enterprise, and he was a man with much power and prestige. My husband needed to feel that way about himself. It was all that gave his life meaning."

"Do . . ."

"Miss Fielding, you haven't told me why this is so important to you?"

Amanda was so blunt and straightforward that Laura decided it was best to be completely honest with her. "Do you remember a Rachel Sims who disappeared on Hodges Island a few weeks after Samuelson drowned?"

"Of course, I remember that incident."

"I was raised by another couple. But I know now that she was my mother. I am trying to figure out what happened to her."

Amanda pursed her lips and ran her index finger across her lower lip as she stared across the table at Laura. "Rachel once worked for us, in this very house. Did you know that?"

"No, I did not know that," Laura admitted. "When did she work for you?"

"In the early 1950s. She came over to do our housecleaning twice a month. Then our money ran out, and we had to let her go."

Laura debated how she should ask the most important question that was on her mind. "I don't know who my father is," she said slowly. "An elderly woman told me she always wondered if my mother got pregnant by some prominent man who was later responsible for what happened to her on Hodges Island."

"I think what you are asking me," Amanda replied bluntly, "is did my husband father a child by Rachel, and did he then dispose of her to protect what was left of his own reputation?"

"Yes," Laura admitted. "That is what I was wondering."

"My husband had many vices," Amanda explained firmly. "Among them was a weakness for young women. He was a heavy drinker and womanizer. The possibility that he might have fathered a child outside of our marriage would come as no great surprise to me. I suspected as much with another woman in a different part of the state. He sent her money for a long time, but he never told me why. Still, in Rachel's case, I just don't think so."

"Why?"

"I wouldn't put it past my husband. But I would be very surprised if Rachel consented to such a relationship. It just wasn't like her. I had a very high opinion of her, as did my son."

"Your son?"

"Yes, we had one child, Jack."

"How old was your son when my mother did your house-cleaning?"

"About Rachel's age."

"Where is he now?"

"I don't know."

"I don't understand."

"My husband was a brutal man," Amanda explained. "He treated our son terribly. Finally, Jack had enough of his father and left home. I haven't heard from him since. I think he blames me for not protecting him when he was growing up."

"When did he leave home?"

"The summer of 1952. He had an argument with my husband. I came downstairs the next morning and found a note on the kitchen table saying he was leaving and wouldn't be back. Two months later, my husband committed suicide."

"May I ask *how* he committed suicide?"

"As I said, after the quarries closed, he would sometimes go out there and sit for hours in his old office, surrounded by the ruins of his business. One day he didn't return home. They found him slumped over his desk, a gun in his hand and a bullet in his head."

><><><

When Laura returned to Farmington the next morning, Finley immediately started the regressive hypnosis process. The session was virtually a replay of his first attempt to use hypnosis to probe into Laura's subconscious mind to expose her earliest childhood memories. The major difference in the two sessions was this time he used the name "Anna" that was on her birth certificate, instead of the name "Laura" the Andersons had given her later in life. As Finley directed her more deeply into the hypnotic trance, he used the same image of the lilac bush as it changed in a reversed seasonal pattern to gradually expose earlier memories.

"Anna," he said gently, "concentrate on the beautiful purple flowers of the lilac bush as they shrink back into the branches, only to disappear completely, then reappear again. I want you to reverse that seasonal cycle until it becomes a blur of purple and gray."

Finley studied her face carefully and then asked, "Anna, where are you now?"

"I'm . . . I don't know."

"Where are you?" Finley asked again.

"I'm on . . . a swing . . ." she whispered softly.

"Is someone with you by the swing?"

*Her mother's voice was soft, gentle.*

"Gone . . ."

"Is someone with you by the swing?" Finley asked.

"Gone! Gone!"

"Was it your mother?" Finley asked.

Laura started to cry softly. "Gone," she repeated sadly.

*She waited by the swing. Every morning she waited.*

"Don't want to go!"

"Is someone trying to take you away?" Finley asked.

*She stretched to look out the car window. Then she started to cry. She cried until she fell asleep.*

"What happened to your mother?" Finley asked emphatically. "Do you remember anything at all about the way your mother disappeared? Were you there?"

*They were running away from the angry voices.*

"Men! Angry men . . ."

"Who were they?" Finley asked.

*Her mother was afraid. She could feel it.*

"Run!" Laura screamed.

*Where's Jesse? What's taking him so long?*

"Jesse . . . Where is . . . Jesse?"

"Anna, did Jesse have something to do with your mother's disappearance?" Finley asked.

*He should be here by now.*

"Where is Jesse?" Laura screamed. "Where is he?"

"It's okay, Anna" Finley said firmly, but gently. "I'm going to take you out of the hypnotic trance now. I want you to reverse the pattern of the seasonal cycles and follow the changing colors of the lilac flowers as the years pass. When it is May of 1974, I want you to open your eyes. Only I want you to retain the memories you had as a very young girl. I want you to carry those memories with you. I want you to feel them inside of you even when you are back in the year 1974."

Laura's eyes suddenly blinked open.

"We visited some of your childhood memories, when your name was still Anna," Finley explained. "Do you remember what you just experienced?"

"Yes, I do," Laura replied slowly. "Only it was different."

"In what way?"

"Somehow I slipped right past my childhood memories. I really thought I was my mother, and I was walking out to the old quarry buildings on Hodges Island, as she had done before she disappeared . . . Dr. Finley, is it possible that I'm sharing some of her thoughts and memories?"

"I suppose it's possible," Finley replied. "I have patients here who swear someone else, often their deceased relatives, inhabits their bodies and their minds."

"You said before that most of them are psychotic."

"Yes, I did say that. But I don't believe that's always the case. The human brain is a very complex thing. We shouldn't underestimate its powers. I'm inclined to believe that under certain conditions we might be able to share the memories of previous generations. After all, we do inherit so much from our ancestors. Why not some of their memories, at least under certain conditions?"

"What are those conditions?"

"Perhaps after traumatic and unexpected deaths. Maybe that's what you're experiencing now. There is, however, another possibility," Finley cautioned her. "You have learned so many of the details of your mother's life and disappearance that you could be vicariously identifying with her to the point where you could be creating memories out of what you have learned about your mother."

"Did you leave me with a hypnotic suggestion, as you said, or did you remove it completely?"

"I left you with it. Whether or not it takes is another question altogether."

"Whatever you did, I felt like I was my mother—and I was walking on Hodges Island the day she disappeared. I was there. I felt it. I was her."

"There might be something to what you were feeling," Finley admitted. "During the regressive process, you mentioned the name Jesse three times. That should not have happened from Anna's point of view, if you were sharing her subconscious memories. The name itself could only come from you or your mother."

As soon as she returned to Point Tyson, Laura drove out to Albert Felstuhl's farm. She stood next to a barbed wire fence while she waited for him to turn off his tractor and walk across a recently plowed field to join her.

"I was worried about you the other day when you went over to Hodges Island," he said, leaning on one of the wooden fence posts. "But some people in Max's Café told me they had seen you after the tornado came through. I figured you were okay."

"I got wet and a little muddy, but I survived," Laura replied.

"What brings you out here today?"

"I just wanted to ask you one more question about what you saw the day Rachel Sims disappeared."

"Okay."

"You told me you didn't see anyone else out here that morning. Is that correct?"

"That's right. Only Grant Sims. But that was quite a while after I saw his wife walkin' 'cross the riverbed."

"Are you absolutely certain there was no one else in this area the day she disappeared?"

"Well, I believe you asked me that same question the last time we talked. I thought a lot about it afterwards. As I searched my memory, I realized there was one other person I might have seen that morning. But I can't imagine he was involved in any way in her disappearance."

"Who was he?"

"Sheldon Andert. He probably walked down this road that morning, the way he did every morning on his way to town. Then he'd walk back down this same road in the afternoon. He did that every day, so I didn't think much of it when you asked me that question."

"I thought he walked a circular path around town."

"He lived with his mother and father about a mile east of here. While they were alive, he walked this road every day. After they died, he moved into his place behind the old drugstore. That's when he started walking in a circle around the town."

"Why are you so convinced he had nothing to do with her disappearance?"

"Because that wouldn't be like him at all. Town kids used to tease him mercilessly because he was so different. They would poke him and hit him. He just stood there and took it. He wouldn't know how to be violent even if he needed to protect himself. It just wasn't in him."

"Did you ever see him go over to Hodges Island?"

"No. But I suppose he might have."

"Why do you say that?"

"His father worked in the quarries for a time. He'd take Sheldon with him to do small odd jobs around the place. Cleaning up and things like that. Nothing very complicated. Sheldon knew the island, and I guess he might have gone over there. But I never saw him do it."

"Did you notice anything different in his behavior after Rachel Sims disappeared?"

Felstuhl pursed his lips and searched deeply into his memories. "Well, now that you mention it," he said, "I do remember something a little unusual. My wife noticed it first. There's another gravel road that runs along the other side of my property. One day, she saw Sheldon walking over there, and she brought it to my attention. She wondered why he had changed the route he always took to town."

Laura looked up and down the gravel road. "How far did Grant and Rachel Sims live from here?" she asked.

"A half-mile east, right off this road. Barn burned down when lightning struck it, but the house's still standing. Place has been abandoned since Grant died. Ralph Sather owns the property now. He told me he's going to bulldoze the house when he has the time."

><><><

Laura steered her car onto a deeply rutted driveway. The house at the end of the driveway reminded her of Klinger's farm, except that it was even more buried in thick trees, bushes, and tall weeds. To her left, she saw the charred remains of a barn protruding above the weeds and tall grass. To her right, an ancient horse-drawn plow with long wooden handles was leaning against the trunk of a dead tree.

She parked the car and got out to survey the abandoned farmyard. The only structure that remained was the house, which had turned a pale gray, making it look like it was slowly disappearing into the countryside. On one side of the house, three posts and two rails from a split wood fence were also disappearing into the brush and weeds that surrounded them. The rest of the fence was apparently already buried in the brush, or it had been dismantled and hauled away. A frayed rope, swaying slowly in the breeze, was tied to a limb of a dead tree near the house. A wooden birdhouse was attached with rusty wire to another dead branch on the same tree. The birdhouse had turned the same pale gray as the farmhouse.

As Laura walked over to what remained of the porch, she saw that the front door and most of the windows were missing. Staring into the doorway, she was suddenly filled with a rush of undefined memories. They were all fleeting sensations, but they triggered powerful emotional responses.

*I've been here before! I remember this house!*

As she stepped cautiously onto the porch, the floorboards groaned and creaked, but they felt solid beneath her feet. On the other side of the open doorway, sunlight and shadows intermingled on the floor of what appeared to be the living room of the house.

Dust particles were drifting gently in the sunlight that poured in through the holes in the roof and the broken and missing front windows. What she had felt before was intensified many times over as her eyes surveyed the interior of the farmhouse. She felt an almost overwhelming sadness, intermixed with contentment, even a glimmer of happiness.

*I have been here before!*

As she walked from room to room, the feelings evoked by the old farmhouse were overwhelming. Each room seemed vaguely familiar. Something in her past seemed to be struggling to find a way out of the shadows and into a more conscious level of her memories. She stared at the dust drifting across the sunlight, while she tried to remember what had happened to her in this house.

*It's all so familiar!*

She was not able to bring those memories to the surface. They were just out of reach, tantalizing her, teasing her, but remaining evasive and unknowable.

When she walked back outside, the sun was hanging above the western horizon. She made her way cautiously through the thick brush to the tree where the frayed rope was hanging from one limb. In the grass, she spotted a piece of wood with two holes that had been drilled at opposite ends. Another frayed and weathered piece of rope had been inserted into one of the holes and secured with a huge knot.

*It's a swing. A child's swing.*

She picked up the piece of wood and examined it closely, while she ran her fingertips across the coarse, rough surface. From somewhere, she heard a voice speaking to her from out of the past. The voice was so distant and faint that it seemed to come from another world.

*It's my mother's voice. She spoke gentle, reassuring words on this very spot of ground. Then, suddenly, she was gone.*

Laura did not know if they were real memories, or memories she had fabricated out of the photographs and stories she had seen and heard about Grant and Rachel Sims. Still, she felt as though she could hear her mother's voice as she stood next to the frayed rope dangling from a dead tree limb.

*When you are older, Anna. Then you can swing higher. Then you can swing as high as the clouds in the sky. But not now, my precious. Not now.*

As she ran her fingers across the weathered piece of wood, more faint glimmerings of fragmented memories started to work their way through the darkness and into the light. She no longer cared if they were real, or if she was creating them in the deepest part of her memories. She struggled to find the words to describe what she was feeling. Suddenly, those feelings poured out of her in uncontrollable torrents of pain and an overwhelming sense of loss and sadness.

*She had waited by the swing, crying for her mother to return. Every morning she waited. Sometimes she wandered through the house, from room to room, looking for her mother. The man with the beard and kind eyes would hold her and try to comfort her. She could not stop crying. She kept looking, hoping, waiting. Always she would go back to the swing. Her mother was never there.*

*It seemed like she wandered through those rooms and the yard forever, looking for her mother. She was standing by the swing when the man with the beard and kind eyes picked her up and hugged her so hard it hurt. Then he handed her to someone she had seen with her mother. The woman put her in a car, and she knew they were taking her somewhere. Maybe they were taking her to her mother.*

*She stood up as she felt the car moving beneath her. She stretched to look out the window. The man with the beard and kind eyes was standing there, crying. He kept waving at her until she could see him no more. Then she started to cry. She cried until she fell asleep. She dreamt about her mother and the swing.*

Before leaving the area, Laura revisited the Hodges Island Dam. She paused in the middle of the walkway and looked down at the water flowing past the concrete and stone structure. The river's current seemed even more sluggish than the first time she had walked across the dam.

When Jesse Willert told her about the poem her mother recited to him in the church cemetery, she was sure she had heard it before. It brought back a flood of undefined, overlapping memories that she could not connect to any period in her life. She only sensed that somehow the poem was connected to Hodges Island, the old riverbed, and the dam.

*Did my mother bring me out here in the days before she disappeared? Did she show me the blossoming lilac flowers on Hodges Island and recite the poem? Did she take me over to the dam?*

Something about her first visit to the dam evoked feelings of things buried so deeply that she could not find words to express them. She only knew the dam was a place that struck fear into the deepest part of her memories. It was the same kind of fear she felt every time she awoke from the reoccurring dream that haunted her from the time she was a young girl.

Those feelings were reawakened when Bertha Mickelson described how she had seen Rachel Sims walking by the dam with her young daughter strapped to her back. Somehow that description attached itself to the memories that were buried in the dream and to the things she learned from people in Point Tyson who knew her mother. Slowly, the sunlight penetrated the darkness of the dream. Fragmented pictures and thoughts began to attach themselves to those feelings, and to something that happened near the dam many years earlier.

At the time, she was too young to even know the words to express what she had seen and heard. Now she could find the words.

*There were voices. Loud, angry voices. Her mother was afraid. She could feel it. She too became afraid. Then there was another sound. Another angry sound. Her mother became even more afraid. Then her mother was running. Running away from the angry voices. They needed to get far away. Far away from the angry voices.*

Laura parked her car in the alley behind the old drugstore. Except for a single light that glowed brightly from a pole in the middle of the alley, the area was dark.

Someone had turned on the jukebox in Max's Café, and the lyrics of a 1950s Country ballad that lamented a lost and irretrievable love drifted across the night air. She could not remember the singer, but the song seemed somehow appropriate as she walked past the dust-covered windows and empty stores in the alley behind Point Tyson's Main Street.

As Laura approached the back door of the abandoned drugstore, she saw a soft light glowing behind thick curtains that covered what she assumed had once been the pharmacy area. She knocked on the door and waited. A few seconds later, a thin, frail man in bib overalls opened the door and looked out at her.

"I'd like to come in and talk to you," Laura explained. "I'm Rachel Sims's daughter. I believe you might know something about what happened to my mother on Hodges Island in May of 1952."

# CHAPTER EIGHTEEN

Laura spent much of the next morning in the historical society basement, searching through the records for the one elusive clue that would tie everything together and explain what had happened the day her mother disappeared on Hodges Island. She was preoccupied with some church documents on the table next to Schlepler's drawing, when she sensed a slight movement in a window located high in the basement walls. Looking up, she saw nothing unusual. She continued to read through the church documents. Moments later, her attention shifted to Schlepler's drawing.

*What did he sense in my photographs of Hodges Island that motivated him to draw this? What is he trying to tell us here? Is it a raven, or is it something else? Maybe it's just a generic symbol of death hovering in the night sky? Why couldn't he have made it simple, like the scarlet "A" in Hawthorne's novel? Although the "A" was imbued with ambiguity, its original meaning of "Adulterer" was clear from the very beginning."*

Another thought suddenly occurred to her.

*Maybe it was not meant to be seen as a bird? Maybe it was meant to be something else? With its long wings extended downwards, it looks like a huge letter "M" in the night sky. Is that what Schlepler was trying to tell us? Was he trying to say that the person responsible for my mother's death is someone associated with the letter "M"?*

She looked at the drawing again, and a flood of words with negative connotations beginning with the letter "M" raced through her mind.

*Murderer? Madman? Monster? Maybe all the above? Or maybe the letter "M" is an initial in the first or last name of the person responsible for my mother's disappearance?*

She quickly skimmed through some of the church documents on the table. "That's it!" she exclaimed excitedly moments later.

Laura thrust her hand into her purse and pulled out a pen and writing pad. She scribbled a quick letter and sealed it in an envelope. She wrote Dr. Finley's address across the front of the envelope and affixed a stamp. Then she gathered up her belongings and quickly rushed upstairs and outside to her car.

><><><><

Laura parked next to the weathered, greenish-brown mailbox on Point Tyson's Main Street. She quickly climbed out of her car and inserted the letter into a tiny slot on the side of the mailbox. Then she drove around the corner to the telephone booth to call Dr. Finley. When she entered the booth, however, she saw that the telephone had been removed and a handwritten note, "No longer in service," was taped to one of the glass panels.

*Did the telephone company do this? Or was it someone else?*

She debated whether she should find another phone, but decided instead to drive out of town in the direction from which she came. A huge dust cloud formed behind her car as she drove along the dirt road that ran parallel to the Lonely Willow River. She parked the car on the shoulder near Felstuhl's pasture and stepped outside. She paused for a moment to lean on the car door and gaze across the riverbed at Hodges Island.

The sky was clear and blue, with only a few white clouds overhead. She speculated that it was probably a similar morning in May of 1952 when her mother had set off on a short journey to Hodges Island, a journey that would end so tragically.

*What was she thinking as she approached Hodges Island? Was she planning to tell Jesse what she knew? Was she planning to tell him everything?*

Laura learned a great deal from Reverend Sinclair and Sheldon Andert. Sinclair shared some of Alfred Kron's notes that revealed the dead man's growing suspicions that Rachel Sims's disappearance was not an isolated incident, but rather was connected to other suspicious events in Archer County in the early 1950s. Kron's own demise in a hit-and-run accident appeared to be one of those suspicious incidents. Sheldon Andert's memories were often fragmented and disjointed, but they were even more revealing, as he had first-hand information regarding the disappearance of Rachel Sims that he harbored for over two decades. From Schlepler's drawing and the Sentinels of God Church records stored in the historical society basement, Laura found the final piece she needed to solve the elaborate puzzle that was her mother's life and disappearance.

*It's all starting to come together.*

She now understood most of what had happened when her mother was seen for the last time walking across the dry riverbed. She had narrowed the possibilities significantly. There were only a few more loose ends to tie together. To do that, she needed to check out something near the old quarry buildings, something she had learned from Sheldon. No one would believe her unless she had every detail straight in her own mind. The motives of those who were responsible for the disappearance of her mother on Hodges Island would be quickly dismissed unless she had irrefutable proof.

Laura walked down the embankment and across the riverbed, stepping on the rocks and dryer areas that formed a rough path to Hodges Island. Tadpoles were swimming in some of the puddles of water that had accumulated during the spring rains. In some areas, the tadpoles had already made their magical transformations into small green frogs that hopped into the brush when they heard her footsteps.

As she approached the large granite boulder, she was convinced her mother had taken her to that very spot a few days before she disappeared. Laura was convinced her mother let her touch the flowers on the lilac bushes, while she recited a poem she had learned from her own mother.

*If I should go, and you should stay, remember me when the lilacs bloom, though I am far away . . .*

She glanced at two ducklings swimming in a large puddle of water in the riverbed. Above the marshlands, a hawk hovered in the sky as it drifted along the air currents. Laura watched the ducklings retreat into some reeds, apparently startled by the hawk. Then she parted the bushes next to the granite boulder and started her journey to the center of the island.

As she walked down the dirt road, small animals rustled through the underbrush. She passed a mound of black dirt, where armies of ants were spilling out of the top of the crater and marching with military precision into the wet carpet of dead leaves that covered the island. She paused for a moment to run her fingers over the moisture that had gathered on the leaves of a bush next to the path. She listened to the breezes sweeping through the trees, and again she wondered what her mother must have been thinking the day she walked this same road.

*She must have been worried about Jesse Willert, and what he needed to know so he could get on with his life. It must have pained her terribly to see him so disillusioned, so broken. She must have agonized over what she planned to tell him. She must have been searching for a way to help him put those old feelings to rest so he could find someone else to share his life. And there were the other secrets as well, the secrets he needed to know should anything happen to her.*

Minutes later, Laura arrived at the center of the island where the fallen and decaying stone and wooden quarry buildings were partially concealed in the thick foliage. The gravestones protruded out of the ground on the embankment to her right. Sheldon told her it was a cemetery for men without families who died during a mysterious epidemic at the end of the last century, and other itinerant laborers who died or were killed while working in the quarries. Sheldon said he knew some of those men. He said they were buried in the company cemetery because no one cared enough about them to claim their bodies after they died. He told her something else about the cemetery too, something that shed a great deal of light on what had happened to her mother.

*There is only one way to find out if he is telling the truth.*

Despite Pete Solvie's warnings to stay on the main road, she walked over to a dirt path and made her way to the top of the embankment. Once she was standing on the embankment, she realized the cemetery was unlike any she had ever seen before. The gravestones were not polished granite stones with names and dates of birth and death neatly inscribed on the surfaces. They were unpolished granite blocks that were so badly cracked and chipped they were apparently discarded as unusable as building stones.

*But they were good enough for the graves of the itinerant laborers who died while working in the quarries.*

The names on the gravestones were also unlike any she had ever seen before. They were carved into the coarse granite surfaces with obvious haste and little concern for details. Even the last names on many of the stones were omitted. The dead workers were identified by first names like Bill, Pete, and Joe. Others contained initials like WS, TJ, and BR.

*Their bodies were discarded here, their lives apparently considered as insignificant as the cracked and flawed stones that mark their graves.*

She speculated that Frank Carver, the owner of the quarry, probably didn't want the workers who chiseled the inscriptions and buried their coworkers to take much time away from more profit-making activities. It was all done with great haste and little reverence or respect for the dead.

Laura walked slowly across the weed-strewn cemetery, remembering what Sheldon said he saw there. The graves for Ole and Joe P were exactly where he said they would be. The unmarked space between the two graves was also exactly as he described it. She stood there for several minutes, staring at the unmarked space. Then she walked back down the path and over to the other side of the dirt road to the quarry buildings.

*This was where it began. But she was not alone. Schlepler was right when he sensed that "someone was watching" her.*

Sheldon was reluctant to tell Laura what he had witnessed that May morning when he spontaneously changed his normal routine and walked over to Hodges Island where he once worked. When she told him she was Rachel Sims's daughter, he relented. What he said confirmed much of what Laura already suspected, while providing important details about what happened to her mother the day she disappeared.

*When Sheldon heard footsteps approaching, he hid in the shadows, near the corner of one of the fallen buildings. Through the bushes and vines, he watched as a young, dark-haired woman left the dirt road and walked into the clearing. As she approached the area where he was hiding, he could tell it was Rachel Sims. He had seen her before, walking along the gravel road by Albert Felstuhl's farm. He sensed that she was nervous and apprehensive.*

*While Rachel Sims apparently waited for someone, she spotted something in the grass. She leaned down and picked up a baby bird and a nest that had fallen out of a tree. She placed the bird in its nest, and said something to it as she put the nest back on one of the branches. Then she picked some flowers off one of the lilac bushes and tied them together with a pink ribbon she pulled out of her hair. She held the bouquet up in the air and admired it.*

*Sheldon tried to be very quiet as he watched from the shadows. But when he took a short step backward, he heard a soft, muffled* creaking sound. He had stepped on a board that was concealed in the grass.

She heard it, too. "Who's there?" she asked nervously. She waited, then walked cautiously in his direction.

Suddenly, two large birds burst out of the brush and flew into the sky. Startled, she tripped and almost fell, but she steadied herself by grabbing a tree branch. "Jesse, is that you?" she asked, staring once again at the area where Sheldon was hiding.

She took another step in his direction and reached out to part the brush. She paused when she heard a sound behind her, over by the dirt road. A bearded, heavy-set man wearing a black, round-brimmed hat suddenly stepped out of the trees at the opposite end of the road from where she had entered the clearing.

"Rachel!" he said sternly, folding his arms across his chest. "What are you doing out here?"

She was startled, frightened. "I was just out for a walk," she said nervously.

"You've been seeing Jesse Willert again, haven't you?"

"Yes," she admitted apprehensively.

"You are a married woman, and yet you are meeting another man on Hodges Island. The sin of adultery is a very serious sin, Rachel."

"I have not committed adultery!" she insisted.

"You have also committed the sin of disobedience," the man reprimanded her.

"I have only disobeyed those who would not let me have my own life," she insisted.

"Come with me, Rachel," the man said, striding over to where she was standing and grabbing her forearm. He pulled and dragged her down the dirt road. "I want to show you something. Something that will hopefully enable you to see the error of your ways."

"Please!" she pleaded as she dropped the bouquet of lilac flowers she had been holding. "Please, let me go!"

"Not until you see what happens to those who commit the sin of adultery," the man said firmly.

"I have not committed the sin of adultery," she insisted. "But you! You have violated one of the most sacred of all the commandments!"

As the bearded man in the black, round-brimmed hat dragged Rachel Sims down the dirt road and out of sight, Sheldon walked slowly, cautiously out of his hiding place. He waited for a few moments, listening to her crying and pleading.

*Sheldon followed them for a time at a safe distance. He hid behind trees and bushes along the way so the bearded man would not see him. He listened to Rachel Sims plead for her life. He listened to her beg the man to let her go back to her husband and daughter. He heard her call out the name "Jesse" time after time after time. He listened to her agonized cries, her desperate pleas for mercy. Finally, when he could stand it no longer, he turned and rushed down the road in the opposite direction.*

*He came back later and found a newly dug, unmarked grave, lightly covered with dead leaves, in the cemetery for itinerant workers. He knew what it meant.*

*That was the beginning of his nightmare. For over twenty years, he felt guilty, terribly guilty that he had not intervened to help Rachel Sims escape from the man in the black, round-brimmed hat. For over twenty years, he heard her voice, her desperate pleas for help as he walked around the small town of Point Tyson.*

Laura stood by the abandoned quarry buildings, playing and replaying in her mind what she had put together from her conversation with Sheldon Andert and her own efforts to expose the person who was responsible for her mother's disappearance. Sheldon said the brim of the man's hat cast a shadow across his face, and he never came close enough to where he was hiding. So, Sheldon could not positively identify the man who dragged Rachel Sims down the dirt road toward the southeastern end of the island. He added, "All of the men in that church had beards and dressed alike." But he said that he thought it was Reverend Turner because he "had seen him drive his horse and buggy down the gravel road many times, and it looked like him from a distance."

Sheldon explained that he did not go to the authorities with what he knew. He said he was afraid they would not believe him if he told them he saw someone from the Sentinels of God Church, most likely Reverend Turner, dragging Rachel Sims down the dirt road. Sheldon was convinced they would think he was the one responsible for her disappearance.

His reason for being on the island would also have been highly suspicious. He said he "saw a huge jackrabbit hop across the gravel road and head out for Hodges Island," and he decided to follow it. Once there, he impulsively decided to revisit the old quarry buildings to see if they looked the way he remembered them, even though he had not been to the interior of the island in years.

He knew his explanation would not convince very many people. So, he kept his secret until Laura told him she was Rachel Sims's daughter. Then he finally revealed that he thought it was Reverend Turner who had dragged her mother out of the clearing and down the dirt road.

What Sheldon told Laura made sense. Reverend Turner, the leader of the Sentinels of God Church, would have seen it as his sacred duty to punish a young woman he believed had violated the Eighth Commandment. The members of the church viewed adultery as one of the most serious of all sins. Whereas men like Nathaniel Klinger who engaged in such immoral activities might be easily forgiven and their adulterous behavior covered up, women who committed adultery were considered a threat to the entire church community. In Turner's mind, Rachel Sims needed to be punished severely for what he thought were her sexual transgressions.

*Perhaps the punishment exceeded what he had anticipated when he intercepted her on Hodges Island. Perhaps Turner had intended to scare her, not to kill her, but something went terribly wrong and she died at his hands elsewhere on the island.*

Still, Laura was not convinced that Sheldon had it right when he identified Reverend Turner as the man he had seen on the edge of the clearing. Nor was she convinced that Turner had the motive to punish Rachel Sims so harshly that she died. Laura knew too much about other things that had been going on in Archer County in the early 1950s, things that did not involve Turner. In fact, he was the victim of others who were becoming more powerful than the governing hierarchy of the Sentinels of God Church.

Laura was also convinced that Bertha Mickelson had it wrong when the elderly midwife speculated that perhaps some prominent married man in the community had murdered Rachel Sims to keep her from exposing him as a common adulterer who had fathered an illegitimate child.

*The motives that led to the disappearance of my mother were much different, and more complex, than anyone in Point Tyson had ever thought possible. The gossip about her leaving with a well-dressed man in a car with Iowa license plates was a well-orchestrated cover-up, nothing more.*

Laura stood by the abandoned buildings for some time, trying to put the whole puzzle together in her mind. She was so lost in her thoughts that she did not notice someone approaching until she heard a slight noise behind her. Turning, she saw a stocky, muscular man step into the clearing.

Laura had never met the leader of the New Sentinels of God Church. She had only seen his name on a church sign and heard him deliver a fiery sermon to those who attended the political rally in Pelican Lake. Still, there was no question that the man who was walking toward her was an older Very Reverend Samuel Morton, previously known as Zechariah Samuel Morton. According to a document she found that morning in the historical society, he was the former Church Treasurer of the Sentinels of God Church. Zechariah Morton, who defrauded the Sentinels of God Church in the early 1950s, and Samuel Morton, who transformed the New Sentinels of God Church into a lucrative television business and powerful political force, were the same person. He was the letter "M" in Schlepler's drawing.

Laura sensed immediately that Morton was positioning himself so she could not flee past him and escape down the dirt road.

"Why couldn't you leave well enough alone?" he asked Laura sternly, menacingly. "Why couldn't you just let it go?"

"Because what you took from me was the most important thing in my life," she replied firmly. "I was a very young girl when you murdered my mother and left her on this island."

"How did I accomplish that incredible feat of deception?" Morton replied scornfully. "Others will tell you I was home that day."

*Keep him talking! Keep him talking! Then look for an opening and make a run for it!*

"Although you were in the process of separating from the Sentinels of God Church," Laura explained angrily, "you came out here dressed as one of them, in case anyone saw you. Perhaps you were even hoping that Reverend Turner would be accused of the crime. After all, he caught you red-handed, defrauding the church to support your business and political causes. What better way to pay him back? You were being groomed to take over for him some day, but that wasn't good enough for you. You wanted it all, and you wanted it right away. Nothing was going to stand in your way. Nothing! My mother saw you murder Norbert Samuelson. That's why you had to make her disappear."

"Your mother slipped away so quietly that day she probably didn't think we saw her," Morton replied tersely. "But we did."

*Keep him talking! Wait for him to lower his guard!*

"Where do Jonathan and Esther Anderson fit into all of this?"

"They were too close to Rachel. We feared she might have told them everything. We looked, but could not find them."

"And Grant Sims?"

"It was obvious he knew nothing. As for your mother, she was a temptress and an adulterer. She deserved the fate that befell her. She was not worthy to live among us."

"I'm surprised you didn't have the others who work for you come out here today," Laura replied sarcastically.

*Move slowly back to the road! Watch for an opening! Then run! Run as fast as you can!*

"They were only told to scare you away. I wanted to put it all to rest. You would not let me."

Laura had felt her mother's pain so often over the past weeks, and now she was confronting the man who had caused most of it. His dismissal of her mother's life and her own pain was unbearable. The anger that had been building inside of her rushed out like water pouring over the top of a swollen dam.

"You hypocrite," she said angrily. "You pose as a man of God because it gives you power and control over the lives of other people. But you are a fraud. You find hate where you should find love. You have nothing in common with the good and decent people who try to improve the lives of all those who are less fortunate. My mother's sins, whatever they might be, were nothing in comparison to the sins of self-righteous hypocrites like you who pompously preach as though you are superior to all others, while you exploit the naïve and gullible for profit. My mother was superior to you in every way."

"You definitely have your mother's temperament," Morton replied calmly.

"Yes. But I have something my mother did not have the day you murdered her," Laura replied defiantly. "I sent a letter explaining everything that happened the day she disappeared . . ."

"You mean this letter?" Morton said. He reached into his coat pocket, pulled out the letter, and held it up for Laura to see. He smiled slightly when he saw that Laura realized she had been terribly outmaneuvered. "It's a very small town," he added.

Laura suddenly bolted and tried to run past Morton, but he reached out and grabbed her arm. Morton had been relatively calm throughout the encounter, but he started to perspire and breathe heavily. Laura felt his wet, clammy hand on her forearm. She tried to pull free, but he was much too strong.

"Now you can join your mother," he muttered angrily.

Laura felt herself being pulled and dragged down the road toward the other end of the island. She fought to break his tight grip on her forearm. When she dug her feet into the road, he picked her up and carried her, while she fought to free herself.

"Your mother was a temptress and an adulterer!" he said angrily. "Her soul and your soul belong on this island!"

*Rachel Sims struggled to free herself from Morton's powerful grip as he dragged her down the dirt road! She had to get back to Grant and Anna! They would never know what had happened to her! But he was too strong! Where was Jesse? She called out Jesse's name again and again! But there was no answer!*

Laura continued to yell and struggle as Morton half carried, half dragged her down a path adjacent to the dirt road. He set her down as they approached an area that was thick with brush. He kept his arms wrapped around her arms and waist as he pushed her deeper into the thick foliage.

*Rachel Sims continued to struggle against Morton's powerful grip! It could not end here! Not like this! Again, she thought of Grant and Anna! She had to get back to them! Where was Jesse?*

Through an opening in the brush, Laura glimpsed what appeared to be a huge, gaping hole in the earth. She fought with all her strength to avoid going any closer to it. She felt Morton suddenly stop, apparently positioning himself to push her into the hole. Simultaneously, she caught a glimpse of an arm reaching in her direction. A hand grabbed Morton by the shoulder and spun him around.

Laura was vaguely aware of a struggle as she fell to the ground and hit her head against an exposed tree root. She heard Morton yell something incomprehensible. Then she slipped into unconsciousness and was surrounded by darkness and more unintelligible sounds. In the darkness she saw her mother reaching out to her. She reached out her own hand, but she could not touch her mother's hand. Her mother's hand was unreachable, even though it was tantalizingly close.

*Mother, I cannot reach your hand! I cannot . . .*

Slowly, soft sunlight penetrated the darkness, and Jessie Willert's face came into view. He was kneeling, looking down at her. She raised her head slightly and saw that Morton was lying face down near the dirt path.

"Are you okay?" Willert asked gently.

"I think so, yes," Laura stammered. "What are you doing here?"

"Your visit the other day brought back some old memories," he explained. "I was driving out to the grove where Rachel and I used to meet. I saw your car and was worried about you being out here alone. What happened here?"

"I figured out . . . what happened to my mother," Laura gasped. She paused to catch her breath. "She was walking in the riverbed near the dam. I was strapped to her back. She saw Samuel Morton and Jerry Harston drown Norbert Samuelson on the walkway. They put his body back in the boat and overturned it farther out on the river."

"Why did they kill Samuelson?" Willert asked.

Laura took a deep breath and spoke more slowly. "He was going to expose Morton's illegal campaign contributions, money he had defrauded from his church. In return, Harston promised to grease the skids for Morton's television ministry. Samuelson's expose would have destroyed both of them. So, they lured Samuelson out to the dam, drowned him, and made it look like an accident."

"Rachel saw all of this?"

"Yes. They caught a glimpse of my mother and me in the riverbed, looking at them. They had to get rid of her. Morton learned she was going to meet you on Hodges Island, probably from your sister, Becky. I think she went to Morton thinking he, as a member of my mother's church, might convince her to stop seeing you. Later, your sister realized something had gone very wrong, and she felt responsible . . ."

Suddenly, Laura heard footsteps and heavy breathing coming from the dirt road. Looking in that direction, she saw Morton rushing toward them, holding a thick piece of lumber with a metal crosspiece hanging loosely from the end. He raised the weapon high over his head and yelled something incomprehensible.

Willert pushed Laura out of the way as Morton charged at them. Laura fell to the ground. She quickly rolled over and looked back as Willert stepped deftly out of the way, barely avoiding Morton's frantic charge. Morton's momentum sent him crashing into the thick brush. Laura heard a shrill, sustained scream, then a muffled thud, and silence.

Willert walked cautiously over to the area where Morton had disappeared. He parted the vegetation and peered into the underbrush. As Laura approached, he held out his hand for her to stop. "He's at the bottom of one of the quarry holes," he explained, grasping her gently by the shoulder and leading her away.

"That's what he did to my mother," Laura replied tearfully."

"Rachel is down there?"

"No. Morton later removed her body and buried her in the cemetery for itinerant laborers," Laura said, struggling to control her emotions. "It was safer to make her disappear completely. Then, to divert everyone away from the crime scene, he started the rumor about her leaving with a man from Iowa. And there were others. When they broke their promises to help him resurrect his business, Frank Carver threatened to expose them. So, they faked his suicide. Alfred Kron got too close to the truth, and they made his death look like a hit and run. I would have been on that list if you hadn't come out here when you did."

"When I got here, it was all over," Willert replied.

"What do you mean?"

"Morton was lying by the road, and you were lying right here."

Laura struggled to comprehend what Willert had just told her. "I heard a struggle. I saw a hand. *Someone* stopped him . . ."

She glanced at the area where Morton had disappeared. A single sprig of lilacs was lying on the ground next to the huge hole in the earth, apparently torn off a nearby bush during Morton's ferocious charge.

*The long, black whirlpool enveloped Rachel Sims for what seemed like an eternity. Drifting and rolling and spinning ever downwards. Pulling her ever deeper into the vortex. Beyond time, beyond space.*

*On all sides of her, there were misshapen reptilian forms seemingly trapped and floating in the black, spinning walls of the whirlpool. And always there were the voices whispering seductively to her from the darkness.*

*Then she saw the light at the end of the vortex. The light that beckoned to her with its comforting presence. The light that encouraged her to end the struggle or risk losing her spirit to the misshapen forms that surrounded her. But as she held out her hand to the light, she saw that she was still clinging to the bouquet of lilac flowers.*

*From somewhere in the darkness, she heard strange voices begin a haunting, mournful lament that built to a crescendo pitch and faded away altogether. Then she drifted deeper and deeper into a dark, silent world where the light could not reach her. A dark, silent world filled only with the beautiful purple flowers of the blossoming lilac bushes.*

# CHAPTER NINETEEN

*May 1977*

"A federal grand jury today completed an investigation into the affairs of former Congressman Jerry Harstad. Harstad will face several criminal charges for his activities before and during the time that he was a United States congressman. Other charges are pending."

Laura turned off the car radio as she approached the sign indicating the Point Tyson City Cemetery was two miles east. She glanced briefly in the rear-view mirror at her young, dark-haired daughter who was sleeping in a toddler's safety chair in the back seat.

After she parked the car, Laura unbuckled the young girl from the safety chair and carried her through the cemetery gates. The little girl awoke as they walked down the path toward the Lonely Willow River.

As they approached Charlie Flanigan's cabin, Laura saw two cardboard boxes next to the front door. Charlie immediately walked out of the door and tossed an ancient thermos jug into one of the boxes.

"Spring cleaning?" she asked.

"Nope," he replied. He pushed one of the cooking pots deeper into the box. "I'm movin'. County's takin' over this place, an' they've asked me ta leave. I'm givin' this stuff away. Rev'rend Sinclair'll be by later this afternoon ta pick it up." He looked up at the young girl and smiled warmly. "Now, who might this be?"

"My daughter, Rachel," Laura explained. "My husband had to work today, but I wanted her to see this place when the lilacs were blossoming."

"She's a cute one, that's for sure."

"Where are you moving to, Charlie?"

"St. Paul. I gotta cousin who'll put me up for a spell. Least 'till I get a job. That is, if there are any jobs out there for a fella with not much in the way of brains, an' no real skills ta brag 'bout."

"Bet you're going to miss living out here," Laura speculated.

"Ya, it's gonna take some gettin' used ta," he agreed. He paused briefly from packing the boxes to look upstream and then across the river. "Prob'bly gonna be wakin' up in the mornin' for a while an' lookin' out the back window of my cousin's place at a buncha garbage cans. But that's okay, jus' so long as I don't have ta sleep on the streets. Say, have ya been up on that hill yet?"

"No, we just got here."

"Well, then ya'd better come with me. A lotta changes up there since ya was out here for that fun'ral last fall. A lotta changes."

Laura followed him up the hill to where the path branched off in two directions. At the top of the hill, he pointed at the graves of Grant and Rachel Sims. A new granite cemetery stone had been set in the ground on the other side of Rachel's gravestone. A single sprig of lilacs had been placed on each grave.

"That's the stone Jesse Willert selected 'fore he died," Charlie said. "Matches the other ones, too, dec'rations and all. It's the way he wanted it. An' now that Rachel Sims is act'ally buried here, maybe they can all fin'ly rest in peace."

"Maybe," Laura agreed. "Charlie, do you remember when I told you that Rachel Sims was my mother?"

"Ya. I remember you tellin' me that."

"Jesse Willert was my father. He didn't know about me until a few years before he died. He was still very much in love with my mother. That's why he's buried here."

Charlie seemed confused, but deeply touched by what Laura had just told him. "Well, I'll be," he muttered.

Laura had been holding her daughter, but she set the little girl down to give her arms a rest. The young girl immediately walked over to the three graves and knelt to study the flowers more closely.

"Say, I was jus' thinkin'," Charlie said. "Ya live in the cities, don't ya?"

"Yes, I do."

"Mind if I bum a ride with ya. I was gonna leave tomorrow, but if you're goin' that way, I might as well go with ya. I don't have many things ta take with me."

"I'd be happy to give you a ride to St. Paul. But only on one condition."

"What's that?"

"You have to tell me the truth about who put the flowers on these graves for all those years. Was it you?"

Charlie's face grew red. "Ya, I brought many of 'em up here," he admitted sheepishly.

"How come, Charlie?"

"I heard the stories they was tellin' in town 'bout your mother. I didn't like it. I jus' thought she needed sum'un on her side." Charlie looked down at the three graves. "I met her husband one time when he picked out these cem'tery plots. He was a very sick man. He tol' me how much he loved his wife. He could hardly talk 'bout it. That's why he put a stone with her name on it in the ground next to his."

"I think it was a beautiful thing you did," Laura reassured him.

"But I gotta tell ya sumthin' else," he insisted, "though ya prob'ly won't believe me now. I didn't put all the flowers up here. Not by a long shot. Many mornin's I came up here and there were lilacs scattered all over this hill. If it wasn't me, it hadda be sum'un else."

"The Lilac Lady?"

"Who else would've done it?"

"Did she also save my life the day I was almost killed on Hodges Island? Or was it you?"

Charlie ignored Laura's question and started walking back down the hill. Laura and young Rachel followed him over to the toppled tree that had fallen into the Lonely Willow River. Laura looked down at some of the wrinkled leaves that had piled up against one of the branches. Uncertain at first, then almost as though directed by the winds, the leaves slipped steadily through the maze of branches and small rocks in the river's shallows, finally floating free of the shore and moving steadily downstream.

Charlie continued to look at Hodges Island as a breeze sent a flurry of purple lilac petals out over the river and into the current. "Maybe she just wasn't ready ta leave yet," he said softly. "Maybe there was something else she had ta do. Maybe that's what it was."

*And so, the Lilac Lady walked the riverbanks at night, with flowers in hand, for reasons known only to her and the wind . . .*

## THE END

# ABOUT THE AUTHOR

DENNIS M. CLAUSEN grew up in west central Minnesota. There, he gained a close, intimate knowledge of the small towns and the lives they harbored. They provide the inspiration for *The Search for Judd McCarthy*, which was a best-selling paperback original when first published under a different title in 1982. *The Sins of Rachel Sims* (2018) is a sequel to *The Search for Judd McCarthy*. Clausen is also the author of *Prairie Son* (1999), an award-winning book of creative nonfiction. This work recreates his father's struggles as an adopted child to survive the Great Depression in a farm home where he was treated more as a worker than a son. In addition to his creative work, Clausen has authored textbooks, including *Screenwriting and Literature* (2009), which explores the relationships between writing screenplays and writing novels. For over thirty years, he has been teaching literature and screenwriting courses at the University of San Diego and has written editorials and columns for various newspapers. He enjoys writing stories that combine and transcend traditional literary genres. He has several other works in progress.